Christopher Green is Professor of Art History at the Courtauld Institute.

One Man Show is his first novel.

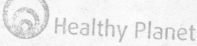

One Man Show

A Fictional History

Christopher Green

An *Abacus* Book

First published in Great Britain by Abacus 1995
This edition published by Abacus 1996

Copyright © Christopher Green 1995

The moral right of the author has been asserted.

A CIP catalogue record for this book
is available from the British Library.

ISBN 0 349 10686 X

Typeset by Palimpsest Book Production Limited,
Polmont, Stirlingshire
Printed and bound in Great Britain by
Clays Ltd, St Ives PLC

Abacus
A Division of
Little, Brown and Company (UK)
Brettenham House
Lancaster Place
London WC2E 7EN

This is a novel, and a history. Histories are plausible fictions based upon more or less verifiable facts. This is a history based upon a more or less plausible fiction.

· 1 ·

Vincent's Chair

Everyone has heard of Jack Driver. I suppose he is the most famous British painter of the twentieth century. Not many people have heard of me, though the professionals have – the art professionals. I'm an art historian. I was the one who put Jack Driver and his work together again. I can't claim much. I was only ever good at getting the facts right. You've probably noticed already that my style, if I have one, is not much more than serviceable. I write efficient prose, and make a virtue of it. At least I do when I publish things, which has been often. My word count must be approaching a million by now, and I've never knowingly wasted one.

This is going to be another professional job. And this time I really am going to get the facts right. I mean the facts about how we salvaged Jack Driver from the past. I've put together the *oeuvre* catalogue; I've edited the writings and the letters: this is different. I've got no career to worry about now, I can go back to all those other facts, the ones that matter. Early retirement gives endless opportunities for little revenges; against myself among others.

It is necessary to begin by setting out my material (that's how to start professionally). First, there are my jottings, or rather my tappings, because they aren't like an old-style diary, they consist of four three-and-a-half-inch double-density disks, and are the result of nightly tapping on the little laptop I had then. Sometimes I let myself go when

I tapped. *Wrote* as opposed to wrote. Allowed myself to be honest, self-exploratory, on occasion *emotional* in prose, even sometimes to be something embarrassingly like *literary*. That was when I tapped in what I felt, what I really thought about people and what I *really* thought had happened. I don't know how often I was honest. You will have to be the judge of that. Now and again, I tried to write down my 'beliefs', etc., as if one day I would become Enormously Distinguished. Those were the times (very rare, fortunately) when I was least reliable of all.

Then there are two extensive and extraordinary hand-written texts that Felicity left behind in the house in Barnes (I mean Felicity Driver, of course). And then there are the critical writings produced at the time in the press (both the national and the art press); especially the writings of Graham Copley. I know that Copley – at least early Copley – is unfashionable now, and that the new populists, including Graham himself, of course, hold his nineties criticism up as *the* model of the 'socialist' elitism we've all finished with, but it was *very* fashionable then, in 1993/4. Things have to be very fashionable to become very unfashionable. And it was, after all, Copley's early writings that gave Driver the visibility he needed for his big exhibition and his fame ever afterwards. I'll use them sparingly, in quotes. I hate the stuff too: it's like chewing toffee with bad teeth.

Then, finally (you have to bring things to a close when you're writing professionally), there's the catalogue that was produced for the Tate/Coverlie's exhibition in 1994, which was, incidentally, the first of the Tate's fully privatised shows. We're all so used to it now: if you're going to do 'a professional job' with the public in this market society, bring the market professionals in. But then it was quite a scandal for a public museum to 'let' space to the trade to organise its shows. Sir Simon McKenna (the then director) and two curators resigned on the issue. Remember? You wouldn't: it elicited widespread indifference, naturally, despite the deafening noise on the arts pages of the broadsheets. Anyway, the catalogue consisted of my extensive *catalogue raisonné* of the work shown, and a squib of an essay by Graham. Not the kind of private life exposés they go in for now in the new market-forces scholarship. Serious stuff. I'll only be giving you excerpts, but, of course, I've used my *raisonné* contribution to check the facts when they are particularly factual (titles, dates, that sort of thing). After all, I was an excellent cataloguer. You can always trust me.

I never did believe much in drama; it's not at all professional. But I shall start with the telling of something that I found very dramatic indeed. Felicity's account is the best one to start with; it's at the beginning of the text she dated 20 May 1994.

20 May 1994
I need to speak to you again, Jack. We've got out of the habit. But so many things have been happening. You need to know. The last few months, you've come back alive so much. More, lots more than the other times we've talked. I've seen the old paintings surface again, the ones from the sixties, and you've come back to me with them. I know you hate me being nostalgic. Nostalgia is a sin worse than gluttony or sloth or even envy, that's what you used to say; I've not forgotten. But it's not nostalgia, I promise. I can talk to you again, even better than before. So listen.

It really started when I came back from my day teaching in the studios at Chelsea. They haven't changed: the littleness of the spaces and the smell and the students trying not to be like anyone else and ending up the same.

You have to understand first what I've done with your chair. The chair you fought and fought. You see, I've left it in the sitting room, under Peter Frew's collage about Charlie Brown, Peanuts and Death. I know you

wouldn't approve. I've left it there to remind me of·
everything they tell me I need to forget: the hopelessness
of your illness. You fighting without weapons. It stands
as it did when you sat in it, on its ridiculous wheels,
beside the two Mies van der Rohe Barcelona chairs,
all black and chrome like them, but different. I've left
it there for me to see. It's my own *memento mori*. But
everyone knows it's your chair, and everyone respects
it enough never to draw attention to it. Or I thought
they did.

I had mucked my appointments, you see, and I
was in a hurry to sort it all out. A bit flustered. You
remember Graham Copley (the critic I said was awful
but necessary)? Well, I agreed he could come and see
me that evening, and I forgot about Roland Matthias.
There's a name you haven't heard of yet. Nor had I
until two weeks before. He wrote to me. One of those
stuffy, well-behaved letters postgraduate students send
when they hope you can write their theses for them. But
at least we've moved on from art-student dissertations
on Jack Driver and the 'Rock' Decade to Ph.D.s now.
Roland Matthias has chosen you to make him into Dr
Matthias. *Uncovering the Early Jack Driver: the Work
before 1971*, that's his title, all of it. It made me smile
when I remembered your attitude to being 'uncovered'.

Anyway, I forgot I had agreed to see him that evening
when I agreed to see Graham. Your silly Felicity doesn't
get any more competent. I need you to be angry with me.

Getting into the house was not easy, especially for
me flustered and hurrying. Next door was being ripped
apart by builders. I skirted the mounds of rubble,
avoided tripping over the scaffold, made a mental note
to deliver another volley of complaints about the skip
in my parking space, and felt distinctly relieved when I
found that Brenda was still at home. She grumbled about
the Hoover sighing, said she'd done her best with the
builders' dust in the circumstances and reported that the

three visitors were in the sitting room. *Three!* I began to worry about my sanity as well as my competence. How could I have invited three? Anyway, I opened the sitting room door determined to be charming and in control, whatever the odds. But I only saw one person at first.

Your chair was out of its corner. It was on the *Yomut* in the middle of the room. And someone was sitting in it. Just as you did, when I came back late. In the middle of the *Yomut*, seething. But this person was startled, not seething. Mortified in my *memento mori*.

He was not at all like you. He was thick all over. Thick body. Thick thighs. Thick hairy wrists under neat cuffs striped blue and pale green. Thick jowly neck over a collar and tie. A lively tie on a stolid person.

If a stolid person can hover while sitting, he hovered, somewhere in between staying there in your chair and getting out. Suddenly I wasn't flustered, I was dignified. You would have been proud of me. I simply said: 'Who exactly are you?' And he said: 'Roland Matthias.'

It was when he smiled that I trusted him. That was when it started, because it was then that I decided that I was going to let the pictures be seen; though I didn't really realise it at the time. I knew he was the right person: dull, obedient but obsessed with you. Why else would he have sat in your chair?

'You wanted to feel what it was like to be Jack,' I said, and he nodded. And then I told him to please get out of your chair and put it back in the corner, carefully.

She goes on, of course, to tell Jack – it really *is* remarkable how she writes as if she is talking to him – how it was that there were three people waiting for her. But I shall explain that myself; I can't let her text go on uninterrupted any longer. I hope you feel, as I do, that it is rather brave and honest of me to let the world read her unadulterated opinion of me: thick of feature, dull of spirit and obsessed. Not far off the mark, in actual fact. But I was not in the wheelchair out of respect for Jack Driver; I was there because of the other two, most of all because of Graham.

I'm going to start by trying to recall, now, what happened when I arrived that day. I shall try to get the facts right, but, remember, it was over twenty years ago. I've always told my students to be suspicious of recollected accounts, especially when they are too much like narratives. This one probably will be.

Felicity Driver's house was not at all special. She lived there with Jack Driver through the last twelve years of the painter's life, and she stayed there, in fact, until she died. It is situated in a leafy suburban road in Barnes: Edwardian, gable-fronted, tile-hung, with a little roofed porch to make even an art historian like myself welcome. Brenda, a large rubicund woman in her late forties, who had been the cleaner there since the Drivers moved in, opened the door to me. Mrs Driver was not back yet. Would I wait in 'the lounge'. There was someone else for her too.

The someone else was Diane Schwartz, the Bond Street dealer. I remember being disturbed to find her there; she had a formidable reputation. At that moment her group of galleries was attempting to negotiate an agreement over the rich remains of Driver's legacy, though I could not have known it (and I had no idea just how rich that legacy was). The agreement was, of course, aborted almost instantly, because of Coverlie's irresistibly powerful playing of a strong hand which was to have such far-reaching effects on the future of so much. But to my eyes then she was a figure who could well become the key for any future dealings regarding Jack Driver.

We shook hands in a room which at first seemed as unexceptional as the exterior of number 71 Horley Road, SW13. There were, however, clear signs that this was somewhere different. On the walls were uncompromising contemporary images: collages and photomontages, a drawing in a chipped white frame, a couple of signed artist's proofs by Richard Hamilton. This much you can trust me on: I remember what I see, and that room didn't change for years, even after the nineties. Driver's taste was visible, though significantly there was not a single trace of his own hand. On the floor was a splendid Turkish *Yomut*, and upon it, between two immaculate Mies van der Rohe chairs (reproductions, unfortunately) was Driver's wheelchair. I remember having predictable thoughts about Van Gogh's chair in the little yellow house at Arles.

Diane Schwartz was certainly formidable; she never missed an opportunity. She was quick to establish that my speciality was the early Driver. We talked about the late work, the work he did when he was very weak, when he could hardly move his hands even to eat. By that stage, as we all know well enough now, Felicity Driver was doing an enormous amount for him: cutting up the press images, pasting, photographing, even painting whole passages, though everything, every decision, came from him in the wheelchair. We agreed that the work weakens at the end, even if Felicity always did remain secondary, in the background. And we agreed that it is the work of the sixties that counts.

That was when the questions began.

What did I know about the missing early pictures? Did I agree that there were early pictures missing? Did I think Felicity had the answers? Was I here to get them from her? There was no missing the point: the market was going to be a factor in anything I found out. So it was, but not in the person of Diane Schwartz. I would soon learn of Coverlie's deep involvement.

I tried to outline the situation as I saw it then. Yes, there were missing pictures. The catalogues of the London shows of the sixties – the Brook show of '61, the Delaney show of '61, the 1964 Tate international, the New York breakthrough shows of '59 and '63 – were full of titles that never turn up again. Certainly titles could have changed, but one had to remember that for Driver the title *was* the work in a centrally important sense; and a check of the measurements made it clear that those panels and canvases do not reappear under new titles later. My figure for the missing pictures was – again I think this is an accurate memory – twelve; hers was significantly lower: seven, maybe eight (this is the sort of thing that I don't forget). We could not guess the real figure. Eighteen were, in fact, to resurface. They were all, of course, shown together for the first time in the Tate/Coverlie's retrospective of 1994. It was they above all, most would agree, that remade Jack Driver's name.

Our question and answer session about early Driver was interrupted by the arrival of Graham Copley, assiduously playing the role of leading critic. As he never tired of saying, he was the one who had 'reread Driver's achievement for the nineties'. He probably said it to me then; I was already intent on being the one to put Driver's achievement 'in order for posterity' (though *I* kept my intentions to myself). He championed Driver as the great Anti-Genius, the one who finally revealed the irrelevance of individual talent. I had my own agenda, something I shall clarify for you shortly. I certainly didn't clarify it for him then.

It was Graham who turned our attention to Jack Driver's wheelchair, and it was the chair that fastened the bond between myself and Felicity Driver.

'Felicity,' he said, 'keeps Jack alive by letting his chair stay here. I think of Vincent.'

So, of course, had I (clichés will out). I remember reflecting on the curiousness of the fact that it was those who wanted to relegate the Geniuses to indistinct points in the prevailing complex of signifying systems who tended to call them by their first names, as if they knew them personally. Graham Copley, of course, was still a teenager when Driver died, but Driver was always 'Jack' to him, just as Van Gogh was always 'Vincent'.

At this point, I need to bring in my jottings. They are, after all, much closer to the event, but before I do so, I want to introduce you properly to Graham, and to Graham's version of Driver as the 'great Anti-Genius' (if *anti*-geniuses can be 'great'). The best introduction is to give you a sample of late twentieth century Copley, undiluted. One thing you should know, however, before I give you my sample is that, like all but the newspaper critics of the later eighties and nineties, Graham was not a working critic in the sense that Clive Bell or Herbert Read or even Peter Fuller were; he didn't write criticism for a living. His profile was high, yes – he was a constant presence on the late-night media – but he published his pieces in relatively obscure periodicals for the like-minded, and already, even then, drew a monthly salary cheque as an academic (a rising young academic, who was the single cause of a new dimension of trauma among his students, as I can testify from the couple I knew).

The sample of Copley I've chosen for you is an extract from the text of a Radio Three interview given just before our meeting (Radio Three was the cultural arm of the old-style public service BBC). The interview was published at the time in *Art Data*, from which I give it to you verbatim. The interviewer, Dick Fearnshaw, is DF; Copley is GC.

DF So, to sum up, in your view his [Jack Driver's] re-emergence in the public eye, his re-emergence as the major British artist of the late fifties and the sixties is the result of his growing relevance now, as the century nears its end.

GC Certainly. He died an embarrassment to British modernism, he's emerged as the key to British postmodernism.

DF Why the key?

GC You used the phrase 'the public eye', and you talk about Jack as a great individual. This is the language of modernist hagiography. I reject it. What matters is the way he painted for much *more* than the eye: the way Jack foregrounded language, visual practice, as a signifying system ranging across both the visual and the verbal. He operated right outside the boundaries imposed by the gaze of the hegemonic formalist. That's why the art establishment sunk him without trace.

DF The curatorial and academic establishment, yes. But he didn't sink without trace. He *was* a great individual.

GC Jack was a man of courage and integrity, I agree; but his practice, his work was not *about* him; it was not about Jack Driver. It exposed the sham of the whole modernist star-system: I mean the idea that paintings are about the giant individuals who are their authors, that there's some unbreakable lifeline between the interior of the artist, the great artist, and the interior of the spectator – us ordinary punters. [Laughter]

DF But how do paintings which are so spectacularly individual, how can such a distinctive image as *Catch Me* be about anything but Driver?

GC OK, let's take *Catch Me*. Does it mean that we are ever going to catch him? Is that really a possible reading?

DF Our listeners might like to know that *Catch Me* is the centrepiece of the eagerly awaited 'Concise Retrospective of Jack Driver' now on in the upper gallery at the Whitechapel.

GC Let's look at *Catch Me*. A veil of drips and spatterings – Pollock quoted (you have to remember Action Painting had just arrived in Britain at the end of the fifties). Boxes unfolded in repeated rhythms – Cubism quoted. Three Teddy boys, part drawn like a Giles cartoon, part documentary photograph. A cutthroat razor in frightening detail, open, like a heraldic device, beneath one of those mock-Egyptian Odeon façades that have become sex cinemas and bingo halls. The single word 'HOT' in lights across the top. The words 'CATCH ME' across the bottom.

DF Makes one think of Pop. The moment of *This is Tomorrow*, Richard Hamilton, 'Slip it to me'. Though Driver wasn't actually part of the Independent Group, was he?

GC No – and that's the point. You see, the consumerism, the Pop imagery isn't there in the same way at all. That's why we can still relate to him, when Kitaj and Hamilton – artists like that – seem as far out of sight, and mind, as Ford Zephyrs. He admired Hamilton and he followed the activities of the Independent Group, but he wasn't *with* those artists. This picture isn't *about* the mass media, advertising – it's about the multivalency of language. It's a barrage of signs, a babble of . . . It's a Tower of Babel for the nineties. And behind it, Jack disappears . . . Behind a screen of contradictory utterances. How can you say just what *is* him in all this?

DF An important question.

GC You can't. That's why Jack Driver is so relevant. He looked at Pollock and De Kooning, all that self-expression, that putting yourself in the painting stuff, and he decided to disappear. Those Jackson Pollock drips, they're always there in Jack's pictures of the early sixties, but he makes them say it's all a fraud. No one's behind the drips, not Pollock, not Jack Driver.

DF Well, Pollock certainly isn't there.

GC It was right. I believe it was right that he should *actually* disappear and then die. The slowness of his dying was itself a statement – the slow erasure of himself. His dying was the other side of his painting. It stood for the death of that boring old Romantic cliché, genius.

See what I mean? I don't eat toffee any more, but it turns up in those selections, concealed inside chocolates, and I find myself having to chew my way through it anyhow. I won't expose you to too much of it, but you have to have a chew from time to time. He wouldn't be heard dead nowadays uttering phrases like 'the multivalency of language' (they were old-fashioned even then), but you have to admire the fluency with which he used them twenty years ago. If anyone has been the complete professional, it has to be Graham.

So the scene is set for getting back to what really happened, as my jottings record it from the nineties. My attitudes may seem a bit quaint now, and my writing veers between the pompous and the hysterical too often, but I make no apologies. This is the evidence. I shall not edit myself. This was the way I wrote it down.

I was, after all, a young postgraduate student with ambitions, and secretly (it had to be secretly, given my off-pink surroundings) I believed that what has happened would happen: that (just conceivably) Labour might come in four or five years' time (it was just after the '92 election), but would certainly go very soon afterwards, that free market individualism had finally triumphed, that what they were soon to call the eurosceptics would restore the Great National Tradition (what we call now the 'Natural Condition of Britain'), that the unstoppable PR machinery of the Tory Party electoral war-machine would clear the path for true-blue stability into the next century and beyond, that the crises and upheavals and the austerity of the early nineties would be forgotten as the newspapers chattered about the return of mild weather and the 'controlled maintenance' of boom conditions. Then, in the nineties, as I plotted my future, I was convinced that this could only mean ultimate success for those like me who, unlike Copley, believed in Genius and Art, that the social historians and the deconstructionists would be driven into oblivion by the triumph of populism and the middlebrows. I could not have imagined that I would end my career accepting early retirement from the rigours of lecturing to audiences of three hundred undergraduates at one of the more run-down universities which will never win research status. I could not imagine that the deconstructionists would find ways to adapt, that the late, the 'new millennium' Copley would be fashionable even when early 'critical theory' Copley is so unfashionable; that he, not I, would crown his career with a professorship at the New Heritage Centre for Cultural

Studies (the NHCCS), free of all teaching responsibilities, heading teams of postgraduates on projects of the highest prestige and the most impenetrable irrelevance, supported by private funding from the likes of Diane Schwartz and Coverlie's.

Then I cared. I might have been a careerist (and known it in my moments of honesty), but I cared. Now, I don't think I care at all about Genius. If it exists, it changes nothing. Copley, of course, has found the cleverest ways of theorising it. He uses the word as easily as he once used the phrase 'death of the author'. Now in the second decade of this twenty-first century, in this era of the 'Great Traditions', the return of Genius was, I suppose, inevitable; and I suppose I could have predicted that it would not be the clerks of culture like me, the ones who believed in it, who would become its acknowledged champions and reap the benefits.

So, then, to my unedited jottings from the day I met Felicity. This is the whole of my long entry (one should call it file, of course). I was still in a turmoil; in a state I can only describe as shock laced with elation. I started with one of my heavier statements of 'belief'; after all, this was the moment when I thought my career had at last begun. It was a statement about me, Driver and Genius.

Today what I write down here matters. I must be clear about what I believe. I believe in ideas to which no professional art historian can confess today, that is without being frozen out of a career. I believe that individuals can change history. I believe in Genius. I know I have not got it, but I shall be its servant willingly. I shall itemise and chart its creations; I shall do it with a rigorous refusal of imagination. Geniuses are all imagination; those who serve them must live and work without it. I shall deny myself imagination in the name of imagination.

But, as I make my catalogues and my charts, I shall never say this. I shall mouth the names Barthes and Foucault and

Lacan and maybe Bakhtin. I shall acknowledge (tacitly) the 'death of the author'. But I shall not let the Geniuses die. I shall serve Jack Driver well.

There, that's said. Now I can try to put down what happened today. Such a day.

How can I put it down? There was too much, and too many feelings, bad as well as good. But mostly good. I shall try to do it by taking one person at a time. Everything centres on the people: Diane, Graham and above all Felicity. You see, I call them by their first names. All of a sudden I am on first-name terms with these *figures*. And they *are* figures. I begin to believe that soon I shall be a figure myself. Except they made me feel such a fool, at least Diane and Graham did . . . Not Felicity.

Diane

The French have a word, '*serviable*'. Something between servile and amenable . . . very amenable. Diane reduced me to that. How could I have allowed her to do it?

There's her appearance. She's a woman tending to the dumpy, but there's something about her square jaw and ruler-drawn slit of a mouth which is formidable. She smiles a lot but never smiles. The mouth becomes a wider slit, and the red of her lipstick becomes a little more visible, but that's all. She tries to make up for her basic inelegance by smooth presentation. Her streaked blond hair is piled up in stylishly cut ridges and plateaux, she wears speckled tortoiseshell glasses shaped so as to save the upper part of her face from ordinariness, and she dresses to straighten up the dumpiness. She's beautifully packaged.

She speaks American with an English accent. She says things like: 'OK, let me run this by you', and 'It sucks'. But she also says 'Delighted to meet you', and 'Cheerio'. She seems to have gone to Wycombe Abbey in the middle of the Atlantic. She filled me with fascination and deep apprehension.

Her technique with me was to flatter and terrorise

alternately. She terrorised me by telling me how nervous I was.

'You're nervous, aren't you?'

'Why should I be nervous?'

'Felicity makes people nervous. So do I, I guess.'

'I promise you I'm not.'

'Well then, there's no need to keep on the move all the time, is there? Take it easy.'

And she terrorised me by damning my opinions. I filled a pause in the conversation by praising Graham's writing on Driver. 'A critic one has to take seriously,' I said. That was when she said: 'It sucks.' And she said a lot else. It went something like this:

'You don't think I'm very bright, do you? You think dealers don't give a damn about ideas. Well, I'm very smart indeed, OK? I know all about your namesake, that piss-artist Roland Barthes, and I know about the death of the author and all that. So don't try patronising me with your opinions. You can come right down off your intellectual's pedestal. Graham Copley is a creep. He's not interested in Driver or Driver's painting; he's interested in Graham Copley, star deconstructionist, mega-media-man of critical theory and all that crap. Well, I wish to God *he'd* disappear into the nearest signifying system.'

She had a good line in steamroller rhetoric. And it *was* rhetoric, because she completely reversed her position when Graham arrived. Greeted him with cries of appreciation that bordered on adoration:

'Fabulous to see you. Your piece on Damien in *Art Data* was just dazzling,' et cetera, et cetera . . .

Everything with Diane is tactics. I saw it but I succumbed like a baby. The flattery was irresistible – and I never could resist flattery. It went with the offering of temptations. I was seriously tempted. First, she went on about the importance of my thesis. Then she thanked me for the authoritativeness of my answers on the missing early pictures.

'No one,' she said, 'has looked at the matter with the seriousness and knowledge that you so obviously have. Fabulous. So impressive. I thought I knew something about the problem, but really, I have to defer.'

And yet it's obvious that all she wants is to be in on whatever I might discover.

And then she started talking about the exhibition she wanted to put on, and how 'right now, you, Roland Matthias, have put yourself in the frame for writing the lead essay for the catalogue.' Me writing 'lead essays' in major catalogues. How do I resist this kind of thing? My heart actually fluttered, as they say hearts do when there's temptation about.

I would have agreed to anything for that woman. Why? I know for a fact that she didn't mean anything she said. I knew it then. She only says things to see what they do to people; and usually she has a pretty good idea what they will do. But I ended up her meek and willing servant.

Graham

So my idea of Graham was wrong, completely wrong. He is not beetle-browed, lantern-jawed and aggressively highbrow. Not to meet. He is a loose person. It's in his appearance. He has a long body, a long face, long floppy fair hair and his features are loose, as if they're not sure how to configure themselves. He smiles a lot, loosely. He likes having jokes; sometimes, I think, with himself, privately. I had the impression a lot of the time that he was having jokes at my expense, privately. I think I know what he would have been like at school: the kind of boy who got you into trouble and sailed through everything himself trouble-free. He could have made a profession as an *agent provocateur*, if he hadn't had the academic conference circuit and critical theory. He was not at all what I expected. But I knew he would make a fool of me, and he did.

It was the chair that made it so easy for him. Jack

Driver's wheelchair. But if there hadn't been the chair, he'd have found other ways to make a fool of me, I suppose.

He began with the 'contrast' between this smooth chrome and leather, technological chair for the late-twentieth-century disabled, and Van Gogh's ('Vincent's') uncomfortable little rush chair in his room at Arles. He then remarked how 'interesting' it would be to see if it had all the working parts in order after so many years, and if it was actually as 'technologically well adapted to the creature comforts of an immobile painter' as it looked.

So he got it out of the corner, and began wheeling it around, casually, making comments like: 'doesn't turn too smoothly to the left'. . . 'has a squeak . . . can you hear the squeak?' It amazes me that he could be so brazen, that it simply didn't occur to him that Felicity could come in any minute. Perhaps it did and he's just like that, brazen.

Then came his descent into childishness. First there was a stupid Goldilocks routine: 'Who's been sitting in *my* chair?' et cetera. Then, inevitably, he sat in the wheelchair himself. The effect was to start him making infantile jokes: 'Here's the big question: who's the best driver, me or Jack?' He found them killingly funny. I laughed out of politeness, a predictable failure of moral fibre. And all the time he was asking about me and accepting the two-faced adoration of Diane. And being cynical. Yes, it was the cynicism that was the most surprising. I never thought he would be cynical. In his writing he's the kind of critic who's always on about being 'tough and uncompromising', etc.

'Diane's an admirer, aren't you Diane? I love admirers. Simple, unalloyed worship of talent. After all, the prices rise with every phrase I make.

'Are you sure you didn't make that name up . . . Roland Matthias? Has class. Distinctly marketable. Good move, Roland. I approve of strategists.'

And so on. Picking on my name was going too far, I

thought. But he makes a practice of going too far. He went far too far when he started manoeuvring Driver's chair in the middle of the *Yomut* and talking about wheelchair slaloms. That was when he dared me to take over and sit in it.

'Your turn.'

'Me?'

'In you get.'

'I'm not having anything to do with this. Count me out.'

'Christ, man, you're shit scared.'

I *was* shit scared. I am shit scared just remembering it. And then he had me. He said: 'If it were Vincent's wonky little cane chair in Arles, you would sit in it, eh? Like *becoming* God the Genius, God the Holy Madman. Come on, if you care about Jack, you have to *be* Jack too.'

And he ushered me in, and I sat in it. Just like that. Then Diane joined in. She pushed me. 'To give you the authentic experience,' she said.

Why did I feel nothing? I should have felt good and serious things. It should have been a profound moment of identification. It was like in my religious phase, when I tried to have visions: nothing happened. Why do I only ever disappoint myself?

Graham disappointed me; I disappointed myself; but Felicity was not at all disappointing.

Felicity

Felicity is wonderful. I've started having fantasies about Felicity. I'm not inexperienced with women (of course you're not, Roland). But I've never been at all good at seduction. I can't imagine seducing her. She's an *older* woman. I have to imagine *her* seducing me.

The best fantasy is when I'm sitting with her looking at reproductions of Driver's work, and I say something penetrating and moving, and she turns suddenly with a glint in her eye and kisses me full on the mouth, with infinite passion. And then I feel her slender hand on my thigh. And then I become glassy-eyed and tumescent.

It's a poor way to go on when it's Felicity 'in the frame', to use Diane's phrase. Felicity is perfect. And she has a splendid dignity. Afterwards, immediately afterwards, here in this little hemmed-in room, with that crass thug Gerald playing his CDs on the other side of the wall . . . thump . . . thump . . . thump . . . I could only ask again and again: how is it that I know Felicity . . . that *I know Felicity*? How can I ever get close to Felicity . . . *really* know her? Will she let me?

And then I began to eat. I went to the biscuit tin. I should never go to the biscuit tin. I put the chair up alongside the imitation Art Deco wardrobe; I climbed up on it; I got down the biscuit tin. I eased open the difficult lid, and when it had clattered off on to the table I didn't even wait to look at them; I ate every one of them, all the chocolate digestives, the ginger-nut crunches, the jaffa cakes and the gypsy creams, every single one of them. Slowly. So as not to make crumbs. I wanted to eat every tiny speck of sugared carbohydrate. I ate to block the desire, to sate myself. And I ended immobile in the window, with the light off, looking down on to the noisy knots of pub-leavers under the yellow lights. The desire still there.

I had a moment, immediately before the biscuits, when the desire really wasn't there. Just a moment. When there was no sweaty little need to fantasise. This house packed with paperbacks and CDs and ageing young students is full of desire. But even here I know I should protect Felicity against desire. For her, it's out of order. But I feel it. Even the whole biscuit tin didn't block it. I shouldn't feel it. There's nowhere for it to lead, Roland. Be careful, Roland. Very careful.

Can I describe her without getting glassy-eyed? I think so. I need to summon up all my self-control. Here goes.

Felicity is tall and slender. There's a slight awkwardness about the way she moves, as if she's always aware of obstacles, but she never moves without grace. She has the face of a once and still beautiful woman. The lines are well on their way across her forehead and beneath her eyes, but they give a calm refinement that becomes her. She has large grey-green eyes, and a mouth that turns up at one corner in the beginning of a smile, even when there is no smile beginning. I expected an air of sadness. There is none.

Yesterday she wore tight jeans, with a show of studs; she dressed young (I suppose for teaching). Her ears, neck and wrists were costumed with discreet and striking modern jewellery. Not expensive, but good. She has a lot of hair; it is tossed up all around her face but is somehow under control. It completes her.

I can be quite literary sometimes. Not a bad description, after all. Perhaps I should be a little less prosaic in the professional stuff.

For Felicity I have to try to tell it as it happened. And I have to try to remember what she said: the exchanges between us in the actual sequence as they occurred. Truman Capote is supposed to have had 100 per cent recall; I don't have much better than 60 per cent, I suspect, but I must try, and the illusion that it happened like that might convince me after all that it did. I shall keep away from the fantasies. Be factual, it's always the best way. People like you, Roland, need to avoid fantasy.

For her to come into that sitting room with me in the chair! And for her to say what she did, with that very special note of understanding in her voice.

'You wanted to feel what it was like to be Jack.'

How could I not have smiled? It wasn't that she was right; she was a long way off the mark. I felt nothing but shocked discomfort. It was the fact that instantly I felt easy with her. Diane was right there behind me pushing, but she might as well not have been. Felicity zeroed in on me alone. Just me. I made contact with her. I knew it. She was not angry. She did not even seem surprised. The chair made the contact between us, and when I smiled it was fastened, tight. I knew it.

Then things happened fast. There were muddles to be unravelled. She unravelled them by very charmingly telling Graham and Diane that I had come a long way and that she really owed me the time. She put me first and asked them to go. And they went. *Tant pis*. Oh my God! *Wasn't* it good to see Graham and Diane deferential and acquiescent?

This is where I have to remember what was said. She got us both drinks (she drank *pastis*, very odd). We got through some preliminaries; they were necessary of course. Before she asked me:

'Did it give you pleasure to sit in Jack's chair?'

I just answered, 'Yes'.

'You wanted to pretend for a moment?'

I think I said: 'To imagine.'

Her eyes became hard and I had the feeling that she was physically closer to me.

'Well, if it gave you pleasure to pretend to be Jack, let me tell you what it was like to be Jack . . . how it was when he lived in that chair all his waking hours.'

I protested – that's the word. 'Please,' I said, 'you must believe me. I know how much he must have suffered, and I admire more than anything how he went on working.'

I sensed a very slight but definite stiffening of her whole body. I really did sense it. She ignored what I had said completely.

'First there were the secretions. He oozed. He seethed with smells. The incontinence began years before he died. Then there was the littleness of every part of him: the little wrists, the little bony shoulders and chest, the stringy hands, the feet that turned kind of inwards on the chair rest, the little eyes behind the brows which seemed so unnaturally big and shaggy. Even his eyes seemed to shrink. And he wasn't old. Not at all old.'

When I interrupted she told me to shut up and listen. She

started talking about his 'bloody-mindedness', his 'desire
to hurt everyone'. Especially her. I tried to say how he
was remembered as a generous man, a big man, not the
stereotype of the egocentric artist at all.

'Shut up. I said listen. People remember him from before
the illness. Sometimes I remember him from before the
illness. The years I knew him when he was still a strong
man. That was when I could really talk to him; when
I really knew him. He was a great teacher, you know.
He could be cruel, but he won respect. He knew lots
of things . . . the most surprising things. He knew how
to make Molotov cocktails and he knew about discourse
theory long before it became the thing that everyone had
to know. He read every day, a couple of hours a day,
wherever he was. Foucault even in the late sixties. It made
a change from Marshall McLuhan and all that. Nietzsche,
Marx, Bataille, Breton, Joyce, Lawrence. Imagination can
remake the world, he used to say. But MS changes people.
It changes the personality, that's what the specialist told
me. I wasn't to worry, it was a normal part of the
illness.'

I thought I should say that I had looked up the effects of
the illness myself. After all, I knew what she was talking
about. I really did take the trouble to find out. She was not
pleased, very abrupt.

'Will you stop interrupting. Just listen. The specialist
said that some MS patients become euphoric. Jack became
euphoric, yes, but he ended up becoming almost vicious.
He hated himself and everyone. He hated me. Not so much
when we worked. That was OK. That was why we tried
to work. To make things good again. But at the end we
worked less and less. He hated all the time. Do you know
about the Lady Chatterley case?'

Lady Chatterley's Lover – D.H. Lawrence. Well, of
course I do. I'm a sixties specialist, for Christ's sake.

'Yes,' I said. ' "It sets upon a pedestal promiscuous and
adulterous intercourse", isn't that how the prosecution put

it? Sex for the working class at three and six a time.' Stupid to be flippant. This was not the moment to be flippant.

'It was an intensely serious thing for Jack. The winning of that case. Nineteen sixty, was it?'

I said yes.

'And when I met him he used to love reading out loud the passages where Connie Chatterley and Mellors . . . you know, the copulation scenes. That word 'fuck', he revelled in Lawrence's relish for it. The irony is that in the end the book became a kind of goad . . . a provocation. I suppose it's obvious it would have happened. He thought of me as Connie, and himself, you see, himself as the husband who cannot give pleasure, tenderness any more. Lawrence's word was tenderness. At the end he hated me for my health . . . for his impotence.'

Then I said: 'I'm sorry, I didn't know it was like that.' And she said: 'You knew he died in that chair, slowly. I leave the chair in the corner not to remind me of him – I don't need the chair to remind me of him – I leave it there to remind me of just *how* he died.'

It's true. It sits there like a skull in a *vanitas* painting. And I lifted it right out. I touched it. I broke all the taboos.

There was nothing I could say. She broke the pause. She put her hands on my shoulders and she said: 'Let's forget about the chair. You're here to talk about Jack before I met him.'

The marvellous thing, the thing that is going to make my career came then, when we had been talking about the people of the fifties and the sixties, the people he admired: Reyner Banham, Robert Melville, Lawrence Alloway, David Sylvester. Again, I must remember just how it happened.

It started when I said how surprised I was that there were no Drivers on the walls, in the house. Her answer was a question.

'Have you ever heard of the Cardinal del Monte?'

'The Cardinal del Monte?'

'Jack told me about him. He was one of Caravaggio's early patrons, but his taste was rather specialist (I've looked it up since; it's all there in Haskell). He went in for very special parties: prelates and boys in drag. He liked those pictures of pretty Roman youths. Well, the Cardinal del Monte owned *Amor Vincitatis*. It's a famous Caravaggio, you must know it . . . a kind of rent boy on a soiled bed in the pose of Victory. But he always kept it behind a curtain. He only looked at it when he wanted that kind of experience, and he only showed it to the friends he trusted. That's the way to handle the really strong pictures. Jack never hung his strong things in the house. He kept them in the studio.'

That was the moment when I had the courage. It amazes me that I had it. To say as cool as you like: 'I suppose he kept those early pictures back in the studio, I mean the ones that seem to have disappeared.' I don't always disappoint myself. She didn't even hesitate.

'Yes. He kept them. They're still there; in the old studio (she meant a studio I didn't know about in Soho; I may be the only one who knows about it, the only one she's told). Sometimes,' she said, 'I go and see them. I've never taken anyone before. I'm going to take you.'

2

On the Brink of the Twenty-first Century

Fortune smiles, for once. I am going to be able to tell the rest of the story far more fully than I ever thought possible.

A fortnight ago I ran into Peter Frew, *Sir* Peter Frew, I should say, sometime confidant of Jack Driver, old friend of Sir Simon McKenna and retiring president of the Royal Academy. This part of the story is stuffed with knights and peers (mostly people who have now become knights or peers). I was never a person of any importance to McKenna, but Peter Frew was and he is a friend of mine because he always remained loyal to Felicity. McKenna and Frew were, as they say, 'like that' (you'll have to imagine my 'thick' index fingers linked to give the sign required). McKenna selected Frew's first major show when he was the 'dynamic young director' of the New Centre for Contemporary Art in Leeds in the late seventies.

I told Peter about my project and I especially impressed on him the importance of getting the facts right about McKenna's resignation from the Tate. The catalyst, of course, was, as everyone knows, the Tate/Coverlie's exhibition of Driver, and especially the splash created by the emergence of the lost early pictures. So I argued that I am the one who can get all the facts together once and for all. Indeed, I am the *only* one.

He could not have been more co-operative. He has let

me see all the correspondence between him and McKenna for the whole of that period. It explains a great deal. It is, in a word, dynamite. McKenna told Peter 'everything'. He has given me permission to use whatever extracts I think necessary. The Tate archive, I might add, has never allowed me to see a single box of the relevant papers.

If we are to get to grips with the Tate/Coverlie's affair, I have to take you a few weeks further on in my relationship with Felicity, and I have other introductions to make.

Along with Simon McKenna, there is my fellow post-graduate in the art history department of Queen's, London, June Sutcliffe; she was the more junior of the two curators who resigned with him. You will not have heard of her. Happily, she dropped out of sight and mind afterwards. (You might think it insensitive of me to say 'happily'. But the fact is that she now grows blackcurrants, apples and pears in Somerset and helps sustain the 'Great Tradition' myth of a land of happy families. She had to suffer, though, before she attained her present sated condition. Once she went through multiple disasters in full public view – as we shall see. Now she is a happy single parent who has recently become a happy single grandparent far away from the inner city.)

And then you will meet Miranda Browne of Coverlie's, now of course Lady Roache, a leading Tory spokeswoman on the arts in the Lords. Miranda Browne/Lady Roache, besides making her hyperactive career under the banner of common names rendered superior by the simple addition of an 'e', is a Great Cultural Power. I remember her as a girl with other powers. I am proud to confess that, in my mind, the Tate/Coverlie's affair is code for another affair, mine with Miranda (exhausting and deeply destabilising though it was). Felicity never really came out of fantasy land, except once. Miranda was not, of course, an older woman. She liked 'fun', and made sure she had lots of it. She certainly would never have used the earnest word 'affair' (with all those connotations: a 'serious affair', etc.) for the 'fun' we had, though she did admit to liking the idea of us being 'lover' and 'mistress' (her tastes, ultimately, were deeply old-fashioned). No, she preferred the word 'fling' to 'affair'.

It may seem inappropriate to bring in this kind of ephemeral material, but none of it is irrelevant in my estimation. I am dealing in facts. All of this material is factual, elements in the network of facts I am trying to knit back together again. I can see no reason for leaving any of it out. A cataloguer includes everything.

Perhaps it's best to open this chapter with the necessary introductions, at least for the leading players: McKenna and Miranda. In the covering letter he sent with the correspondence, Peter has done the job for me as far as McKenna is concerned. It needs me to gloss it before you read it, but it does the job rather well in my opinion.

Peter Frew, you have to realise, is the kind of artist who trained when painters were *visual*, when all the talk was of literal flatness and painting as painting. I'm talking about the mid-sixties. It was not advisable to be articulate; instead a kind of monosyllabic *bonhomie* was encouraged. He was, however, educated well enough (at a minor public school in Wiltshire) to know how to write sentences with abundant sub-clauses. I suspect he still knows how to parse. There is, therefore, in his letter-writing a curious mixture of the simple and the sophisticated. He pretends to bluff directness, and he intersperses everything with 'fucking' and 'bloody' because he thinks it's authentic, but he has his own line in rolling rhetorical prose which can be very eloquent indeed.

So, here's how Peter introduces his old friend.

Dear Roland,

Before you read these letters, I want to say something about Simon as I knew him. The old bastard needs to be saved from his declining reputation. I hardly recognise the McKenna who runs that spectacular museum in Los

Angeles, and dispenses wisdom from his beach-house under layers of Piz Buin total sun block, as the fine man I knew. I only wish the fuckers in power when he was obliged to leave could have had the sense to prohibit his subsequent export instead of expediting it.

Simon was glamorous and he never knew it. No, he never *let* on he knew it. He didn't need to dress up to be glamorous, he just was. If you had a drink with him in a pub (I mean before his face was all over the press) you spent your time trying not to notice that you were being noticed (by women, mainly). People would keep turning and glancing, or shifting their places so that they could glance a bit better.

Everyone wanted to be with him, the jammy bastard, but he behaved as if he was no more interesting than anyone else. The thing was, he treated you *normally*, that's very flattering for most people from someone so special.

Well, he certainly was special, and in those years just before he got the Tate job and just after, he gave us hope. For artists like me who wanted to believe that the institutions were not just back-scratching clubs for time-servers, he was all about hope. People said it at the time: he was the John F. Kennedy of the art world. The way he behaved when the chips were down shows we were right to trust him. Of course, the Tory version of culture has turned out to be all *about* glamour: the glamour of the fucking 'Great', the glamour of fucking 'Knowledge' and the glamour of the for-ever-fucking 'Classics', all marketed by the glamour of the glamorous places which house fucking 'Art', by the fabulous sums it attracts, and, not least, by the glamour of its supporters, the super-rich who, I know we should be awfully thankful, take time off between faxes to buy our pictures (there are some who do that by fax too, sight unseen). Simon, who had all it takes to be one of the new culture's leading ambassadors, but who hated glamour with grim passion, did what he had to.

Grim passion. That sums it up. Simon was passionately

engaged with us and with art. Not art as something 'Classic' and 'Great', just as something some people did that mattered. There aren't a lot of you word people who can feel, like he did, how much it takes to go on doing what we do, us image people. But his passion had no lightness in it. Everything was in deadly earnest. He never got further than smiling, even at the best jokes, although he does have a wry sense of humour. I *have* heard him laugh. He *is* physically capable of it. But he can't let it go; it comes out like hiccups. Causes a lot of embarrassment. My belief is he doesn't think he ought to do it. Time is short; matters are serious; great issues are at stake. Back in the nineties he was bloody right.

I still love the old bastard, even though he's gone and got himself hooked on American money. I don't think he could resist it. It wasn't the money, it was the Americans and Culture. Americans are so *serious* about fucking Culture. And they *would* fuck it, if they could find out how (maybe some of them *have* found out how). Anyway, it's *that* serious. They make it seem tough and wholesome and bloody hard work too, in between the black-tie receptions. The super-rich are mostly American now, of course, but you have to give it to them: they've left it to *our* Heritage industry to turn Culture (read 'the Classics') into the glamour end of entertainment.

Simon was right: you have to go to America and leave us to play with ourselves if you're going to be serious and passionate about art. Europe either imitates America or drowns in Heritage. I've chosen America too – I freely admit it – I chose America nearly fifty years ago. You can stay in Britain and be American – a lot of us do.

Anyway, my message is simple. Take Simon seriously. He's not a manipulator. There are no Byzantine plots. The others were the plotters, and they knew bloody well that the one thing they could be sure of was that Simon was above plotting. It's dangerous to be sincere *all* the time, like Simon was and still is. He means what he says. He worries. He cares. That's what I know about him: he bloody cares. And you can use these letters, because we both agree that you care.

Just to reassure you. I phoned Simon the other day. He gives his blessing. He said: I hope he tells people everything. So do I.

Yours ever,
Peter

PS Come and eat a crust with Daphne and me one evening. You can see what I've been up to. I'm making collages again. They remind me of Jack. Such a long time ago.

PPS I hope you've got to the bottom, finally, of the so-called lost pictures. As you will see, they puzzled Simon, and, though I didn't make enough of it at the time, they puzzled me. They still do. At least some of them. But Jack was an unpredictable bastard when all's said and done.

You have to respect old Peter Frew. His painting's like him: big, bluff and highly sophisticated, but beginning to age a little. And even though he takes time off to stick together the odd collage, his heart is still in acrylic and white cotton duck on very large-scale stretchers. He's transatlantic, like Diane Schwartz's way of speaking the mother tongue, except he's sixties/seventies transatlantic and she was nineties transatlantic.

He also knows how to look at paintings; he has what they used to call 'a good eye'. He's one of a very few who have kept a genuinely open mind about the 'lost' pictures, and I don't mean just about what they might be about.

So to Miranda. It's more difficult to introduce Miranda. I often wonder if Miranda ever existed. I never really found her credible. I always suspected she was the product of somebody else's dream and had somehow been inserted into my life by mistake. If this were a novel, she would be just the kind of character the marketing people would insist on bringing in (classy, sexy, exaggeratedly glamorous – to use Frew's word), if it were not for the fact that she was so complicated, and in the end, so baffling. I suppose the best way to introduce Miranda is slowly, so that you can get used to her (I didn't have the chance, and never recovered from the shock). And the best way to do that is to go back to how I was introduced to her the week after I met Diane, Graham and Felicity.

It happened in the presence (symbolic at least) of Sir Simon McKenna. The venue was a small reception at the Tate to inaugurate the rehang of a couple of galleries. After the success of the Whitechapel's 'Concise Retrospective', *Catch Me* was made the centrepiece of a new display of Driver in a couple of the rooms on the right of the Duveen Gallery. Felicity, naturally, was invited (she had loaned one or two things for the occasion), and she asked me along, because, as she put it, there were 'developments afoot'. I had not yet seen any of the lost pictures. They were still a mystery to be penetrated. She said the great revelation would come when these 'developments' had started to develop. And there was someone in particular she wanted me to meet. This was, of course, Miranda.

The first thing to get straight is some of the facts that matter about the Tate occasion, so I shall start by giving the 'background'. I've still got a certain amount of documentation to help my memory – press cuttings and so on – but I've warned you (along with my students) already, recollections like this are always to be treated with caution.

The date of the Tate reception for the new 'Jack Driver Room' was 21 April 1993. I remember my excitement when Felicity made sure I was asked. I remember thinking that this was the date that marked once and for all the end of the neglect from which the name of Driver had suffered since his death in 1987; indeed, since some years earlier than that. The company was certainly select enough. John Duncan, then Minister of Heritage, was there (he's now

Lord Kierhaven, of course); Lord Troy, chairman of Coverlie's, was there (I remember being surprised by how accessible he was). Then there were major collectors of contemporary art: Derek Strange, Constance Pierpoint and several others; there were major critics, including Brian Merritt and, of course, Copley; and there were several prominent academics too, including my supervisor, Professor Kit Moss. The sheer quality of the guest list made inescapable the importance of the occasion.

Miranda came as part of Troy's entourage. She was his protégée: the youthful director of Coverlie's Contemporary. But she had the presence to stand apart. I was aware of that the moment I set eyes on her. Felicity, I now realise, made a point of ensuring that when I was introduced to her, June Sutcliffe was not there. She led me from one to the other (I remember June conspiratorially telling me of 'great things afoot', 'a giant sponsorship deal' which would 'hit the newspapers tomorrow or the next day'; she was so naïve about it all, but I don't think she deserved what happened to her). That evening Miranda was as I shall always think of her, whatever her present-day House of Lords image: petite, young, exuberant. She was arrayed in a shimmery off-the-shoulder dress in extremes of black and crimson which yet was in perfect good taste; she was alert and at ease. She was also – and this is really true – interested in me and my work. She made me feel good.

It was Miranda, together with Felicity, who told me about the 'developments' that were about to develop. This is the situation, as I was given to understand it then. I was not, after all, alone in knowing about the lost pictures in the Soho studio. Miranda knew about them, so did Lord Troy, and so also did June Sutcliffe and her boss Sir Simon McKenna. No one but Felicity knew the specifics – exactly how many, exactly what was there – and she had no properly catalogued record. Driver was not the kind of artist who kept records. No one had yet gone to the Soho studio, and no one had seen a single one of the lost works 'in the flesh'.

The plan was for an exhibition concentrating on the first twenty years of Driver's career (before the final onset of his illness), including for the first time the lost pictures; it was to be sponsored by Coverlie's with unprecedented generosity for a show of what qualified as contemporary work. The Tate was to be the organiser, with June as the resident curator. Coverlie's involvement was to stretch to the financing of an especially ambitious catalogue which was to be edited by Miranda. I was to work with Miranda, integrating my knowledge of the known early work with the newly discovered material to produce a comprehensive catalogue and commentary. I was to be paid a salary to do this, and to be known as Coverlie's Visiting Scholar at the Tate Gallery. An office, properly equipped with computing facilities for the creation of a database, was to be set up by Coverlie's, liaison with the Tate to be ensured by June. It was she who was to oversee selection of the show (though 'in partnership' with Miranda). No mention was made that evening of a different kind of commercial relationship between Coverlie's and the Tate, or of anything but a normal sponsor's relationship between them.

The Tate/Coverlie's deal was, of course, to provide the impetus for a controversy whose political repercussions continued for two or three years. What, you might ask, was my position then? About a year after the exhibition I tried to answer my critics by writing a letter to *Art Data*. Here is the most relevant passage from it:

'I write in answer to the steady stream of criticisms of me and my involvement with the Jack Driver show at the Tate Gallery. I would like to make my position in regard to the political aspects of this exhibition clear once and for all. I am not interested in politics, *except insofar as they impinge on and are infused by the art which is my historical interest* [I went in for italics a lot in those days]. I am committed to

the furtherance of art, artists and history, and the how and
the why of the institutions through which I work are not
my concern. They are (sometimes) necessary evils.

'Everything I have done in the mounting of the Tate
exhibition, and the writing of its catalogue, has been *for*
Jack Driver. This is a position entirely consistent with that
of Felicity Driver, as she has repeatedly said. I regret many
of the developments that are still going on as a result of the
politics around the exhibition (I should emphasise, *around*
not *of* the exhibition); but I do not regret the exhibition. It
has been an immense success, and it has established the
name of Jack Driver for the future, once and for all . . .'

At the time, when the project was just starting, it was
claimed that McKenna himself was 'thrilled' with the
whole thing. I saw no sign of uncertainty in anything he
said or did. According to Miranda, the minister was there
on the evening of 21 April 1993 to seal the deal and he
had McKenna's 100 per cent backing. Why shouldn't it
have been like that? I had no misgivings. None. Everything
seemed so natural. As the 'recovery' became day by day
more keenly anticipated, and the enterprise of Coverlie's
was put into gear to power the art market back into
profit, it was clear enough that confidence would be
boosted by just this kind of collaboration between a
great national institution and a leading 'player' in the
marketplace. It was all so logical. The way I like history
to be. The virulence of the reaction of the more doctrinaire
of my supervisor's colleagues at Queen's came as a real
surprise to me. With Felicity's unreserved support and
co-operation, everything, then, seemed set for success.

Later that evening I met Sir Simon McKenna for the
first time.

He did not mention the exhibition, he simply said: 'Interesting to meet you at last. Kit Moss has been talking about
you. A safe pair of hands, he told me. I am sure he's right.'

*   *   *

There seems no better point than here to bring in the first two letters I want to use from McKenna's correspondence with Frew. They expose the heedlessness of my optimism.

McKenna is sombre. He is full of foreboding. He may not have been a plotter, in on the second-level agenda that had already been prepared, but at some level he knew the worst, even then.

A further brief gloss is required here. McKenna addresses Peter as 'Rag', because (Peter told me), the (bad) joke was (when they were first friends) that Frew was a 'rag' to everyone – everything from a toerag to a red-rag-to-a-bull rag.

16 April 1993

Dear Rag,

I feel unremittingly low. I see nothing but black. I have real need of all your colour. You have to keep my spirits up.

I often think now that I shouldn't have taken this job, and I can't go on with it. I've become a quisling to you all. I betray you and myself every day of the week from eight in the morning to ten at night. This job gets longer and longer. And the worst thing of all is that they've chosen Jack to be the thin end of the wedge, Jack who was so good at saying what needed to be said against them.

I had that smooth barrister Duncan in my office on Tuesday. I told you how he's used his friends to get Coverlie's involved with my plan to do Jack's show as it should be done. How do you justify an auction house committed to the winning of its 10 per cent plus 10 per cent (or more) on the highest possible prices sponsoring the exhibition in a national museum of *any* artist, let alone Jack? I did manage to make the point that we were in danger of becoming Coverlie's very own advertising agency. But he shrugged and said: 'Everything has to be seen in market terms nowadays. And what you're really advertising is Jack Driver. That's a good thing, after all. Surely the Tate has to be in the business of marketing the best in British art.' And then he said: 'We have to work for the next century, not this.' Chilled me to the marrow.

It's a fight just to retain curatorial control over the show. And I feel for poor, trusting June. She's bright and committed. I had no choice but to leave her in it. If I'd chosen anyone else for the job, she'd have been devastated. But she hasn't a chance against Miranda and Troy. They're people one can't help liking, even respecting, but that's why they're so formidable. It's so very nice when they're nice to one. Even austere, aloof Simon likes it. After all, they too care about Jack. And Miranda has talent; I promise you. It's true, even if I can hear you giving me hell for saying so. One's defences drop so low.

Sorry to burden you with all this, Rag. But I need you to keep my morale above sea level and my purpose firm.

I hope you won't stay out there in Dorset too long. All those deep blue people might invade your palette. Come back soon. I need a word.

Yours,
Simon

PS Come to the reception for Jack's new rooms on Thursday. It's only a three-hour drive. It looks spectacular. He was such a strong man, and such a good artist. But most of all, come to see the birds of prey gather in all their shapes and sizes. If I lose my rag, I'm there for the taking.

17 April 1993

Dear Rag,

Don't come on the 21st. I'd rather see Jack's rooms with you uninterrupted. There are some good aspects of this job. I don't want to lose them. One is the pleasure of looking at things one cares about with friends one cares about.

Simon

The two of them were, as I said, very close. After the

sombreness of 'Simon', the elation of my jottings offers a strong contrast. My jottings are as ever (when I'm not stating my beliefs) a record of something close to what I actually felt that evening; and they are the best evidence in my possession of what really happened. But I have to confess that I am beginning to wonder about the accuracy of even my jottings now. Why trust them more than my well-documented recollections? After all, why did I write them? *Was* it to say what I *really* felt and what *really* happened? And who did I write them for? There could have been only one person. Me. So this is me on me tapped out for me on my laptop. Is one always entirely honest with oneself?

It is so important to remember and to remember accurately. Felicity was with him. She knows what he did and how he spoke. She can bring me close to him. I have to get her to talk and then I have to remember. Everything.

She talked in the taxi (I haven't been in a taxi for such a long time. Christ, they're uncomfortable things). She talked about the late pictures in a way I could never have imagined. [Please note, for future reference, there's an article in this, an important one.]

She was all in a glow. Relaxed. I didn't have to get her to talk at all, she just started. She wasn't looking at me, she was looking at the shops and the pubs and the people going by as the taxi jerked and vibrated its way to the Tate. There were lots of pauses, and I interjected a few times (I can't get myself to shut up when I should), but my interjections didn't change anything. As I remember it, this essentially is what she said. It might as well have been a monologue.

'You're going to see two of the later pieces. They've hung them like pendants either side of *Catch Me*. They're the ones I've lent. The critics get cagey about the later pieces. But these haven't been shown before, and even Graham says they're good. I've never really been able to do Graham-speak – I actually can't understand how it works and what the words mean. Though everyone seems to be using them now in the college. They're ordinary words but they mean something entirely different when he uses them. You have to go on a course to be able to do it. At college they only just tolerate me not knowing; you're supposed to now. I don't see why I should. Anyway, he said something like: "They have all the heterological unpredictability of the best early work."

'I'm not quite sure what "heterological" is, but they certainly are surprising. And I'll tell you something. They're the ones from the end of his life I had most to do with. They came from the very last six months before they took him into hospital to die. I made sure Jack got them done. He needed me to. They're the only two I've kept from that time. I destroyed the others. I didn't feel they were properly his; he wasn't enough involved in them. Couldn't destroy these. They still surprise me.'

She was full of herself. Happy.

'I know the official line. I'm responsible for it, so I should. We did the late pieces together. I was the dogsbody. Did the processing and some of the more physically demanding painting and all that. Well, OK, that's true, and you could say we did do these two that way as well. But Jack needed me much more for these. Mostly he just sat there watching me, and I knew when he was with it and when he was against it. Everything came from him. And on the good days he did things. His hand is in them. Often. But these two are only hanging in the Tate this evening because of me. Sometimes, you know, I think I could have conceived them myself – he was so much inside me. The conception of them is surprising, but it follows on from the series of bodies falling through the air in tourist resorts at night with arc lights playing across them in the sky. You'll see what I mean. This was the next thing to do. The bodies float, they're buoyant. And it's dawn with the lights still on. A violet dawn. I could see what to do next as well as he. Almost as well, anyway. So you see, these are the two of Jack's last pictures which are the closest of all to me. I'm glad I kept them.'

She touched me. She goes in for touching people. Not just me. It isn't a sign.

'There,' she said. 'You're the very first I've told that to. You can publish it if you like. One day. When this is all over.'

Really good material. But there's not the time to make anything of it just yet. So much is going on. I've got my work cut out. Late Driver will have to wait. There are such *major* things going on.

The reception was a succession of 'major' events featuring 'major' figures, but again I lived down to my worst expectations. I am not a comfortable person among the enormously prestigious. I am the original tongue-tied idiot, who can only think 'awesome', and shrink inwardly away from it all. Is it possible to *learn* how to behave normally in OTT situations?

I have secret hopes that Miranda can teach me. I would love to be taught anything and everything by Miranda. And the thing is, I think I'm going to be. It all conspires to say so. It's like being thrown into some long-running blind date. But I'm not complaining. May it last for ever.

Before I met Miranda, I floundered from one sweaty handshake to another, incontrovertibly confirming my inadequacy with a succession of luminaries. Queering my pitch everywhere for ever. After I met her I was an irresistible combination of wit and fluency with the looks of the filmogenic. The trouble is I can't quite recall with whom I was pathetic and with whom I was amazing. The fact remains, however, she enhanced me at a stroke. And there were, in fact, one or two actual strokes that I couldn't help feeling might have been significant. She's another toucher, Miranda. There's lots of kissing and hugging and clutching, but once or twice I'm sure the touches were significant. We shall see. Let's hope I've been experiencing something more than just well-honed social skills.

And she's rich. And she knows lots of the 'right' people. She is, after all, the niece of Sir Harold Browne. Enough said. I realise you've decided that you don't care about money, Roland, that you're going to be a Great Scholar, and that means being above money and influence. But be honest with yourself, Roland. It does make a difference. It isn't half attractive. There's no need to *refuse* money and influence. That makes being ethical downright stupid. The thing is not be motivated by it, but not to refuse it either. That's what being above it all means, surely. I've decided not to say no to *anything*. I'm ready for *all* opportunities. OK?

I shall revel in how it all came out, or at least began to come out. Here it is, the conversation as it happened between me, Felicity and Miranda. I think it went like this:

'Here, Miranda, is my great find. Roland, meet Miranda Browne, Coverlie's star of the contemporary firmament. We three have a great deal to discuss together.'

'Hello [this is Miranda, of course, I was as usual struck dumb]. You and I are going to be seeing rather a lot of each other. I'm really looking forward to it.'

'Well [she immediately assayed a miracle cure and I could speak], so am I, if we really are going to.'

'I haven't told him yet, Miranda. Shall you, or shall I?'

'You should know that Felicity is being very brave. She is giving away all her secrets. She is letting out all those lost early pictures to make the kernel of what is going to be *the* Jack Driver exhibition. This is the moment. There never was a better one.'

'He knows about the pictures. He doesn't know about the exhibition.'

'But the exhibition's where he's going to make his name. It's where, Roland, you and I together are going to make our names. Agreed?'

'I don't know what I'm agreeing to [it was lovely playing dumb; she played up to it beautifully].'

'You're to be the art-historical know-how that makes a professional job of putting this exhibition together and producing the catalogue on Driver to end them all. I'm to be your unforgiving editor. And it's all going to be in the venerable name of the Tate gilded by the bottomless pit of Coverlie's money. *D'accord?*'

'Oh, I'll agree to that. Anything else?'

'Lots. But most of it can wait. Come and meet my crotchety old boss. He's young and charming really. Well, young*ish* and charming. Coming, Felicity? I'm taking him over to meet Troy and Duncan.'

And she did and I did. So at least I know I was amazing in the presence of Lord Troy and the minister. With Miranda at my elbow I can do anything.

And I *shall* do 'lots'.

On 22 April 1993, the Tate issued a press statement. Variants on it appeared in all the broadsheets:

A retrospective is to be held next year of the neglected but major British artist Jack Driver. It will feature a significant number of hitherto unexhibited and unpublished works from the important early period of Driver's career, and will seek to establish him as among the most radical and inventive artists working in Britain during the late fifties, the sixties and into the seventies.

As we approach the twenty-first century new opportunities exist for all the arts. This exhibition is to set in operation an entirely new kind of partnership between a national museum and the private sector. Coverlie's is to take a key role in the financing of the project and above all in ensuring the highest levels of scholarship in the catalogue for the exhibition, which is to be researched by a newly designated Coverlie's Visiting Scholar at the Tate Gallery. The young historian selected is Roland Matthias of the Department of Art History at Queen's College in the University of London, who is

to work with Miranda Browne of Coverlie's. Dr June
Sutcliffe will curate the exhibition.

The *Independent* quoted Sir Simon McKenna thus:

'On the brink of the twenty-first century, I see this as
a watershed exhibition, our way into an exciting and
secure future.'

Jack, are you listening? You sometimes didn't, when
you didn't want to hear. There was and is no alternative.
I think I know what you would say. Something like:
　'We are different. These people are nothing to do with
us. They're alien. We have to define ourselves *against*
them. We cannot be seen to depend on them. Socialism
can never be compromised by their money. Neither can
I. My pictures are commodities freely bought and sold.
But I sell no obligations with them. I am obliged to no
one. I sell because I live in a commodity culture and I
cannot work if I do not sell. But I sell no more than the
material object, the area of canvas and the image upon
it. And I have left the image there to act, to redefine, to
subvert. It sows doubt and confusion, and it leaves me
with nothing. The Lord Troys and the Miranda Brownes
are against us. They cannot be with us. Leave the images
to do their work. We can have nothing to do with them.'
　Close enough? But the world has changed. You have
to understand. Socialism is in hibernation; perhaps for
fifty, a hundred years. Perhaps hibernation is death. It
feels like it. You saw the beginning and nearly the end of
what now seems to be set to go on for ever. Remember
what you said in seventy-nine, when Thatcher got in?
Give them two years. Give them two and a quarter
million unemployed. Give them the heat of the unions
backed by the solidarity of anger. They will be swept
from power. And then what you said in the Falklands
election: this means nothing, patriotism unhinges the

working class, they go blue, but not for long. You saw them in a third time before you died, with even the miners broken. You must have begun to realise. I've seen them elected again, when everyone said they were finished. They're still here, after forced devaluation, continuing catastrophic unemployment, crisis after crisis of their own making. And who says they can't come back next time? Nowadays they're sold like any other product by their friends in advertising and PR, and no one else can sell themselves so shamelessly. The world has changed, once and for all (you wouldn't even recognise the left of the Labour Party as Socialists). I have to live with, not against them. If I don't, your work and you will disappear, like the Socialism you thought would always be the future.

So I've signed my pact with the Devil and the deepest of the deep blue seas. I've seen what that cold fish McKenna, with all his laudable principles, refuses to see (even though he's deeper than most in the deep blue sea), that we have to *use* them to get under their skins. Their money can make the pictures continue to act, and if the pictures continue to act their values will continue to crack. You would have seen that it is the only strategy, I know you would. Forgive me, Jack. I know what I am doing, and I shall do it with all the commitment I have left in me. I shall bring you back through this exhibition. You the Socialist, in your work. Just be grateful that you don't have to shake the hands of Troy and Miranda and the Tory Ministers of the Crown. Leave it to me. Trust me.

I have begun to trust people. When I met Roland, sitting bolt upright in your chair, I trusted him. Brenda agreed with you – she always took your side. She called him 'shifty'. 'The one in the corduroy jacket,' she said. 'The shifty one. The one who kept saying thank you.' But I trusted him, and I was right.

Roland isn't a Troy or a Miranda. He isn't one of them. He could be one of us. He lacks strength. But he wants to have it. He lacks many things. He has no flair; he has sacrificed imagination to something he calls discipline. You wouldn't have given him house room as a pet, Jack. But I think I can make him become strong. And anyway, now, in this world, for your future, I have no choice. I need a Roland. If not this one, then another.

Dead artists need their cataloguers. If you won't listen, I have to be brutal. They do. Even you do. This exhibition always needed its Roland. To make you and everything you did factual, to make it all *real* again. There have to be properly recorded events, people, pictures, places, dates. All with the proper apparatus of substantiation. I have been the substantiation. I have supplied the events, the people, the places; you have supplied the pictures, which I authenticate. You need a Roland to make things dead so that they can come back to life again. Me and Roland are going to bring you back to life out of the fifties and sixties and seventies.

And me and Roland need Miranda and Coverlie's, do you see? And we all need the Tate to bring you back to life in the Grand Manner. The only appropriate manner. So we all need your inaccessible friend McKenna. He's still a Socialist. I know it. But he regularly sups with the Devil. He has to. He is doing his best for you, but he cannot do *the* best for you without Miranda and Coverlie's. It's the way it is. The nature of things.

If you don't believe me, then take a look at him. You could have done in the presence of your own pictures, the day I gave Roland to Miranda at the beginning of all this. But *you* wouldn't have accepted the invitation. Not your kind of thing at all. Important people in dinner jackets and long dresses because they were 'going on somewhere'. Well-connected people, trained to be nice to each other and in certain circumstances to those who show the proper respect. Well, McKenna sopped them all up with his charisma and was entirely consumed by them in return. Even he has sold his soul. You wouldn't have resisted in the end, Jack.

And what has it given you, my capitulation and McKenna's? It's given you *your own rooms in the Tate*. Already. Even if you would have thrown their embossed invitation straight in the pedal bin, I bet you would have sneaked in to have a look at your own rooms in the Tate. You'd have bullied me until I got you there, and then you would have had me push you all round a hundred and more times before you asked to go home.

It was hung by a brown, furry, bright-eyed creature called June Sutcliffe, Dr June Sutcliffe. I know you always want to know who's done the hang. I'll say it for you: 'The way they hang the work tells me about them: what they've learnt.' I think she's not learnt too much yet, but she *is* learning. It's not that easy to hang well in the new 1930s neo-classical Tate – they've stripped it all down to its architectural basics. The received wisdom when they did it a few years ago was that it's ravishing. Be that as it may, *you* never did sit well in that kind of frame. Makes it look as if they've tamed you at last.

Thank God, she didn't make you look too tamed. She hung you in terms of contrasts. Early and late together, confrontationally. You as unequivocally you alongside you *and* me – when I was doing things for you. I let her hang those two collages that made you smile, the ones we called *Floating Towards the Ocean: Sunrise I* and *II*. And she hung them like side panels bracketing *Catch Me*. It was the best thing she did.

My success was to put Roland and Miranda together. Almost as successful a juxtaposition as hers. Thick, stolid, dependable Roland in his unsuitable suit and compromise tie, and slim, flighty, ruthless Miranda in all her top-notch regalia. He with his 'pleased to meet you', and she with her 'really thrilling' and '*molto bene*'.

They went rather brilliantly together in the neo-classical setting. Better than I could have hoped.

I don't know whether you'll ever forgive me. That evening I consigned you to Roland and Miranda and to the public relations strategies of the great and the evil who masquerade as the great and the good.

But I did it willingly. I did it for you. And I knew I did right.

Felicity, of course, from her text of 20 May 1994. Felicity treating with Jack and the Devil. Well, I suppose we all were.

The principle of contrast works well, don't you think? Me with and against Miranda; early with and against late Driver. I've constructed this chapter according to the principle of contrast. The next chapter will be, however, a single homogeneous whole. Or as nearly as can be. Another contrast. I shall turn back to me on me for me: to my laptop tappings. And this time, since I should be behaving much more to type (as a cataloguer), I shall give the sequence of extracts that I have decided to present as exactly as possible; I shall date each extract as conscientiously as I did at the time.

Let us continue to believe in the facts. You should ignore my moments of scepticism. Academics need to have them, even in early retirement. But I assure you they pass.

3

Cataloguing the Past

15 June 1993

Today I sat looking at lists on my VDU. They seemed so complete. I felt meticulous, exact, in control. There was the number, the title, the date, the medium, the measurements (in inches and centimetres), the technical observations (if any), the provenance (sometimes no more than 'artist's collection'), the exhibitions (where, what, when), the literature (with page numbers and plate numbers).

I've just begun. The lists are developing. They will get longer, as fact piles on fact. And every item will be checked, so that there is not a single error. I have started with the pictures that I have worked on already. The pictures in the Soho studio will come soon. I am to be allowed to see them imminently. I shall need to scrutinise, measure, check catalogues and books, read articles and ask questions. I shall have to ask Felicity many, many questions. And then they will be answered and the lists will be completed, absolutely, without possible omission.

So far just the preliminaries. But already so many satisfactions.

Just one omission. One uncertainty. I can never ask questions about the one who came before Felicity, Louise Jay. Felicity's eyes warn me off. The secret is to ask only the questions that can be answered. So I do.

There is no state of contentment to equal certainty. Graham said to me: 'Make the catalogue. We can all

feed off it. No one else has the stamina to do it.' But I
don't need any stamina for the job. No job could give me
more than this one. I understand now that what I love are
the facts. First, I am mesmerised – Driver hypnotises me –
then I have to know everything that can be listed, tabulated,
checked and cross-checked about what mesmerises me.
Facts are wonders. I shall always be a cataloguer. It is
my *métier*.

   Miranda and Felicity have mesmerised me. I shall
catalogue them.

1. Miranda Mary Frances Browne

Born 9 April 1963

h.63in.; w.122lb.

Brunette, pale of feature, with a slight tendency to darkened
olive on the cheeks and temples; traces of dark down on
forearms; tiny crescent scar on right cheek

Eyes: wide, as if surprised; coffee brown (Costa Rica)

Build: slim and flexible

Voice: never *entre deux*; soft and suggestive or loud and
excitable (sometimes aggressively shrill)

Dress: never *entre deux*; overstated or understated; expensive;
taste for lipstick in delicate shades of pink or sudden shades of
vermilion and crimson

Provenance
The Brownes of Withenshaw, Wilts., on father's side; the
   Hankey-Dawes (Lord Clowberrough), on mother's side
Educated Benenden and St Andrew's
Coverlie's Diploma
MA (Hist. of Art), London
Coverlie's Contemporary (from 1992)
Unmarried

2. Felicity Katrina Driver (née Ryan)

Born 2 February 1950

h.68 1/2 in; w.147lb.

Brunette with faint streaks of grey (some traces of dyeing); dark complexion, with freckling of the arms (evidence of determined summertime exposure to the sun)

Eyes: direct, uncompromising; green/grey; brows, thick and shapely, subtly expressive

Build: elegant yet strong

Voice: measured and firm; almost never raised

Dress: young; usually tight jeans or full skirts; likes open-toed sandals which can be thrown off; little make-up, except around the eyes

Provenance (established with difficulty)
Joseph Ryan (heating engineer) of East Croydon, Surrey, and
   Kay Warner of Lytham St Annes
Carshalton Grammar School for Girls
Kingston Technical College
Camberwell School of Art (BA 1971, 1st class)
Married Jack Driver (painter), September 1971
No children

Well, there are the facts. All of the facts? Without omission? Two women presented as two objects. Objects of what? My gaze (it would be said). My imagination. My appetite for facts. These facts feed my fantasies as much as the facts about Jack Driver feed my fantasies. My fantasies of control.

   I see no harm in listing them.

16 June 1993
I have to confess (it's even more necessary to confess when it's to yourself): there is a hidden agenda behind my last entry. I'm humming to keep my courage up as usual. I needed to satisfy myself that cataloguing is an OK activity, bona fide, and certainly the right activity for me.

The reason, of course, was/is Graham. He knows now he's been left on the outside. He knows that Felicity, Coverlie's and the powers at the Tate have decided to put together *the* Jack Driver exhibition without a word in print from Graham Copley. And he is not pleased at all. I am his target, his comeuppance figure, his fall guy, the one who is going to pay for the sudden, catastrophic decline (as he sees it) in his fortunes. He, after all, was the one, he never tires of insisting, who 'reinvented Jack Driver. Reinvented him for the nineties.' How could I be in and he be out?

Graham's trained his heaviest guns on me. And yet, at the Meredith opening, he made a point of coming over and saying all these supportive things.

'So,' he said, 'what's it like to be taken to Felicity's bosom? To be the new confidant?' And I said (ineffectually), 'Terribly nice.' Whereupon he said, 'Terribly nice? My dear, she'll eat you alive.' And I said, 'She's a vegetarian.' And he laughed like a drain.

'You *are* getting relaxed, Roland. You're making jokes.'

She isn't actually a vegetarian; there's no evidence of it that I know. But wasn't it a good joke? Made me feel quite talented for a moment.

Then there was more on how important I was becoming: 'You are now *the* source, *the* intermediary between Driver and his audience. You're the one who's finally broken through Felicity's defences. *Félicitations.*' And then all that stuff on the 'contribution' the catalogue would make, and 'the need' for people like me with the 'stamina and the dedication' to do the work. And yet he's gunning for me. And he knows I know it.

Because the fact is that, even before the Tate's press statement (even before I knew my new role in the world), last week's *Format* carried an article signed Graham Copley which was targeted straight *at* me. There can be no doubt about it now; someone told him what was in the air and he tried to shoot it down before it could get going. There was not a single mention of my name (why give me free publicity?); but I was the rabbit in the headlights all right.

> The word is out that an official catalogue covering much of the work of Jack Driver is to be commissioned by the Tate Gallery and Coverlie's. It is to be published to accompany a major exhibition of Driver's work from the late fifties into the late seventies. Quite apart from the question of bedfellows – is it quite *moral* for the Tate Gallery to get into bed with *professionals*? – the notion of a catalogue on Jack Driver seems to redefine the limits of the inappropriate.
>
> To catalogue *any* of the work of Jack Driver is to destroy it, to squeeze all the force out of it, to render it limp, debilitated, impotent, to leave him (the *indestructible* Driver) in the enfeebled condition that finally killed him (the fallible body). A catalogue is a sclerotic condition forced upon the catalogued. Paintings, especially Jack Driver's paintings, can never be reduced to their mere, factual objecthood. Because, in Max Ernst's phrase, they are beyond art [actually Ernst said beyond *painting*; accuracy isn't Graham's strong suit]; they are also beyond death.

I have to defend myself to myself. And there's only one way. To keep repeating the satisfactions of the job.

But there might be another. To cut up Graham's article and make it into a nonsense collage. Rob it of its power. So here it is, in pieces. For my own delectation.

'*Everything* in Driver is political.'

'A moment in which the historically codified regimes of art practice were disrupted and collapsed.'

'As Kristeva says, all transgression of conventional rules, even on a formal level, is necessarily [wait for it] political.'

'His statements are Baudrillard's hell of connotation.'

'Radical transgression . . . heterologically transgressive . . . radical interdiscursivity . . .'

'A hell where significations have become so plural that they can never stabilise, a hell of "residues, superfluities, excrescences, eccentricities, ornament and uselessness".'

'He was bored by genius and bored by art.'

'Driver's work goes beyond even the last vestiges of empiricism . . . Driver's work constitutes a signifying activity which is simply not tied down to the fine art network . . . Driver's work closes off even the *possibility* of explanation . . . Driver's work is a postmodern phenomenon of radical [wait for it] interdiscursivity . . .'

'A polyglot heteroglossia . . .'

'Driver in the nineties leaves no more room for the diagramming of synchronic structures. The body of utterances that makes up Driver's corpus operates indefatigably *against* description, explanation, structures of all kinds. He strikes at the very basis of the catalogue, of any syntagmatic project of any kind: at the list, the lexicon, the taxonomy, the very cartography of conventional art-historical practice. That is why he is indestructible. And that is why his work will never be contained in a catalogue.'

I leave the last statement whole. It freezes my heart. It fascinates me. It may be true. And even when I read the argument in pieces, I am withered by the look directed at *me* behind every word. And the onslaught still threatens to overwhelm me with its names and phrases and unassailable technicalities.

I repeat soothing thoughts over and over again, and go on humming to keep my courage up.

19 June 1993

Much better to swamp my brain with the life-enhancing, bona fide activities surrounding Miranda (h.63in.; w.122lb.) and Felicity (h.68 1/2in., w.147lb.).

Curious. Why has Felicity insisted that I have an office in her house too? She's squeezing me into a corner of her living room, so that I will be in regular sight of that chair. It's all so obviously unnecessary and so obviously inconvenient. I have my own corner in the Tate library, and I have a perfectly good office in Coverlie's headquarters building, even if it is only accessible by the most rickety staircase to have survived in all the West End, and only just fits me, a couple of filing cabinets, a few bookshelves, the computer and Miranda, when she honours me with a visit (which is increasingly often).

What an odd life I shall lead, between Bond Street and Barnes, my briefcase stuffed with files and photographs and three-and-a-half-inch disks. I shall travel between alternate VDUs and the women that preside over them; between the domain of Miranda and the domain of Felicity, each with its keyboard and its screen. Pursuing Jack Driver back to the sixties, and even to the fifties. Consuming my millions of bytes with lists. Trying not to think of Graham Copley, even torn into pieces.

Tomorrow I see the lost pictures in the Soho studio. Miranda will be with me. But Felicity will be the mistress of ceremonies. I shall meet Driver as very few have been able to for near on thirty years, as even the brilliant Graham has not.

Felicity will introduce me.

She says that there is more than the paintings to meet in the Soho studio. She says he is still there, in the paintings. Sounds a fairly ordinary sentiment; the kind an artist's widow might share with one. But she also says – and the way she says it tells me that she is both not serious and *deadly* serious – she also says that he is ready to enjoy visitors now.

20 June 1993
The address is 2 Orlando Street. It's an ordinary early nineteenth-century brick house off Charlotte Street. Not

Soho really. Pretty close, in fact, to Bloomsbury and Queen's. Very appropriate, the lost Drivers have gone to ground in Fitzrovia, not far from the haunts of Wyndham Lewis and Roger Fry, Omega and all that.

The ground floor of the house is a bookshop run by a severe man with an Asterix moustache (despite the season, he was dressed in an enormously bulky coat with a tartan scarf, like a French yeti of Scottish origin). He seemed somehow stranded among his old copies of *The Golden Bough* and his primers on the tarot. He and Felicity exchanged nods (otherwise he didn't move a muscle) and we were ushered through into a yard full of builders' materials. As we exited, his voice followed: 'Take care.' He spoke vintage Etonian.

The studio, if it can be called that, is a long shed-like structure, reached by a wooden external stair from the yard. It has skylights and big windows overlooking the yard, but it's too hemmed in on all sides by walls to be well lit. The skylights are covered in mesh and scabby with dirt.

In the twilit interior Felicity had arranged five canvases around the three sides of the space facing the door and the windows. They were standing on untidy foam cuttings and behind them other canvases were stacked. The floor otherwise was a mess of rags and tins, as if someone still worked here, or no one had cleaned it up after Driver's death (but that's not possible, so someone *does* work here . . . Felicity?). The walls are dominated by visible plumbing and messages (ancient as far as I could see), written or painted directly on to the cracking brown surface: 'Camilla tomorrow, 8.15 . . . Tube to Embankment, change to District via Earl's Court, Fulham Broadway' . . . various telephone numbers . . . and then, in small, deft letters, but in a red that shouts out, the single word: 'Viva'.

I wondered aloud whether Driver was responsible for the graffiti. After all, he couldn't have written anything much at the end of his life. But Felicity said he got the place before the illness, indeed before she had met him, and only

worked here briefly. The Barnes studio, the one converted
from the garage at the bottom of the garden, became the
working studio. This became a store for the litter from the
past. Here ranged around it was some of that 'litter'.

I have to remember it exactly as it was. Going from left
to right as we looked in from the door off the stair, there
were the following (the titles are as given by Felicity, I
have indicated where they are consistent with exhibited
works):

1. *Star in a Sunny Sky*, 1960 (the one canvas against
the left-hand wall – I *think* it's 1960, taking account
of the fact that the star theme is said to have begun
to interest him in that year; but it's *very* early for such
an American image, so I wonder about that date and the
star theme altogether). A single star as if lifted off the
American flag, set on a Mediterranean/Californian sky
blue, above a pair of nylon stockings (empty and wrinkled
but evidently manufactured for young legs) which are
juxtaposed with a rather stiffly presented man's tie, with
severe stripes. Below on a dull grey ground, the words:
'Shoot the stars.' An extraordinarily prescient work if it
really is 1960.

2. *Let Go*, 1961 (against the facing wall, with two other
canvases) (exhibited with this date at the November 1961
show at the Delaney Gallery). Two open palms (hands)
above an open palm tree; an aerial view of the Pentagon reduced to something remarkably like a post-Cubist
geometric abstraction, splattered with Pollock drips. The
letters that make up 'Let go' disassembled among the
elements of the picture, to be reassembled by us.

3. *International Style*, 1963 (exhibited with this date in
the 1964 Tate International). Hovering De Stijl planes in
primary colours, floating across and part obliterating fragments of dancers, sixties dancers, depicted in contradictory
manners, part caricature, part flashily painted fashion
magazine illustration, part screen-printed photograph, all

set in a photographic grey space (cf. the Teddy boys in *Catch Me*). The dancing of the dancers does not involve touching but is highly sexualised. Across the bottom, in a joined-together hand, scruffily brushed (cf. early Hockney for the calligraphy): 'A Portrait of the Tragic' (must refer to 'the tragic' in Mondrian, i.e. the world without the perfect resolution of 'Truth').

4. *On a Trip*, 1963 (exhibited with this date at the New York show of the same year and reproduced in the catalogue). Another Mediterranean/Californian sky, this time streaked, as if with rain, by those ubiquitous Pollock drips, above the grim greys of the bare concrete (*béton brut*) of the Parkhill housing estate in Sheffield (very comparable to the use of the Pentagon in *Let Go*, and similarly done as if a post-Cubist abstraction). In the sky, a tiny hot-air balloon floating, bright vermilion against the blue (something I've never noticed in the reproduction). How strange. Makes me think of Max Ernst and balloons.

5. *Six-six Vision on the Big Screen*, 1963 (alone against the right-hand wall – I'm guessing at the date, but it seems to relate to *On a Trip*, almost as a pendant – same large scale, same vertical measurements, same range from Mediterranean/Californian sky to Sheffield grey; not previously exhibited or published to my knowledge). In the grey here, holiday villa architecture, with fragmentary bathers, looking oblivious to the cold of the grey palette. One bather (male) pointing upwards, like those figures that point to the realm of the Kingdom of God in Ascensions and Transfigurations and so on. The red balloon again, floating in the blue sky. And a ladder. This time I think, not of Ernst, but of Miró: the ladder that hangs flimsily down from the Toulouse-Rabat aeroplane in Miró's *Catalan Hunter* (a quote?). Strange that Felicity didn't put this picture alongside *On a Trip* to bring out the relationship. Powerful and surprising. Very odd, these Surrealist quotes. Not sixties at all. Perhaps the most remarkable thing shown us.

Any observations? I was struck by the repeated confrontation of Mediterranean/Californian skies (a dream of sunny skies and freedom) and English grey. And then the balloons . . . What about the balloons?

There may be a major theme here. Keep it in mind.

We were there for half an hour. Felicity said that this was enough for the moment. She believed in seeing things a few at a time. That was the way to absorb them. I was reminded of the Cardinal del Monte and the curtain. She said it was a pity everyone who was interested couldn't see them. But I don't know whether she meant it. I'm sure it was Graham she had in mind. I've noticed with some delight that she tends to enjoy keeping Graham out.

The excitement has robbed me of adjectives. I can only record what was there. Record and describe. And make observations to develop later.

Touch yourself. You're real. It happened, Roland.

Magic.

6 July 1993

I should touch myself again. I look at the walls around me, stuffed floor-to-ceiling with paperbacks, except where the imitation Art Deco wardrobe intrudes on the heavy sense of impecunious seriousness, and nothing seems quite real any more. I live in a fantasy as I prepare my lists. All that is real are the lists. But the fantasy *is* magic. And it has an added dimension.

I'm to have a 'fling' with Miranda.

'Nothing serious. That must be understood. Absolutely. The slightest sign of possessiveness, of wetness of any description, above all of love, and it's finished. Really finished. *Compris?* A fling, Roland, in the freest sense of the word. It's very good for working relationships, I've found.'

That's not Miranda. That's a caricature of Miranda. Or is it? She said something very like that; but the thing about Miranda is that you can never take her out of context.

Anything she does or says, just described or reported, can seem absurd; but it all fits together, and when you're there, you only glimpse the absurdity; now and again. And despite all the excesses, somewhere underneath, there's a calculator working with absolute control.

Take her temper. Her temper is absurd. It's completely OTT; but it works for her. Thank God I met it first at second hand. In fact, so far I've only met it at second hand. Let's try to remember how she used it that first time. The victim was Gerry; the victim is often Gerry, it seems.

Gerry Dworkin is her male secretary/assistant; he is very good with everything to do with computers but relatively incompetent with people. (The world seems to be full now of backroom people with Ph.D.s but without the ability to relate to their fellow human beings; they're all bracingly kept on short-term contracts. Like me.)

I find Gerry rather endearing. He is extremely tall and, because Miranda is relatively small, he always seems to encounter her with head slightly bowed, like an unnaturally tall Japanese. Except he's American. He speaks transatlantic the reverse way round to Diane Schwartz; with infinite *English* deference. That is, he anglicises his preppy East Coast tones in an approximation of what he imagines is an Anglo upper-class drawl. When he and Miranda are together, the impression I get is of tall and short, fast and slow, always out of sync with one another. Yet, generally they get on; and they get on, I now realise, because she loses her temper with him and so he does *everything* for her; and he does everything for her because he loves being frightened by her temper. And, of course, she understands and manipulates the whole complicated psychological process.

It was two weeks ago. She had been subjecting me to her warm, welcoming smile (which is something else I have to reflect on – the uses of that smile), so I was not prepared for the change that would occur when she picked up the phone and dialled Gerry. Everything about her changed. Her usually delicate movements, became sharp and angular. She was all elbows in the small space. Her eyes shrunk to glittering creases in the hollows beneath her brows; her entire face seemed drawn tight. It paled. And her voice came in short, screeching bursts.

It was astonishing how I ceased to exist. She was only aware of Gerry; the need to *tell* Gerry. I can't remember what it was about; what he had to be told. I just remember that within an hour, the phone had whinnied, the deferential Gerry was at the other end, and whatever *had* to be done had been done.

Like everything about Miranda, her temper is immensely cost-effective. It would repay the most exigent management consultancy analysis (one thing I forgot to put in when I catalogued her the other day is that MBA of hers from Fontainebleau; perhaps she followed a course there on 'the managerial uses of the temper-tantrum').

Then what about her smile? That beaming 'you're wonderful' smile of hers? The charm I'm having to get used to at first hand. At least some of the time. It's just as absurd; it's just as OTT. But it works too. I know it works, because it works so well on me. How can it work when I'm perfectly aware of just how absurd she is? She's a caricature and even *she* thinks she's a caricature. She said so. She said so when she made her move.

I should try to remember what happened in the days before she made her move. She used the smile a lot then. And she used other techniques too: flattery and titillation. She started with titillation; went on to flattery and then made her move. Everything she did in her titillation and flattery mode was absurd (and came with the smile). Yet here I am, caught by it. Unresisting. Her methods *are* irresistible.

Her mode of titillation is to talk about other men, when in close proximity. The office being distinctly cramped, she is always in close proximity on her visits. I can *feel* exactly where she is. I'm looking at trannies [this was late-twentieth-century professional slang for transparencies]; she's right there, at my shoulder, looking at them with me. I can feel her breath against my ear, and the warmth of her flexible left thigh very close to hand (she always wears those beautifully tailored business suits for women that move rubber-glove-like with the body). Both my hands are occupied, however: one holding the trannies; the other frozen rigid with excitement. It's like a rerun of my well-worn Felicity fantasies, except with a younger woman making all the right moves.

'Such a pity we aren't going to be printing in Milan. I did tell you about Paolo, didn't I? The single most Italian Italian in my life. Really fabulous. Hair so black it's blue – blue, I promise you; and a wonderful furry mat all *over* his chest. But it's his tight little bum that turns me on. I love tight little bums on men. Such a pity about Milan. What do you think? Talking about blues, I thought the blues for the sky in *On a Trip* were a little over-cool. What do you think?'

If the sexes were reversed, I'd have a prima facie case for harassment. There can't be many female 'bosses' about who 'relate' to their 'subordinate male colleagues' like this. I'm not sure I like being harassed. It's unsettling, her style of harassment. At least, it was before she made her move. It made me feel I was being invited to do something, but left me unable to do anything at all. Electrified but paralysed. Overheated but frozen. I don't know why.

The flattery, though, I like the flattery a lot. Let's hope that at least the flattery continues. It's direct and thoroughly unabashed. Far better than Diane Schwartz's. Why should I doubt it? It's like taking vitamin pills. Builds me up, sustains me. Not much substance, of course, but wonderful for floating on. No need to resist, Roland. Let yourself float, nice and easy.

The time to record was last week, when I suggested that I might write to one or two American universities and offer a lecture, once the exhibition was up and running. That was the best of all, because there might actually be some substance in it. Something I can continue to float on for months.

'We'll be *sending* you, Roland. You don't have to write to anyone. You're going to have a really lovely time being a well-known academic "name". People who put together a major artist, like you are, do become well-known academic "names", you know. No one will be able to even *think* about Jack Driver without breathing your name too. There'll be conference keynote addresses, public lectures, television appearances. Hectic stuff, but thrilling. Tremendous fun. After all, it's odds on now the show will go on to the Modern in New York. We'll *have* to send you.'

'The Modern? The Modern!' [How else could I react but stupidly? It was the first time I'd heard. She almost completely ignored my stupid incredulity, of course.]

'Yes, the Modern. Satisfied? Just think . . . all those special dinners and embarrassingly fulsome introductory speeches.'

'How do you mean?' [That was more like it – a good linking interjection to keep it going.]

'You know: Ladies and Gentlemen, it seems only days since the name of Roland Matthias first emerged into the public eye. Matthias is the new name to reckon with in a field bristling with innovation. After Copley, Matthias.'

I drew the line at that. I actually felt myself flush with delight when she said it – 'After Copley, Matthias' – but the very pleasure of it made me feel uncomfortable.

'It's not a question of Copley or Matthias,' I said. 'We're different. I'll never be a Graham Copley. I'm not a critic. I'm a cataloguer.'

She laughed her sharp little laugh at my discomfort. 'Don't be so magnanimous, Roland. Graham isn't at all magnanimous, I can tell you. You're not *a* cataloguer; you're *the* cataloguer.'

Then, with a careless perspicacity that took my breath

away, she added: 'I bet you've begun an entry on me. You would catalogue anything that breathes, as well as most things that don't.'

But I'm going too fast, because that was when she made her move. That was her cue. Typical of her to supply it herself. There's more to get down, though, before I'm allowed to have the pleasure of remembering how she made her move and how I responded. There *is* more to Miranda.

There are, for instance, the bits in between, the bits when she gets the job done, the bits when she's a competitive bitch of an MBA. Now I think about it, the bits in between were what made it so difficult to know if the messages in the smiles and the titillation and the flattery were real or fantasy. How could I know how to react the way she wanted? One moment I'm electrified or basking. The next I'm being driven by a driven professional. Because that's often what she is: a driven professional.

The chat stops. She even switches languages: her slightly old-fashioned socialite idiom is extinguished by a cold, efficient art-business idiom. She usually signals the switch, but it's always unnerving.

'We've work to do [the signal]. Get on the phone to Strathern's, I must have those valuations for the pictures Ormonde has in his vault. I need them for June tomorrow. Did you get in touch with archives yesterday about *Making It*? I *must* know who has it now . . .' etc., etc.'

All the 'simplys', 'reallys', '*d'accord*s' and so on that are the normal decoration of her chatty mode are ruthlessly excised. She speaks without adverbs and adjectives. Her smile is chilled off her face.

And she makes me do things. She's begun to make me do things (or not do things) that worry me. Little things. But they worry me. I'm 'not to say a word to June'; I'm to 'let June think . . .'; I'm 'not to give the impression to June . . .' It's always to do with 'us' and June. And June's a friend. A colleague even.

In the end, I suppose there's one question to put concerning Miranda: is there anything about her that isn't either merely efficient and cost-effective or absurd – that is, when one's able to step back a little from the heat of the often overheated moment? May there be about her, at some deep, partially concealed level, frailties?

I don't think I'm going to get close enough to find out. But the answer could be, yes. She obviously loves to dominate and manipulate, but she also has a need – a real need – to be dominated. There's something about the way she refers to 'Henry Troy' (with whom she is daily in touch). Verbally, and even in her movements, she makes herself especially little when she talks about Lord Troy. If 'Henry' is to be phoned or visited or consulted, she becomes – as far as she could be – a timorous and small person who wants to be patted and stroked. She seems to need to think of him as supremely masterful. And yet, none of this could be suspected when she is with him. Then, she is more winning in her vivacity than ever with anyone else. She is almost totally made up of her welcoming smile; it continues and continues in one long echo. He is, of course, the single person in her world she cannot control with her titillation, her flattery and her temper. That much is clear. He's a kind of 'daddy' figure for whom she loves to 'behave'.

Then there was the way she made her move. At last, I can get down the way she made her move. The thing is that there was something oddly touching about it, though she couldn't have been more direct to begin with; it wasn't just absurd, even when I think about it now, at a little distance.

'What heading am I catalogued under?' she asked. 'Probables? Possibles? No-go areas? My guess is no-go areas. Well, you're wrong.'

'Wrong about what?' [There wasn't much else to say.]
'Do you find me attractive?'
[After a pause.] 'Yes.'

'Well then.'

I still didn't understand. I had only the vaguest feeling that this was after all the delicious moment which would cure me of my paralysis.

'Honestly, I shall have to spell it out. If you find me attractive, let's have a *thing* together.'

'A thing?'

'A fling, if you like. That's a better word, isn't it? I have my terms though.'

And then she spelt them out. I'm not to fall in love with her. That's the main thing. And I have to realise that her ambition is to have a career before she even *thinks* of getting involved properly with anyone. But meanwhile she likes flings.

None of that was touching, of course. It was merely cost-effective. What was touching was the moment she realised the absurdity of it. I wasn't at all frightened of her then. I wasn't excited either. I almost liked her. Even though – but for the single '*n'est-ce pas*' – her language was at its most stripped-down.

'There you are. You see, all I want is to get things straight. It's the way I am. It's how it has to be in business. You put your cards on the table, *n'est-ce pas*? Just like that. If you're ambitious like me, there's no other way. I suppose you think I'm not a person at all. A caricature . . . an invention of Julie Burchill's. Don't laugh. Don't deny it. I know that's how I come over. Glamorously involved in glamorous money-making activities, offering myself for lovers on the side, but definitely not for love. Well, it's sort of true. Sort of true. But only sort of. And I promise you, no one invented me; there really is something here. Someone with needs. It's just I have to be sure before I even begin to let it out. So I keep myself to myself, at least to begin with. OK?'

What a bizarre, convoluted outburst from one apparently so sure of herself. From one so *successful*.

That was the moment my paralysis was cured and I

kissed her. Wonderful, how she ate me up. Such a strange moment, so passionless and so full of passion.

You see, I can't really get her down at all; she escapes me. I think it's because she's so far away from me, so much from another world. She's all glittering surface effects which act to obscure and mislead. I can't see how so many absurdities can come together, or what there is really there behind them. I can't even guess; she won't ever let me see enough to guess.

(When I say that, inevitably I think of Felicity. Felicity is someone I think of as from *my* world – someone extraordinary, yes, but from my world. I think I might begin to know Felicity, and – something that unnerves and thrills me more than Miranda ever could – I think she might allow me to.)

Miranda and I are not to be seen together as a couple in public. We are, in fact, to live up to the caricature. Whatever 'relationship' we're to have is to be entirely a matter of work and sex; at least that's what she says. In the afternoons. Office hours (which are sometimes to be stretched a bit to accommodate us).

As a sixties specialist, I seem to remember that there used to be a magazine for sex-lovers called *Health and Efficiency*. This is to be all about health and efficiency. How can I call it anything but the caricature of a 'relationship'? There may be pleasure too, though, lots of it. So why complain? There's nothing actually wrong with either health or efficiency. And there must be something about me that turns her on. Excites her. When all's said and done, this has to count in the credit column. Of course it does.

Gerry nearly shot me dead with the look he gave me when we arrived for the inaugural session just as he was putting his screen and keyboard to bed (my office is 'much too cramped'). He clearly knows the routine. What an active little person the formidable Miranda is.

Well, I find them acceptable terms. I have accepted them. As you've always said to yourself, Roland, this is an area in which you are not inexperienced. Looks can be deceptive.

So, I'm to have a fling, and I'm not to fall in love.

I'm a cataloguer. My interest is in facts, nothing more. I told her so.

I can do without love, if she can. For the moment.

7 July 1993

The flexible Miranda has set me to thinking about sex and red balloons in blue Mediterranean/Californian skies.

Surely Driver can't have been as banal as that? Towers, men's ties with severe stripes, opening palm trees, float-ing balloons, floating bodies in the sunrise. Dreams of freedom?

Or are the pictures actually just (just?) about sex?

A quite recent symbol of the male organ in dreams deserves mention: the airship, whose use in this sense is justified by its connection with flying as well as sometimes by its shape.

In men's dreams a necktie often appears as a symbol for the penis. No doubt this is not only because neckties are long, dependent objects and peculiar to men, but also because they can be chosen according to taste – a liberty which, in the case of the objects symbolised, is forbidden by Nature.

Steps, ladders or staircases, or, as the case may be, walking up or down them, are representations of the sexual act.'

(Sigmund Freud, *The Interpretation of Dreams*, trans. James Strachey, Harmondsworth, 1976, pp.472–75.)

Or sex *and* creativity? Remember Jung. An unthinkable thought: is the hidden subtext in the lost-and-found work of the great proto-postmodern, who finally did away with the myth of the potent, creative genius, actually just sex, creativity and . . . Genius? The thought makes me smile.

What an irony to relish. Nothing, ultimately, there in Driver but the finding of the self, in sex.

But then . . . If it really was so, could I actually say so, in print? Even with a long footnote on Freud and/or Jung to give it weight and intellectual tone, as above, it doesn't bear thinking about. No one would/*could* take it seriously. The sacred cows would roll over and die in *herds*. Graham would publicly consign me to blood sacrifice. And the sky would fall out of the firmament.

You can't afford to think the unthinkable, Roland.

· 4 ·

Tenderness

You would understand, Jack. You always understood
about desire. I have started masturbating again. It's
mostly about you, but not all about you. There are one
or two highly desirables who pass through my field
of vision and get rather excitingly mixed up with you
when I fantasise (they do not include Roland). You can
understand, can't you? It was such a long time ago,
now. But I still remember enough. And it's only when
I need to remember that I do it. It's not very often, just
sometimes. I wonder why I feel this is a confession. It
shouldn't be. There's nothing to be guilty about.

If desire atrophies so does imagination. You used to
say that, and it's true.

I masturbated the day I went back to the Orlando
Street shack. I unrolled that stripy mattress and dreamed
a little and did it. It was three days away from exactly
one year ago. It was an important date: 20 May 1993. It
started the habit again.

You see, I hadn't been back to Orlando Street for
something like eighteen months, and your pictures
have been covered up and stacked away for years now.
And when I went back, it was to plier off the staples
and uncover the five I'd chosen to show Roland and
Miranda first. You'll want a list, of course. I can give it
to you later, but it included two of the red balloons that
we used to dream about together. Flying away.

Going back brought the desire back. The shack
brought it back. Climbing the stair (it still hasn't
collapsed); penetrating the darkness; feeling you there.
I remembered so many things and I want to remember
them again with you now. I want to write them down.
This writing down of my talks with you is something
that I need now. It settles me.

I know you understand. Though you always hated
remembering. Be patient with me.

It's obvious enough, I suppose, that, although the text of
20 May 1994 is given a single date, in fact it was signed
at the end of a period of weeks, perhaps even more than
a month. The assumption must be that, throughout this
period, Felicity quite often sat down, probably before
she went to bed, and wrote. Though none of her earlier
'conversations' with Driver survive; she seems to have
done it before, after all. Consider the way she says: 'This
writing down of my talks with you . . .' 'My talks with
you . . .': there could be no other implication.

The extracts I've given you earlier seem to have been
written appreciably before the excerpts I am going to give
you in this chapter. I have been able to establish four
clearly separate sections, in terms of style of address and
content. This is the beginning of what I regard as the last,
and the reference to the anniversary of our first visit to the
Soho studio (there were to be others) establishes without
a shadow of doubt that it was begun on the 17th (the visit
was three days from exactly one year before). It is also
the longest, some seventeen pages in all, and so it cannot
have been written in its entirety at a single sitting. That
the last part of it was not written on the same day as the
excerpt given above is again decisively established by its
content, as you shall see; it is, of course, underlined by
that 20 May date.

I've decided to give you this part of the text quite fully,
though in a sequence of excerpts. In fact, the seventeen

pages of the original are themselves unusually broken up. There are some six hiatuses in the manuscript, that is to say, unexplained gaps of a half-page or so in the writing, as if one part ends and another starts.

She seems to have written with compulsive intensity over a very brief period of three days, and as she did so her mood veered and swung. There are passages where she writes so fast that the writing nears illegibility.

At the time, of course, I was entirely unaware of her state of mind. She remained the warm, approachable and yet slightly distant figure she had been from the beginning. If anything she acquired a kind of serenity: an impenetrable calm which I think I interpreted as a calm which had come with the making of her decision.

The thing about the shack is that everything there is impregnated with the way we were before the diagnosis.

You took me there at the very beginning. The stripy mattress is still the same stripy mattress. The writing on the walls is still yours, except for my 'Viva', which seems to get redder with time. The camping gas is still there on the old trestle table where you used to prepare things. I can smell those picnics of ours: the Campbell's mulligatawny and oxtail soups, the Heinz spaghetti and baked beans, the vegetable mixes I used to do with aubergines (an almost unaffordable luxury in those days) and *petits pois* and onions and peppers and tomatoes, to eat with the sausages from Schmidt's in Charlotte Street.

Charlotte Street is much more Greek and Italian and Indian than it was before. But, of course, you were there to see that Italian place (you know, Tavola Calda it was called) move in when Schmidt's moved out. But it still feels like Charlotte Street. So just walking from Goodge Street tube makes that time come right back.

I'm on my way to see you. I'm back at Camberwell and we're entering a new decade, trying to ignore all that 'Attitudes become Form' stuff (or was that afterwards?). And I'm bursting just with the idea of 'uncovering you'.

The thing is that when I'm in the shack, I feel it's not just the shack, but the garage too and the *baraque* in the Monts du Cantal. It feels like all the places where we worked and made love together and felt good. Everywhere. They were always shabby places impregnated with the smell of my vegetable mixtures and our solvents. I don't get turned on by thinking of the rooms where we roomed or the beds we slept in. I get turned on by the thought of those shabby places. The shacks.

Look, Jack. You're just going to have to accept it. The past is too strong. It's too much my present now. Going back to the shack in Orlando Street has released me. I am going to remember. I am going to be nostalgic. And that's it. You'll have to lump it. You can be nostalgic with me if you want, but I'm quite prepared to do it all by myself. There's no need to sneer. That's all there is to it.

I'm going to sit and remember and write it down. Then there's no danger it will ever be lost, is there?

Let's remember the start of it.

You frightened me – but then I told you that. Your work frightened me; it was so intensely felt and so *intelligent*. And you were unpredictable, abrupt, hurtful. You said my things were 'slight'. You accused me of 'faint-heartedness'. You said: 'There's no ambition in any of this.' And everything I did in that little corner of the third-year studio in Camberwell was for you. I was carrying on a kind of conversation with you in my head and on the canvases, except you weren't with it at all. I thought my work responded to you on every level, and you seemed to hate it on every level.

So, when I caught sight of you in Schmidt's I was shy.

And when you said: 'I'm the only one allowed to buy *bockworst* here; it's the best in London,' I had no humorous reply.

And when you said: 'You must live around here. My studio's just round the corner. Let me give you lunch upstairs,' I was lost immediately. I knew what was going to happen; I knew the 'reputation' you'd got yourself after Louise left you; I wanted it to happen, and the strategist in me started calculating how to accelerate the preliminaries. I was frightened but very excited.

I can't remember how I stopped being frightened, but I know it was upstairs in that warren of a restaurant, in that deserted corner we found, long before the preliminaries were over. You talked to me as if I mattered; as if I was no longer 'slight'. I probably should have remembered your reputation and kept my defences up. But I took them all down, and let my eyes and my body do an awful lot of my talking. I used to think I was good at that. Very articulate.

Then there was Picasso, Françoise Gilot and Carlton Lake. In the shack you kept talking about that book by Gilot, *My Life with Picasso*, as if I was Gilot which, of course, left you being Picasso. I shouldn't have allowed you to get away with that, but you used it to say such enhancing things that I just basked inwardly and let it go on as if you really were Picasso.

'You remind me of her. You're taller, of course. She's quite small, so they say. But you have her kind of supple, firm beauty, and the intelligence in the eyes. You have appraising eyes. I enjoy having them appraise me.'

So much for offering open invitations with my eyes. As you saw them, it was me *appraising* you. It obviously didn't work. Except it did work, in a funny way.

'I don't know about her painting. But Françoise

Gilot is an intelligent woman with her own strength.
She's the only one who could stand up to that arrogant
Spaniard. And walk away. It's not just your eyes that
tell me about your strength. I know people through their
painting. And yours I know all about. It's good. That's
why I'm unkind to you. A teacher is always cruellest to
the best students. And you're a good painter. I've seen
it, especially recently. I wonder if Gilot is as good a
painter as you.'

Fancy me being Françoise Gilot and you being
Picasso. The cheek of it. But then you never cared
about the risk of presumption, did you? Christ, your
ego was powerful then. You seemed untouchable,
you yourself. And yet not many besides poor fools
like me rated you then. You had buried yourself in
teaching and anyway you were dead and gone in the
face of Greenberg and Stella and Newman and Olitski;
and even more dead and gone in the face of all those
conundrums and photographs stuck to gallery walls
and called sculpture. All you had was the admiration
of a few old friends, a few unfashionable critics and us
nonentities, that and your indestructible ego.

The cheek of asking *me* to seduce you. Unrolling
that mattress in that so deliberate way of yours and
reclining on it, then saying, cool as you like: 'Uncover
me.' Maybe it was the hundredth time you had said it
to an appetising young student; there was a practised
smoothness about the way you said it, not a second of
hesitation – 'Uncover me.' And I knew at once that the
'me' to be uncovered was the one that lay behind the
zip; your 'little big man', your 'other me', the one you
said was for touching. I can grip it still in my mind.
Desire has a size and a temperature.

Tenderness. I gave it to you, and you gave it to me.

They say sex is not love. It was then. They were one
and the same thing.

You surprised me afterwards. You were hesitant.

You asked to see me again as if I would say no. As
if you were *afraid* I would say no. And you actually
laughed when I said yes. Laughed with pleasure and
triumph.

I loved you best in triumph.

It was me who found the *baraque*. Give me credit for
that. You probably weren't even aware of it, but you
used to issue orders for the summer, just as if I was
some kind of agency. Finding somewhere to go, writing
the letters, paying the bills, all of that was beneath
you. It was me who had to work and worry at it, and it
was work and worry. You ought to know, Jack. I still
resent it.

And you were so unnecessarily cantankerous about it.

'I want somewhere quiet. No neighbours. At least
three miles outside the nearest village. And I want lots
of nature. You know, birds and bees in abundance. It's
time to plan our summer idyll. You need to be sending
for those brochures, Felicity. Chop, chop!'

Except the first year we went, it was at least an autumn
idyll, not summer with all those school holiday families,
so finding something was a little easier. But there were
lots of difficulties. It had to be spacious and cheap as
well as entirely solitary. Nearly impossible instructions
for any agency. *Gîtes* in France don't come very often
without neighbours, and if they do they're great big
places – *manoires* and *domaines*. They don't come
cheap. They didn't then and they don't now.

It was a real achievement to find the *baraque*. A
place that sounded simply perfect for nearly nothing.
All right, it was nowhere fashionable like the Dordogne
or Provence; it was 'away from it all, in a remote and
unspoilt corner of the Massif Central'. But it came over
as a purpose-built studio specially for people like us (of
whom there are not very many): one big space with big
windows and 'pretty sleeping accommodation for up to

four in a purpose-built gallery above a purpose-built, if basic kitchen', the whole set back from a small *route départementale*, surrounded on three sides by forests 'of beech, pine and fir, full of wild mushrooms, *myrtilles* [blueberries] and wild raspberries'.

You couldn't have been more horrible when we arrived. I still find it difficult to forgive you. I was disappointed too. After all that driving in all that heat behind caravan after caravan in a car packed tight with wood for stretchers and rolled canvases and books, to lurch to a halt amidst stinging nettles and brambles in front of a kind of elongated cowshed constructed of roughly plastered breeze blocks surrounded by walls of conifers and know that this was home for two months. I was gutted too. And all you could do was moan and rant.

'It's ugly, Felicity. *Ugly!* It must be the *only* place for rent in France that *is* ugly. What about all those charming photographs I saw in those bloody brochures of yours? Not one of them was ugly. This is some achievement, Felicity. And all hemmed in by a regiment of firs. Why didn't you *check*? Didn't you *bother* to ask for any photographs, for fuck's sake?'

And it was the best place ever. You always said it was the best place ever. The ugliness was just its way of keeping the secret. And the regiment of trees was just a screen to keep hidden the most lovely, the most alive forest in the world. The place buzzed and hummed with life: all those insects high above, where the light was broken up and re-formed into those little bursts and slivers that were impossible to paint. None of that could ever be represented, but I can still *see* and *hear* it in my head.

You never said sorry for how horrible you were, but I forgive you. Things were too good then to waste time with *real* resentment. Besides, I love your anger. It's a part of the way you were. Before the illness. And before the illness it was just anger; not rage. Of course I forgive it.

I loved the mornings. The broad daylight of eight o'clock making patterns through those rather thickly stitched lace curtains on the unplastered pine planks of the wall. Your head and arm very brown on the pillowcase and sheet. Kissing you. Touching.

Clambering down the gallery stair, avoiding those silly newel posts at the bottom with their over-elaborate turned profiles (there to make us believe an effort had been made with design). Trying to listen to Radio Four crackling over the forest with news of Arsenal and Everton and Manchester United, and of terrible things like oil price hikes and torture and death in Chile. Sitting on the side of the bed as you slurped your instant coffee out of those enormous French breakfast bowls. Catching your mood, grumbling about Arsenal (as if I was actually interested), threatening to pack up and leave immediately 'to do something about Pinochet'. Sitting quietly in front of those still resolutely urban images set up in the big room. Work in progress. Thinking about the day to come and what was to be done, before setting to and doing it. The quiet intensity of doing it together in that sparklingly lit space with its red tile floor covered in pots and rags all mixed up with strands of grass walked in from outside. Our shacks have always been a mess.

The few words exchanged as we worked. The moments taken for touching. The concentration of being and working in such immediate proximity, of knowing that everything I did and you did was instantly scrutinised and judged.

That was the right routine. Work and sometimes tenderness in the morning. Satisfactions taken to the nth degree. Then those long walks in the forest, getting lost under the buzz of the insects. Seeing so much, from the endlessly subtle browns and yellows and reds and grey-greens of the autumn mushrooms, to the umbers, whites and greens of lichen and moss, and the sharp reds of the rowan berries. Seeing and storing it up, though none of it ever seemed to get into the paintings in the big room.

That first year we were there in September and October (to miss the tourists, you said). There was so much in the forest: its fruitfulness was a kind of careless abandon, offered us as if time was short. You said that too.

We learnt about *girolles* and *ceps* and *rusula*. The *girolles grises* were the great secret, hidden beneath moss and rotting branches, and then, when one had been spotted, revealed in hundreds, massed together in dense grey-green profusion, soft and dank to the touch as we picked and picked. We took home bulging, subtly scented bags of them to fry in butter and garlic, and made whole meals of them.

We thought about and talked about city things and city art in this indelibly green place. We painted city paintings for city people. And we lived in a shack on the edge of a forest with the city shut out.

You used to *try* and get us lost. I know you did. You loved the sense of being enveloped in that deep green place with all its secrets. You used to spread out your arms and put your head back and laugh with the feeling of the place. 'Who would have thought that I could feel like Caspar David Friedrich? Here I am *being* Caspar David Friedrich.'

The forest never frightened me. Even when you convinced me we were finally lost, once and for all. It was a benevolent place where we were always protected. If there was savagery there, it was the best kept of all its secrets.

There was no savagery between us in that place. That ugly shack and the forest around it was full of our tenderness.

Is that how you think of it, Jack? Or am I just nostalgic after all? Silly, sentimental Felicity.

To get the facts absolutely clear: Driver's MS was diagnosed in 1978 (he was not chair-ridden till 1981), so the time before the diagnosis that Felicity is remembering in this fourth section of the text dated 20 May 1994 is between her third year at Camberwell, when things first developed between them, i.e. 1971, and the diagnosis, i.e. 1978. My summing-up from the surviving evidence is that the first stay in the *baraque* was between early September and late October 1973 (the Pinochet *coup* against Allende took place on 11 September 1973 – and Camberwell's records show that Driver took the autumn term off from his part-time teaching); the first stay seems to have been followed by three others in the summers (July and August) of 1974, '75 and '76 (he resumed his autumn-term teaching from 1974 to 1980).

The *baraque* is still there, though no longer let as a *gîte*. It was not initially a cowshed, but had some storage purpose for the peasant-cum-forester, Monsieur François Courtine, who owned it, before he converted it for the tourist market (which consisted almost exclusively of the Drivers in this area, and which has almost disappeared now). It is to be found four kilometres outside the village of Saint Genès-aux-Bois, surrounded by the *Forêt domainale de l'Hospice de Saint Genès-aux-Bois*, in the foothills of the Puy Marie. You can reach it easily by car from Aurillac. It's now near enough a ruin. The stinging nettles have finally taken over and last time I was there one of the shutters had been battered in, but the newel post is still there and so is the little gallery where the bedroom once was, though the furniture has all gone.

Interesting to me is the corroboration here of my belief (previously suggested in an article of 1995 in the autumn issue of *Art History*) that Felicity started to work with Driver in the same studio space long before the illness got under way. Other information I now have, as you will see, makes it clear that they worked together in London too, at the Orlando Street studio, probably from as early as 1971.

Felicity the painter, of course, has never had the attention given Driver. But one should remember her relatively well-received shows at Sam Dorey's gallery in 1976 and 1980. She certainly had powers as a painter. And before the illness began to take all her attention, she had an identity as an artist; which was revived early this century by the exhibition of 2000. It was, predictably, always considered subordinate to Driver's, and very closely related, but it has been taken seriously, especially over the last fifteen years.

There are not many instances in the history of modernism of two artists working so closely together and sharing their studios. One thinks of Robert and Sonia Delaunay in Paris from before 1914, and Ben Nicholson and Barbara Hepworth in the Mall Studios in the thirties, but they seem to have been the exceptions. Felicity, of course, has never made a reputation comparable to Sonia Delaunay or Barbara Hepworth.

The forest – a recognisable Caspar David Friedrich forest – does, in fact, feature in the work of both of them during the mid to late seventies, though not from the period of that first visit. It is used as a foil against urban images, much as the Mediterranean/Californian skies were in the early sixties. There has been a tendency, led by Graham Copley, to interpret it as an imagery of entrapment, confinement, capture (Masson's and Ernst's forests are routinely invoked – French Surrealism again, Driver was a surprisingly French artist when you put him in the English context of the sixties and seventies, though not when Bacon is remembered). Felicity's text makes me wonder. Could it not be more an imagery of concealment, of hidden pleasures and beauties? Even (if I recall my speculations about Freud) an imagery of hidden sexual release.

The *baraque* never features in the painting of either of them. Its long, low structure, with its grey corrugated iron roof and its dirty off-white walls, is indeed ugly. Old photographs from Felicity's scrapbooks show that when they rented it, the windows had smart, newly stained wooden frames and shutters, but the effect even then was of holes arbitrarily placed, like missing teeth (see, for instance, Fig.6 in Volume 3 of my full *catalogue raisonné*, the volume in which I deal with the work of the seventies).

One can understand Driver's dismay.

I was in the *ancien étang* just now. I went back there in my mind. I walked up the long path into the forest, stopped at the junction where the five paths meet, walked along the piled-up logs, tripped and fell, let you pick me up to feel your strength, and turned up the middle path on the right with your hand resting on my shoulder.

We walked up past the big patch of *myrtilles* that ripens early, and between those dense, dark plantations protected by rock outcrops where the path narrows and the tractor ruts are full of water, and then suddenly we came out into the great space of the clearing where once, they told us, there was a lake in the very depths of the forest, the *ancien étang*.

We didn't find it till our second year, did we? And when we found it, we couldn't believe its fruitfulness, the sheer extravagance of it: the masses and masses of little blue *myrtilles* on bushes that seemed like forests of fruiting bonsai trees; the masses and masses of raspberries tangled up in their brambles; the blackberries that replaced the raspberries when they finally shrivelled away in the sun; the scent, as if the fruit were gently stewing in the heat.

I went back to it, because I wanted to remember one very particular time, a time that suddenly came to me not long ago, but all mixed up, like unedited snippets of film. I thought that, if I walked all the way there in my mind, the bits and pieces of memory would sort themselves out. And they did.

On that particular afternoon (we set off when the Radio Four news finished, just after three), it's important to remember exactly what I was wearing. I wanted shade for my eyes, so I put on my new dark glasses and that wide straw hat of mine with the silly little flowers attached. But I wanted sun for my arms, because you loved them to get browner and browner, and so I put on my red singlet with no sleeves. I wore that rather capacious brown skirt you called my peasant skirt, and those tie-up sandals that were always being inconvenient.

When we reached the *ancien étang* we sat down together on the grass beside the path and you began to undress me, or that's what I thought to begin with. But you only took off my sunglasses and two items of clothing, first my hat and then my sandals. You were so very painstaking untying the stupidly intricate lacing of those sandals. You made it into a little ritual, one which had to be done in precisely the right way. You made it seem very significant.

Then you lay on your back in the grass, and I lay beside you.

'Don't shut your eyes,' you said. 'They have to stay open against the light, however bright it is. And listen, there are so many tiny sounds, so many living creatures. And touch. Touch with the palms of your hands and with your feet. That's it, lift your knees so that the soles of your feet can feel the grass. Let it scuff and tickle. Don't touch me. Feel the warmth of the ground. Feel it come up into you.'

We lay there silent under the great blue glow of the sky for a long time. Not touching each other, but touching with all of our senses.

Suddenly you're on your feet and laughing. You're a shadow against the sky. I can see no eyes in the shadow.

'Christ, those insects tickle after a while. I had one of those little spiders with the very long legs climb all the way from the tip of my big toe right up to my knee. Took real self-discipline not to end its days. Come on, get up. The ground must be beginning to feel distinctly damp after all this time.'

Then you made a strange gesture, one I almost never saw you make at any other time. It was a kind of pushing motion, as if you were clearing something out of the way.

'Did you really believe I was a pantheist after all? What a thought: Jack Driver pantheist.'

You said it lightly, to make it seem unimportant. But I did believe it. I knew it then with absolute certainty, and I still do. 'Jack Driver pantheist.' Yes.

There are some things, Jack, that you would never admit. Your only way out is to make a joke of it. That was always your way.

At least I've admitted my nostalgia.

One day you will have to admit your Romanticism. Or I shall have to do it for you.

Today is the anniversary of 20 May 1993. I went back to the Orlando Street shack exactly twelve months ago to the day. I sit here in Barnes and I'm back in Orlando Street with you.

Twelve months ago, I walked out of Goodge Street station. I took the usual route up Tottenham Court Road, opposite Heal's past that clock on the National Westminster Bank (it was 1.45 p.m.; I had three hours leeway before they were to arrive). I turned left, then into Charlotte Street and right into Orlando Street.

The littleness of the terrace houses, the griminess of the London brick, the cracked and faded shop fronts,

the cloying smell of restaurant kitchens, pasta and
curry mixed, it was all as familiar and welcome as the
crackle underfoot of the paths of the *Forêt domainale
de l'Hospice de Saint Genès-aux-Bois*. I felt at
home again when I opened the door of the Fabulous
Fabritius's little shop. He was pleased to see me after
all these months; so pleased he actually offered me
a cup of the stewed coffee from his filter machine. I
declined, and went straight across the yard and up the
stairs. I wanted to be back again.

I saw the old mattress and unrolled it. Dust exploded
from it and hung on the dim air. I took one of the old
brushes. I masturbated. I was never very hygienic about
that kind of thing. But, of course, I've told you that,
unless you've forgotten. I don't keep things from you.

And then I began to look at the pictures. One by
one. I heard your voice talking about *On a Trip* and
Star in a Sunny Sky and *Let Go*. You are there in that
place, Jack, in those pictures. You and your voice have
somehow stayed with them.

I heard you say: 'They can mean anything. But, for
me, they meant something very particular, something
only you and I perhaps will ever know.'

Well, in each and every case, I haven't forgotten that
something very particular. Your voice still tells me,
when the image is back in front of me. But no one will
know, shall they, Jack? Not what we know. It's not
the meaning of the images; it's *our* meaning. They can
think what they like. And they will.

I've let the pictures out, all of them. Soon, in a
matter of months, they will be on public view in
the Tate Gallery, numbered, titled, dated, given all
their specifications, catalogued, *raisonné*-ed. My good,
obedient, unimaginative Roland will have done his job
down to the very last verifiable detail. The Graham
Copleys of this world will spin their interpretations,
and the others will puzzle and ponder. People will

talk endlessly about the 'collage principle' and the subversion of convention and the exposure of the very structures of language. We've heard it all, haven't we? But nobody will know what we know about them; nobody will know about us and them.

I let them out into the world again, Jack. But I shall keep their secrets. And ours.

The second and longer of Felicity's texts, the one she left undated, which, as I shall argue later, was clearly written in the months following the noise of the exhibition's opening while the works were all on view, has told me something of what she had in mind when she wrote this last passage.

My response to the undated text (which I read only considerably later) was that my own speculations in my jottings, all those years ago, had actually been in the right direction after all. I felt vindicated, and I relished the impact of what might be exposed. I thought of the ladder, and the necktie, and the red balloons in the sky floating out of sight.

I thought of the idyll in the *baraque* and the forest, I thought of sex and creativity, of Jung and Sigmund Freud and Nietzsche (a name which will return), and of 'flying away'. I thought I must, after all, have been right.

But this is not the moment to release the undated text to your scrutiny. You will have to speculate with me, as I did when I first read the text of 20 May 1994, and wait for Felicity, finally, to give up at least a few more of her secrets.

5

You Can't Trust Anyone Nowadays

The day after I got back from that first visit to the studio in Orlando Street, I wrote something triumphal. The moment seemed like that. What had happened was big and important; it seemed that I too was really to become big and important. Something triumphal was needed from me. So I tried. I wrote about a 'momentous discovery' . . . 'perhaps the most important unpublished and unexhibited group of British paintings in existence'. I wrote about 'uncovering Jack Driver for a new generation . . . in an area of London redolent with the history of Britain's art and artists'. I announced that my belief in 'the persistence of Genius' was vindicated, 'against all that the postmoderns have tried to tell us'. I was satisfied with myself.

Be grateful that I've decided to give you no more than snatches of it. One passage, however, I shall give you whole. It's me being a clever commentator towards the end. Here it is.

I have only one observation to make with regard to the five paintings seen yesterday afternoon. It should be taken as no more than an hypothesis, which will perhaps be sustained by a more wide-ranging rereading of all of Driver's work of the early sixties. It concerns the red balloon to be picked out against the blue skies of *On a Trip* and *Six-six Vision on the Big Screen*.

Could that tiny balloon not be read as an image of sexual liberation? We are after all in the decade that followed upon the *Lady Chatterley* trial. And, if it is to be read thus, could it suggest ultimately that the question of creativity and sexuality did not elude Driver in the late fifties and early sixties, a decade when other artists, like Allen Jones and Richard Hamilton (*Crysler Corp*), were indeed exploring that very connection in terms of a fragmented commercial imagery which is not unrelated to his?

My hypothesis is not that we have here the mere *expression*, in banal terms, of a sexualised creativity conveyed by the simple-minded introduction of a Freudian imagery, but that we have here Driver's *ironic*, knowing invocation of such a notion, through its *representation*.

We have here, I would suggest, a wistful, a poignant game with the idea, not that Genius does exist, but that it *might* exist, because it can be represented.

What do you think of that? Clever, well clever-ish anyway. But hollow. You see, it was the Matthias-as-Great-Art-Historian-in-the-Making's way of dealing with all those unpublishable thoughts about Freud in a manner acceptable for the post-Copley market. In those days, if you were going to be against Copley and critical theory you had to be for it too; and you certainly had to speak the language (hence Felicity's slight embarrassment at not speaking it). You had to speak it even in semi-private, when writing for Posterity (i.e. you).

Pretty thin stuff really. Take something simple, make it complex and slightly mystificatory and above all so reflexive that you can't be accused of an elementary belief in self-expression, and it becomes just about acceptable. Especially if you can unravel tortuous arguments around the term 'representation'. What most strikes me now about the whole text is my absolute certainty – my failure to doubt – and the nudge-nudge, wink-wink intellectual shiftiness. Intellectually I have always been in a mess. *Tant pis* (as Miranda would have said).

It's much better to get back to editing the evidence, the material which, so reassuringly, can always be armoured with nice corroborative footnotes. So that's what I shall do.

The principle of contrast demands something completely different. Where in any of this, you may ask, are feet to be found firmly on the ground? I feel the need for the cooling powers of McKenna's letters. We deserve a good dousing in his scepticism. McKenna certainly continued to harbour doubts. Serious doubts. And he kept 'Rag' informed of them.

Frew, incidentally, was preparing for one of his biannual showings in midtown New York, hence the transatlantic flow of letters that follows.

24 June 1993

Dear Rag,

How have your pictures travelled? Monica said everything was 'impeccable', when she got in from the overnight flight yesterday morning. She said you were beginning to hang the show already. One has one's spies.

Here there are developments. I've seen transparencies of five of the 'lost' Drivers. They include *On a Trip*, which, of course, one has known well enough from the reproduction in the 1963 New York catalogue.

I wondered, while you're there, if you could contact Mackray's and get hold of the catalogue; ours has gone missing in the library here. I gather it is rather a rarity now. I want to compare the reproduction with the painting itself as it now survives. June and myself are to go and see the five for which we have the transparencies (including *On a Trip*) in ten days' time. We're to go with Miranda and her new escort, Matthias (the 'expert' Kit Moss has supplied to act as

Coverlie's stooge). Miranda and Matthias have seen them already. I'd be grateful to have the Mackray catalogue (or a colour Xerox of the reproduction) by then. Please try for me.

I'm sending by separate cover the transparency that's been made from the picture in the studio. Have a look at it alongside the 1963 reproduction yourself. Tell me what you think. No need to return the transparency; it's a duplicate.

One has to confess that Felicity is rather admirable about the whole process of revelation. She rations it. Jack trained her well, she wants things to be *looked* at, not just glanced at. The first five are to be followed by another five and then another, and so on. I gather there are fifteen plus to be seen. You would approve.

And she refuses anything that smacks of sensation-alism. She says she won't have the press in until the arrangements and the texts for the show are completely under control. She wants everything to proceed with the utmost 'level-headedness' (as she puts it). She seems to believe that Coverlie's stooge will supply both the exper-tise (Queen's-trained, etc.) and the level-headedness. The man has a tendency to sweat (damp handshake); not a good sign. I shall reserve judgement until the pressures build. One must be fair to him, of course. But the pressures will build.

Incidentally, how many of you knew the Orlando Street studio? It's odd to me that it has remained such a secret. You were already close to Jack in the early seventies, before I really knew him, so I assume you must have visited him there. Tell me about it. The place interests me too. There is something distinctly mysterious about the way it has suddenly emerged out of oblivion, without anyone ever having mentioned it before. I don't like mysteries. Exactly why and how was Felicity able to keep her secret so well?

Sorry always to be asking favours and questions. Apologies especially for asking a favour which isn't strictly necessary. I know I could have Mackray's faxed direct for the catalogue or the image. But I have to confess, Rag, it's a way of keeping you in on things. So I can have the benefit of your great wisdom, old friend. I know you'll understand.

Yours,
Simon

28 June 1993

Dear Rag,

Very many thanks. The colour Xerox of the 1963 reproduction arrived today in good time. It confirms what I thought, and I'm glad you've noticed it too, although I suppose, with both images in front of one, it's obvious enough. The red balloon wasn't there in the picture when it was shown at Mackray's. One can only suppose that some time, probably soon afterwards, Driver just painted it into the sky. What I didn't tell you is that the picture has a partner. It's called *Six-six Vision on the Big Screen* (a strangely unwieldy title for Jack), and it has another red balloon in the sky, this one complete with a ladder hanging down from it (Miró, Ernst, etc.).

Mysteries. Those balloons, one feels, don't quite gel with one's idea of Driver in the early sixties. There's something surprisingly finicky (and Surrealist) about such an addition (they're painted in a finicky way too by the look of it), and then the imagery seems almost *obvious*. But it is all explicable in the end, I suppose. I shall ask Jim in Conservation to have a close look and tell me if there are clearly late passages of overpainting including the red balloon.

And then there is the fact that someone like you can deny all knowledge of 2 Orlando Street. I find it *distinctly* mysterious that Jack should have had a studio where he kept completely incommunicado from everyone, despite what happened after the departure of the awful Louise Jay and the break with Ivor Selwyn. Felicity says that when she met him he liked to have a place where he could feel submerged from the world; and that anyway he only worked there for a couple of years. But that's what makes one just the slightest bit uneasy about all this: we have to depend so absolutely on what Felicity says and what Felicity chooses to show us as his work. She is the seal of authenticity. It is her word that says what is true and not true. And when these 'lost' pictures are finally gathered together (all fifteen plus of them), they will make up a very significant proportion of the known early work of Jack Driver.

That red balloon has started me asking questions. Did Jack add it? *Would* he have added it? And, if he didn't, what of the other balloon? And then, what of the other painting altogether? Is it his? I've enclosed a transparency of the other painting. Tell me, does it raise doubts in your mind?

I don't like mysteries, and I don't want there to be even the remotest chance that we are putting together an exhibition that is, in some way, to some degree a fiction.

I need to hear soon.

Yours,
Simon

6 July 1993

Dear Rag,

I write with some relief. What you say has helped me clear my mind of the doubts. Thank you.

First – yes, I did intend to infer that Felicity might actually have been in some way involved in *making* the lost paintings. Yes, it did occur to me that she could even have gone beyond adding things and painted an entire 'early Driver' . . . or two, or three . . . One knows well enough that she was, and still is, a good painter, and she was as close as anyone could be to Jack. After all, there's no secret about her role in actually fabricating the last things, even if one has to ask the question, was she ever as good as *that*? The red balloon set me thinking.

The fact is, though, that in the name of Jack, Felicity is capable of anything. Over the last few months I have begun to realise that. One is always struck by her openness and her strength. She has always been so direct. You ask her for something, and she says instantly yes or no; there is never anything like evasion. And yet she is opaque. Her motivations are very deep, and *they* are never on the surface. One sees only the residue: determination and passionate loyalty to Jack's memory. One can only guess at the lengths to which she would go to get him remembered as she wishes. There is a level at which I know she could justify (at least to herself) murder. So why not the painting of one or two early Drivers, pictures that he might have, could have painted himself?

But, yes, I take your argument. Quite apart from the question of whether she's capable of it, how, indeed, could one understand the *psychology* of Felicity actually *doing* such a thing? She was and always has been so insistent on Jack's separate and particular identity, and on his work as what gives that identity form. It defies belief that she could have literally inserted herself into what she thinks of as his very being by painting his paintings, above all the early paintings which so much establish what we think of as essentially *his* work, paintings made not in her company but in that of Louise, who we all know she will never even mention. No, such a thing simply doesn't ring true psychologically.

And I find it a great relief to hear your opinion of the other picture, *Six-six Vision on the Big Screen.* Somewhere in the back of my mind, I would have continued to have doubts (despite the question of capacity and the psychological argument) if you had them. I go along with the idea that it's a surprise (the Transfiguration quotation especially – straight out of Raphael! – and the slightly casual yet expressive, even muscular treatment of the bathers), but an exciting surprise, which is consistent with Driver as you understand him; and I go along with it especially now because I've seen it. We went this afternoon (the place is just what you'd expect from Jack, a tip, a very 'authentic' tip). Seeing the place and the picture has left me with few doubts. Jack Driver did paint it. And the others too.

I still have problems understanding the addition of the balloon in *On a Trip*, but I have no problem now accepting that these two pictures are both *entirely* his. And they're among the toughest things he ever did, especially *Six-six Vision*, which has a rather remarkable force and directness about it. I know it's something one should not say, but it's among his most masculine pictures.

I always was too much the sceptic. Seeing paintings is such a *positive* experience. I can never get enough of it.

I know you're on the other side of the Atlantic, Rag. But don't go away. You keep me thinking straight.

Your friend,
Simon

10 July 1993

Dear Rag,

I knew I couldn't be free of problems for long. There are further developments in relation to the Driver show. I suppose one has to accept them as inevitable.

Queen's is in turmoil (it does happen from time to time, even in safe places like art history departments). Kit Moss was on the phone to me, embarrassed and confused (very much *not* his usual smooth, emollient self). It appears I am to receive a letter of protest about the Gallery's involvement with Mammon in the form of Coverlie's from an 'influential' group of his more 'left-inclined' colleagues. They are scandalised by the involvement of a Queen's student (the malleable Matthias), and 'concerned' about the implications for the relationship between 'scholarship' and commercial interests.

The trouble is that they're absolutely right to be concerned; and I find myself having to defend the erosion of principles which are fundamental for me too.

This is, one knows too well, the first of many toils and travails to come. I shall keep you informed.

Yours in haste,
Simon

13 July 1993

Dear Rag,

Well, here it is, the Queen's 'protest'. It's to appear in the *Guardian* tomorrow. At least they had the courtesy to give me a foretaste.

As you can see, it's headed by that splendid woman Gabby Cabe (who's pregnant again, I've heard, but never pauses for breath let alone to give birth, as far as I can see). And inevitably the ageing firebrand Dick Waldeau is among them.

I'm with them too, except I cannot be.

Your quisling friend,
Simon

The 'protest' was enclosed, and read as follows:

The planned exhibition of the work of Jack Driver at the Tate Gallery is of great interest and could well make a significant contribution.

We are, however, concerned at the sponsorship deal that has been struck with Coverlie's to finance this exhibition. It threatens the entire future of scholarship in cultural history and theory as an independent and disinterested activity, for it could well open the way to a much more direct engagement by the profit-making sector in the promotion not merely of particular cultural values but of particular types of historical and critical practice. How soon will it be before we have Enterprise History to service the Enterprise Culture? The implications for the future of academic and cultural institutions in Britain are profoundly disturbing. Are scholars and curators to become no more than the 'arm's-length' representatives of the great commercial interests in society?

It is our hope that Sir Simon McKenna and the trustees of the Tate Gallery will reconsider what could well prove a disastrously short-sighted decision.

Including Dr Gabby Cabe and Professor Dick Waldeau, there were six signatories to the letter. They were all designated 'working cultural and art historians in the Department of the History of Art, Queen's College, University of London'.

17 July 1993

Dear Rag,

It was really pleasing to hear how well New York has gone for you. Thank God you're back in a fortnight. I need a session with you more and more urgently.

On this side of the Atlantic, just up the river from Westminster, the difficulties do not so much multiply as become daily more boring. I had Kit Moss in my office just before lunch, emptying my coffee machine, and doing his blandest best to convince me that these little disagreements happen among the 'best of mates' in academia, and that anyway academics as a breed are on the point of disappearing *en masse* to the further corners of the earth for their summers over the word processor. He's got his composure back, and insists there is no question of the Queen's Higher Degrees Committee in the History of Art demanding that Coverlie's stooge extract himself from his 'unethical' state of dependency (there was, it seems, some threat that damning papers would be passed from one committee to another – Higher Degrees to academic board to college council – causing dismay and total paralysis and therefore the end of Coverlie's stooge as a viable postgraduate prospect). Coverlie's stooge himself is said to have taken it all with a blithe shrug – 'they would, wouldn't they?' is apparently his attitude – if one can believe that anyone could understand such machinations let alone cope with them. They sound terrifying to me.

Well, I don't believe a word of it. All clearly *is* turmoil at Queen's. But I do believe in Moss's formidable skills as a fixer. It's obvious to me that he couldn't have the position he has without those skills. One has to be a fixer of extraordinarily oily gifts to survive in the new Byzantium of boards and committees they've built in the universities. Let academics like Moss and his 'mates' loose on putting together a bureaucracy and they end up with something so fiendish that only a very few even among them understand it, let alone know how to work it – and they, of course, end up with the real power. I am confident that he will neutralise or divert in some harmless direction the more destructive powers of Cabe, Waldeau et al.

This is, one can be sure, a minor difficulty; an irritation. Matthias will continue to aid and abet the delightful Miranda, who will continue to make things happen with unstoppable efficiency, while Henry Troy continues his talks with that ideologue Duncan about the future of the arts in this country.

One begins to feel that we need a *real* crisis, not a mere minor difficulty, if things are to be prevented from just jogging efficiently towards some unimaginable catastrophe.

Yours ever,
Simon

PS Coverlie's first valuations for the pictures in private collections have come in. They are almost outrageously high, considering the sluggish state of the market. They range from five hundred thousand to one and a quarter million (one and a quarter *million pounds*). I know we're said to be on the brink of a recovery of sorts. But it took my breath away. These are valuations that rival Bacon. Jack would simply laugh, if he didn't cry – he'd probably do both.

At least Coverlie's have a clear idea of the game they're in.

19 July 1993

Dear Rag,

I suppose one could have predicted it. Graham Copley draped his lanky frame over the leather swivel chair in my office this morning, and introduced a further level of difficulty into things.

He was playing hurt and self-righteous. He isn't at all good at playing hurt (he's too obviously armour-plated), but he's very good at self-righteousness. What do you think: should I tell Felicity and Miranda they must find him the space to rehearse his version of Jack in the catalogue? 'If it hadn't been for me,' he said, 'none of this would be happening.'

I had to remind him that Jack was a good friend of mine long before he (Copley) received his A-level results. But he has a point. One knows well enough that his writing has had a crucial role. And it might read sometimes like a parody of itself, but he is the future, he and his kind of writing, not the stodginess of Coverlie's stooge. The man has wit, intelligence and imagination, even if it is all used, one sometimes thinks, for his greater glory at the *expense* of the artists he takes up.

I have almost decided that I shall back him. It will allow me to see just how far we do still have curatorial control over this show.

And I know June Sutcliffe will be for it; she repeatedly says that she can't understand how Felicity has ditched 'a dazzler like Graham Copley' for, as she puts it, 'a dullard like Matthias'.

Yours,
Simon

22 July 1993

Dear Rag,

I *have* to write, even though I know you'll be back in just a few days. You have to know. I think, finally, we are to have a crisis. A real *big* crisis. And sooner rather than later.

Do you remember a man with wire-rimmed spectacles and a very bright bow tie, who rather took you aback at Jessie Noble's by telling you that you were a product of 'the market' and should 'bloody well be grateful to capitalism'? Jason was his name, Jason Furnival. Well, Jason Furnival and a team of a blue so saturated as to be beyond nuance, have just produced, in the name of Heritage, a one-hundred-and-seventy-five-page report with sixteen recommendations, which landed on my desk this morning . . .

This was, of course, the government-commissioned Furnival Report on the future of public funding in the national museums and galleries. This was the report that recommended the takeover of museum temporary exhibition programmes by the 'professionals' of the private sector, meaning, among others, organisations like Coverlie's. 'A previously overprotected and subsidised activity' was to be exposed to 'the healthy climate of the marketplace'. The museums were to become (as they have, of course) merely 'venues' leasing out space to 'suitable ventures'.

McKenna's resignation issue had at last landed on his desk. But he saw only a 'crisis', because he did not know

that John Duncan, Lord Troy and Sir Gordon Creasey
(chairman of the Trustees of the Tate) were already
in talks about a comprehensive takeover of the Driver
exhibition by Coverlie's on the proposed new model.
The illusion of *any* curatorial control for McKenna
(whose description of me as Coverlie's stodgy stooge
I find really hurtful) and June Sutcliffe (who I am sure
you will agree is an opinionated bitch as well as naïve)
was about to disappear altogether.

McKenna should perhaps have taken his own advice a
little more seriously at the end of his letter to 'Rag' of
18 July: 'I shall have to be even more careful now. You
can't trust anyone nowadays.'

The transatlantic flow of letters from Sir Simon to 'Rag'
between 24 June and 22 July 1993 can be rather nicely
glossed by the parallel flow of my laptop tappings.
This is just the kind of complementary evidence that
we professionals most value. You can cross-reference
and corrolate to your heart's content; there's so much
demonstrable truth in it all. We have it, after all, from
more than one side.

But the question returns: given that we can, of course,
trust the private letters of McKenna to Frew (clearly we
can), does the same apply to me on me? As McKenna
said: 'You can't trust anyone nowadays.'

It was something, in fact, that I said too over a fortnight
before him, in my jottings of 6 July, so I have my cue.

6 July 1993
You can't trust anyone nowadays. They're just jealous.
They talk about 'a principled stand', but it's because I've
had the break, that's all. They resent it.

But I shall hang in there. I shan't let them divert me.
The future of Driver's legacy is too important for me
to take any other attitude. I have other loyalties: to
Felicity, to Miranda, to Jack Driver. You, Roland, can

be principled too. You're going to stay with it, Roland, whatever they do.

But I have to admit it, when Rachel Wark had finished with me in the canteen I felt the chill right to the very tips of my extremities, every single one of them. And yet I was sweating. I'm still sweating to think of it: I'm scared sick. I'm freezing and in a fever.

I must have the courage to put it down, every word she said.

The sun is bright through the tall windows and I am just saying to myself that I can remain slumped pleasurably in my bucket chair in front of the white formica table with its coffee-mug rings for another couple of minutes before going back to my checking in the library, when Rachel is suddenly there all intense and threatening.

'So what's Coverlie's Visiting Scholar at the Tate doing visiting Queen's? Just as well you've come, my dear. I was with Gabby this morning. You are in trouble, Roland. I'm not joking, deep trouble, *mega* trouble. Gabby says that Queen's can't be seen to condone what's going on between Coverlie's and the Tate. She says a principled stand has to be made on the matter, that you will have to withdraw before Queen's is implicated any further. She says the full awfulness of the college committee structure will have to be brought to bear. She says no one can withstand that. It smothers people. And quite apart from that, there's even talk of protests to the Dean of Humanities and McKenna and letters to the press. You really are going to be famous now, Roland, and sooner than you think. Notorious might be a better word.'

Well, actually I don't think she said *exactly* that. It's more that's the way it seemed to me she would have put it if the gloves had been off. But Rachel never takes them off. You never hear what's really *behind* what she says. If I was being literally accurate, I suppose what she actually said was terribly reasonable: more like this.

'Look, Roland, I think you should know that Gabby

has begun to make noises about your involvement with Coverlie's and the Tate. There may be trouble. I was with her this morning, and she was talking about asking for the involvement of the college council. There's even talk about co-ordinating a letter to the press. Really, I mean it, you ought to think seriously about where you stand if there is trouble.'

Either way, I was rather quick with the response, and was distinctly pleased to hear myself call her 'a malevolent bitch'. There you are, sometimes I can rise above blandness. Sometimes I can be the masterful man Miranda would like all men to be. 'Some people,' I said, 'don't enjoy the role of bringer of bad tidings, you do, you malevolent bitch.' But all she did was to shrug and smile her overwide smile in her overwide face.

And when, of course, I tried to milk her for the details, her shrug and her wide smile set in, replicating themselves again and again, the most impenetrable of defences. She enjoyed every moment of having nothing else to say.

'How can you expect me to remember *exactly* what Gabby said? You know how fast she talks when she's excited . . .'

'I don't know how the committees do anything here. No one does. It's one of those mysteries only Anthea Althorpe [the department secretary] and her computer understands.'

'I don't know *which* of the broadsheets. But enough of one to make you *seriously* famous.'

I should have realised, Rachel's only a malevolent bitch when you ask her to be. I did, so she told me nothing, just kept on suggesting the worst.

I'm in a pit. It's so bloody cold. And I'm shit scared.

15 July 1993
I'm still alive. The letter appeared in the *Guardian* yesterday, and I'm still alive.

I went into Queen's this morning. I walked through

the hall on the way up to the department and said good morning to the severe receptionist, who looked at me with no more than the usual severity. I went all the way through the warren of corridors to the department library and gave in my books, and the librarian on duty nodded in his usual no-nonsense fashion and signed them in quite normally. I was unchanged, apparently. I was not famous, and I was not a pariah. I was normal.

And then, as I went to coffee, I passed the pigeonholes for students. They were almost entirely empty of course (eerie): the undergraduates have mostly gone home. Except for the 'M' slot. There, all alone, was a note for me, a note addressed in Kit Moss's handwriting and very carefully sealed with Sellotape. Suddenly I was wholly *ab*normal. The note said simply: 'Come and see me. We have to discuss our position. Things are grave.' Things are never 'grave' for Kit. Things are only ever 'problematic'. If things were 'grave', they were on the edge of catastrophe.

I went to the lavatory. It's quiet and safe in there.

Then I climbed the countless stairs to Kit's office and knocked on the door. Naturally, he wasn't in, so I sat miserably on the chair in the narrow corridor contemplating the nameplate that told me 'Professor Kit Moss' *should* be there. It has become such a familiar place, and, even if he does always apologise so profusely when he finally arrives, I shall not forgive him for all the hours I've sat there in that windowless space which Hoovers never seem to visit.

The room behind the door is spacious and light. The chairs are always askew and the table around which he teaches is always piled chaotically with books and papers. There is a splendid view across the roofs of the eighteenth-century square to the grand neoclassical fabric of the college, and then across the cornices and balustrades to the cereal boxes of the tower blocks in the City. That perfectly balanced still life by Marchand that hangs above the mantelpiece is enough to convince one that nothing could ever be really out of place in there. Everything is relaxed and at ease with the world.

The corridor is a constrained, tense place, where I sat tensely.

But I have to say that when, at last, I was in the light of the room, and he was nodding and smiling and almost but not quite winking in that inimitably reassuring way, I would have forgiven him anything. He arrived cooking gently in his perspiration with his bike bag over his shoulder, and I thought to myself, how can this shabby, sweating man with a bicycle have all this power? But despite his trainers and corduroy trousers with shiny knees, he has. And it makes me feel so comfortable.

He has a particular, insouciant manner of swivelling his desk chair that inspires total ease of mind. Gravity seemed never to have entered his spirit. One wondered whether it could actually have been he, Kit Moss, who had written that note.

'Let's not exaggerate, eh? What else would you expect of Cabe and Waldeau? And if we had predicted it, would I have advised you against taking the opportunity? Of course not. All that matters is doing a professional job for Driver and for the history of British art in the sixties and seventies. No, Roland, we tough it out. And I promise you there won't be much to tough out. They've all had their say, and that, after all, is what matters to them. Action is another dimension altogether. These are academics, remember? I know about academics, even *hard* academics like that lot. You know about academics too. What are they going to *do*? They talk. They send letters. But in the end they just trog around.'

Naturally, I played along with it. I protested a little. I was anxious and inexperienced and saw the worst everywhere, but only so that he could be calm, experienced and see the best everywhere. I fed him the cues, and then relaxed more and more as he unreeled the reassuring

lines which are his speciality. He spoke them, as I knew
he would, with total conviction and all the requisite
authority.

'Have you struck off!' He laughed at that idea. 'Do you
think they have more influence on the academic board
than me? And even if they could take it further than that,
what about the college council? Take it from me, I know
about committees. I was working committees before that
lot had read *Peter Rabbit*. After all, I was one of the
architects of the whole structure, for Christ's sake. You
didn't know that, did you?' [I did, of course; he keeps
telling me about it.]

In the end he has taught me how to survive: indifference. What does it matter what they say, they would,
wouldn't they? The point is that I *have* the opportunity,
that I *can* do the job, and that I *shall* do it. That's all. I am
the one who has made the breakthrough with Felicity, and
not just Coverlie's but the Tate as well are behind me. And
anyway, no one can beat Kit Moss at his own game.

'We're in the centre, Roland, where things happen.
They're where they like to be, on the margins, where
nothing happens. They've nothing better to do but send
protests. They *like* to be left just trogging around.'

So twenty-four hours have gone by, and I'm still alive.
And I'm beginning to feel like kicking too.

23 July 1993
I've died again. I now understand utterly that word
mortified. I am mortified. I have it from two directions
at once – Kit and Miranda – Copley is to write in the
catalogue.

Why should I feel like this about it? I should *like* the
idea. Copley is to appear alongside me in a catalogue
which I shall dominate by all the measures that matter.
He is to write a six-thousand-word essay; I am to supply
a seventy-thousand-word run-down on one-hundred-and-
thirty-odd works, fifteen or more of them 'lost' works.

Why should I care? It's no contest. It will still be Roland Matthias's catalogue. Of course it will.

But I was *mortified* each time I heard it. First it was just a possibility, but then it became a corroborated fact.

I died twice.

25 July 1993

I began to feel comfortable again today. I keep on dying and being raised up again, like Lazarus on a yoyo.

I saw June Sutcliffe, and she made me feel good and important. She is such a kind person. And her honesty is transparent. You can really trust her, and I know she's been an admirer of mine for years. She said that everyone at the Tate supported me, and indeed that they were 'delighted' to have me 'involved'. 'For once,' she said, 'the results of serious doctoral research will make the contribution they should.'

And, more than that, she said that McKenna had made a point of 'singing my praises' to her. My feeling has been, actually, that McKenna only just tolerates me. I see very little of him, but he has stopped to say hello once or twice when I'm working in my corner in the Tate library, and beneath the apparent charm I've detected a chill, a disturbing *un*friendliness, an *antipathy*. He is the perfect mandarin, impenetrable, and I was probably imagining things. But all the same it makes a real difference to hear from June, who sees him often, that actually I am so much in Sir Simon's influential good books. She says that he talks about 'this great project' and its 'implications for the future'. She says he remarked that I was a man 'whose professionalism could be trusted'.

I have resolved to be positive and upbeat. Follow Kit. Ignore everything that is negative. Dwell only on the good things. Rigorously deny yourself the luxury of the worst. There may be cautionary tales like Graham around. But if you want to get anywhere nowadays, you just have to trust people in the end.

How else, after all, to see Gabby Cabe's *Guardian* protest, but as the final guarantee that the show will become a *cause célèbre*?

How else, ultimately, to see Graham's inclusion in the catalogue, but as a compliment, and a sure way to lend me and the whole project real intellectual cachet?

There is no reason, Roland, to be anything but satisfied with yourself.

Got it?

6

Pictures Are For Looking At Slowly

Ready when you are. That's not addressed to you; it's addressed to me. It's what I said to myself when I sat down and began this chapter. Do you see? The you was me. I, the writer, have become a you to myself: somebody else I work with who has to be ready when I start.

For me in this record of events, I am now many yous, not just one. There is me as a you to me in two or maybe three forms: me in early retirement (now) making a commentary, me in early retirement recollecting (from now), and me in my jottings (then). There is, besides, the you for whom the writer of my jottings taps, who is yet another me. Remember?

And then there is Felicity's you. Felicity's you, of course, is Jack. But, at the same time, it is not Jack. It is Felicity. Just as the you to whom I addressed my 'ready when you are' is me.

When I became an art historian identity was the name of the crisis, of course. A lot of time was spent declaring its non-existence. The self was dead or had divided like an aberrant amoeba into so many selves that you couldn't talk about it any more. Except muddlingly (see above). It wasn't even single-sexed. It had become like those 'his and hers' hairdressers that were everywhere in the later decades of the twentieth century, male *and* female, or to use their singularly inappropriate word: unisex. The essential *male* Jack Driver – the one who had 'one-*man* shows' in the sixties, before they invented solo shows – was a 'notion'. So was the essential *female* Felicity. So was I. And to put no finer point on it, we were all lamentably mistaken as notions: we were erroneous notions.

The crisis doesn't seem to have disappeared, though the unisex hairdressers have, of course. Men in 'the natural condition' of 'this Britain' have gone back to having their hair dressed with men. We have it done in brown masculine places, styled like rugger changing-rooms (except for the photographs of over-elaborately coiffured heads on the walls); while *they* have it done in lilac and pink places, styled like hugely enlarged dressing tables.

Well, that's enough digression for the moment. I begin today (I am relieved to say) not with me and my (explicitly male) jottings, but with Felicity and her (explicitly female) talks with Jack. It's time to turn to the second of her texts, the undated one. As I've said already, everything about it indicates that it was written just after the end of the story, that is, just after the opening of the Tate/Coverlie's exhibition, which took place on 26 September 1994.

Today is the twenty-fourth anniversary of that day. For me, it is a day for remembering many yous from the past. Or for remembering that I can never, even after only twenty-odd years, really remember them.

Felicity believed utterly that she could remember one. Jack.

So you see, Jack, it was worth it. You had your triumph, and I *know* you were there. Don't deny it. There isn't any denying it. However many recently valeted beautiful people there were holding their glasses out for more of the vintage Bollinger (specially presented by 'Best Vintages Ltd.'), you wouldn't have missed it for the world.

But I suppose just in case I'm imagining things (it would be understandable, wouldn't it?), I'll try to tell you about it. Not so much about the opening. They become more and more ritualised. This one had a procession of the initiates, headed, you'll be flattered to hear, by the only Royal known to take an interest in contemporary art, and the Foreign Secretary. I listened in on a discussion about the mystery of great painting and the privilege of being English. But you won't want to hear about any of that, will you? You'll want to hear about the exhibition.

The show's so *big*, Jack. There are over one hundred and thirty paintings, and fifty-three works on paper. It fills twelve generous spaces in that great cube made up of cubes that they put up in the seventies to the right of the Duveen Gallery. It's been beautifully hung by Miranda, who doesn't need to learn, she simply knows. She didn't let Roland do anything more than say 'ooh' and 'ah', once the decisions had been made. She has all the panache she needs. It's got nothing to do with the kind of historian's things Roland and June know (and fortunately June could be dropped at precisely the right moment).

There's so much space that she's been able to let things breathe and yet, just where some acceleration of rhythm is needed, to bunch three or four things together. And I've never seen you lit so effectively. Miranda's hung the works on paper in the same spaces as the paintings (a risk that June said shouldn't be taken). But it's worked so dramatically. She's grouped them in specially constructed smaller areas, which create pools of shadow, dark spaces in light spaces; the sudden heightened lighting of the pictures allows your colour to shout out.

It's wonderful. Coverlie's has not stinted, I promise. They did quite a lot of special construction work inside the cubes and not just to make possible the showing of drawings and paintings together. All of it's beautifully designed, and finished to the nth degree. Money has to be spent for things to be shown this well. And it has

been. When I came in the afternoon before the opening
I tried to be cool and judgemental, but I didn't have the
heart for it. I wanted to applaud. I simply wanted to
applaud.

And there has been nothing but applause, even from
the *Guardian*, which has put so much into making
a political scandal of what has happened. When it
comes to the show, they have heaped you, buried you,
smothered you with praise. Got it, Jack. I'll say it again.
Very loudly. PRAISE.

Do you want some quotes? Of course you do. OK,
you always said that none of it mattered, especially
the national press. They just printed the first thing that
gelled with their prejudices. You always said that only
what happened in the studio mattered, between us and
the work. But the attacks from the anti-painting and the
flatness people always hurt you. And later on, in the
early eighties, I remember when *Time Out* got at your
little revival show in Tottenham Mews, and told people
not to rake up their past; you refused to speak to me
for the whole morning, as if it was my fault. And the
PRAISE, even the littlest glimmers of PRAISE, always
left you replete and calm. What you really wanted was
for that strange possessive mother of yours to ruffle your
hair and say ever so reassuringly, 'Well done, you're
frightfully clever, Jack. I'm proud of you.' I've always
known it. So here is a nice eulogistic quote from the
Guardian to make your day.

Jack Driver was a Socialist. His work is the subject
of the first profit-led "enterprise exhibition" to be held
at the Tate. He would have fulminated against it, as this
newspaper has. It is unforgivable that he should have
been the tool of so destructive an attack on the principle
of public provision and public responsibility in the arts.
But Jack Driver the Socialist painter of the sixties
and the seventies emerges with his edge still sharp;

his work can still do the business. There is a rough
and ready directness about it, and yet limitless subtlety.
There is ordinariness, and yet everything in it surprises.
Driver's achievement is simply massive.

There are lots of others to give you, but I knew you'd
like the *Guardian* first. The *Independent* talks about
you having 'rescued British painting in the twentieth
century from its provincialism and its mediocrity'. *The
Times* talks about 'an art so much of its time, that it
transcends any time'.

Even the tabloids have noticed you. There's so much
money involved. The *Mail* had a headline: 'Dead
Men's Sales'. Coverlie's are estimating more than eight
million for the six pictures I've given them to sell.
They refer to me (sick-makingly) as 'the millionairess
of Barnes' or 'Bohemia's Merry Widow'. I even had a
photographer advance snapping hungrily as I went to
the off-licence on Thursday, though I have to admit
there was only one. The result was me looking flustered
and slightly guilty (the off-licence) somewhere inside
the *Mirror* and a caption which (I don't understand
why) hazarded a guess at the value of our house.

Don't shake your head like that. There wasn't
any other way. You can't keep money out of things
nowadays. Even art. I told you. I don't need to be rich.
The money's for your Foundation, not for me. You
know very well it's not in me to be 'the Merry Widow
of Barnes', and I never liked the idea of the Côte
d'Azur or the Costa del Sol or even California. I liked
the shacks and the poky spaces of art schools. I still
do. And my pleasures get more and more private, like
masturbation.

The money's for artists and students and the kind
of exhibitions Miranda and her friends wouldn't risk
looking at. We're going to exploit Capitalism, Jack,
if Capitalism exploits us. Getting the money out of
all those people who do like the Côte d'Azur is just

another more direct way of using Capitalism to subvert
Capitalism. You know how I've argued it. There's no
alternative. The images have to have a platform. They
have to work. And yours have been working as they
never ever did, even in the sixties, before Ivor Selwyn
and the Berkeley Gallery finally dropped you.

So stop looking edgy and critical. I told you before:
we have to recognise that the world has moved out of
the reach of Simon McKenna. I'm clearing another
space in which to act. And I know you'll like the name
I'm giving your Foundation. I'm calling it: The Jack
Driver Foundation for Action Through Art, or just ATA,
Action Through Art. That's OK, isn't it?

But the show's the thing. I want to walk round it
with you. I want us to take our time and look at just a
few pieces well. The way we used to. We can take it
one room at a time. One image in one room at a time,
ending as we always used to end by going back to the
beginning, by going backwards through the years in
images. And I shall listen to you again.

Pictures are for looking at slowly. There should
be speed limits in all museums and galleries. 'This
picture must be looked at for not less than five minutes.
Hurrying is an act of vandalism which will not be
tolerated.' Your words.

So let's look. Slowly.

And they (she?) did. That's what the undated text is
largely: Felicity going round the show with Jack, and
letting the images act on her (them), letting them generate
meanings. Her meanings and Jack's meanings. Times,
places and feelings from their past. Experienced there
and then in the show.

It's much longer than the text of 20 May 1994. Indeed,
in my estimation, it could have been written over a period
of far longer than a month; maybe two or three months,
about the length of time that the show was on. If it

was begun just after the opening. My belief is (though it couldn't be proven, of course) that the sections that follow, taking Jack from one room to another, were written after visits, when she went back alone, and looked again.

I like the idea of her looking slowly. Us historians, we're among the busy-busy people who are always going fast. We have deadlines and we have our points to make. There are too few seconds and we aim to fill them all, like packets of six by four file cards or three-and-a-half-inch disks. The lines and the bytes and the seconds are there to be consumed, fast, fast, fast. So are the pictures. I suppose I have to face the irony that Driver's triumph at the Tate was the beginning of all those exhibitions which have pushed more and more people faster and faster past less and less demanding images: people as units of consumption, consuming the marketable in easy-going surroundings. It was a great exhibition, yes (of course it was); it *was* beautifully hung by Miranda; and Driver's work always makes demands. But it opened the way to the 'market-led' 'enterprise exhibition culture' which fills the spaces now not just of the Tate, but of the splendid new 'Tate Museum of the Modern Tradition' across the river from St Paul's, and the Whitechapel and the Victoria and Albert and every provincial gallery in Britain – all those retrospective and 'solo' shows of very expensive artists (either young or dead), all those 'monographic' shows of 'great private collections' formed by very rich and very newsworthy dynasties on Fifth Avenue or Lakeshore Drive or on the coasts of the Pacific or the Mediterranean – all those shows that people 'want to see', and consume so very fast. All those pictures and installations people need only a second to fit into their hierarchies of the 'significant' and the glamorous.

We shall return in not too many pages to Felicity in the exhibition with Jack, looking slowly. Very slowly. But she has left the professional organisation of this history with a problem, because her text has taken us right to the end, immediately. This is, of course, not what my jottings or my recollections do; they're trapped inescapably in the chronology of events, as of course are McKenna's letters to 'Rag'.

I am sorry to say that I have no alternative but to indulge in the kind of temporal oscillation usually reserved for 'ambitious' fiction. Please forgive any ensuing confusion. I am by nature and inclination a narrative historian who begins at the beginning and progresses systematically to the end. But I counted without Felicity.

So (I hope I'm not compromising my professional standards too disastrously) let's go back to where we were before.

Henry, Lord Troy, was the kind of man who believed in team spirit. He was also a good and a generous manager of men and women (he certainly thought of them as different; he hadn't heard of sexual politics, and, if he had, he wouldn't have let on). Not long after the appearance of the *Guardian* open letter, and Graham's invitation to 'come on board' (Troy's phrase), he held a party. It was styled a party to launch the show, but its real purpose was to 'firm up' the sense of *esprit de corps*.

Troy's party wasn't what I thought of then as a party at all. It was a 'black-tie supper'. He held it at his own expense in his club, Clarendon's on St James's Street. To it was invited everyone involved in the exhibition from the level of myself and June Sutcliffe up (including Sir Simon McKenna), and two old critic friends of Troy's to complement the 'young Turk' Graham: the ageing and illustrious one-time sidekick of the Parisian Surrealists in forties Paris, Brian Merritt, and the equally ageing but less illustrious fifties regular at the Colony Club, John Pettigrew.

As far as I was concerned, Lord Troy's management initiative worked well. That evening I bonded with him and his organisation. What I saw was not what I had learned to expect from his liberal detractors. This did not seem to be a man who stood for tooth-and-claw ethics in cultural life at all. This seemed to be a man who wanted peaceful collaboration with McKenna and the Tate, a pooling of expertise. And, above all, this seemed to be a man who could not take visual or literary culture lightly, and who wished Driver well in the best sense. Everything about him said so. Or seemed to.

He was, after all, trained as a painter, something that is still too easily forgotten. Even as a teenager he converted a stable at Fawsey Castle (the Shropshire estate of the Troy family) into a studio, and he was famous at Eton for founding his own art review in the mid-sixties, which published an interview, for instance, with Bernard Buffet (he has had the advantage of a bilingual upbringing; his mother is from a distinguished Lyons silk-manufacturing family). He was a student at Chelsea and the Royal Academy, and even showed twice at the turn of the sixties and seventies (work which seemed at the time anachronistic, but which was undeniably serious: it bore the recognisable imprint of Nicholas de Staël, but took as its subject-matter moments of social intimacy). One of his great friends, of course, was the poet Maurice Fosse, with whom, in the seventies, he launched a dealing and publishing venture specialising in British artists and writers, the 99 Gallery (at 99 Bruce Street, just off Berkeley Square). He illustrated one of Fosse's early volumes, *Caged Carion*.

There were two occasions that evening in the Clarendon Club which acted as especially powerful bonding agents. One was Troy's speech, and the way it contrasted with McKenna's. The other involved a pair of group portraits from the late eighteenth century which have been in the possession of the Clarendon since they were painted; it took place before we sat down to dinner. My jottings offer something of an insight into why these two occasions made such an impression on me, but the real point is that by the end of the evening, I was convinced of the great good will of Troy, and I was convinced of it at the expense of McKenna. I had been taken in.

Across twenty-four years I can see that it could not have been otherwise. An entire society, including its intelligentsia (indeed, *especially* its intelligentsia), has been taken in by the enveloping charm of Troy and his like. McKenna saw it: these larger-than-life people were and are irresistible. It is so delightful to think that one is accepted by them, that one might be just in some minor way like them. Don't we all want to have their vigour, their openness, their appetite for anything and everything, their imperturbable confidence, and their *knowledge* that the world is so much theirs that they will never be betrayed?

I would be taken in again. Of course I would. And you? All of you who are fascinated by culture? You'd be taken in too.

The attractions of culture in the twenty-first century are, after all, the attractions offered by the Henry Troy I knew in the nineties who's still going strong: that ability to appear ruled by the warmth of *feeling*, and yet also, effortlessly, to possess style; that ability to appear challenged and yet not to offer any challenge; that aura of absolute integrity; that sense of power slowly matured over centuries; that *smell* of money; those discreetly worn but nevertheless *visible* signs of class: the highest class. Like modern culture, Henry Troy was and is a quality product perfected over time, a product displayed for our admiration but for nothing else. We are allowed to *appreciate* him, to see him shine like something a long way out of reach behind a Bond Street shop window. We are not ever allowed to *know* him.

I never *knew* Henry Troy. But I was continually flattered by the thought that one day he might allow me to, invite me to, and that in some obscure fashion I might myself acquire a spare scintilla or so of his lustre.

My only consolation lies in my jottings, for they are

evidence that, if I was taken in, it was not altogether on every level that I succumbed.

Somewhere in me, a rather feeble and frightened sceptic survived, even as I threw in my lot with him and his world.

30 July 1993

There was a moment in the Clarendon Club *pissoir* tonight when I was overcome with confusion. I stood trying to pass water. I was in between a lord and a knight who were successfully passing their water under impressively high pressure. They crowded me and the water wouldn't come, not for me.

They must be thinking, I thought, what a strange little man, to come to the WC and then just to stand there with his organ in the expensively freshened air *not peeing*. Nothing was said for a very long time. There was just the sound of their shushing and of the silence of my incapacity. Two things were absolutely imperative: to start peeing and to think of something *suitable* to say.

Both came at once.

'I'm surprised Felicity isn't here,' I said.

'This is the Gents,' Troy answered, and started to make a strange shuck-a-shuck-a-shuck sound, which was his version, it seemed, of chuckling. I was reminded of Graham's jokes in Driver's wheelchair. The juvenility of the celebrated is something to wonder at.

'No, no . . . I'm surprised she hasn't been invited tonight,' I added redundantly.

'You can't invite presiding geniuses, can you, Simon? Of course, Jack was *the* Genius as distinct from the presiding version. I'd have invited *him*. Isn't that right, Simon? Got wonderful facilities for the disabled here, you know. We can manage wheelchairs without the slightest difficulty.'

At that point considerable commotion was caused by the fact that Brian Merritt inserted his long question-mark-shaped person into the immaculate but compact space of the Gents. Merritt is a shambling and disintegrating figure. He has entered his early eighties and clearly believes that no one will know that he is Very Distinguished unless they know him to be Very Old as well. Leaving decaying critics waiting in lavatories is not an option for well-bred people, so all three at the *pissoir* called it a day, variously zipped and buttoned up, and edged out in apologetic Indian file sideways into the passage. Our conversation about Genius was at an end.

I dwell on this scenario, because it reminds me of the awful difficulties in my life. I am not very important. Let's be honest, Roland – not very important at all. I am a menial in all this. And I am uncomfortably positioned in the *pissoir* of the art world between extremely important persons with the power to dish me and with, very probably, rival agendas.

(Am I to believe this? Have I, an individual dedicated to facts and implacably opposed to the exercise of the imagination, actually coined the appalling metaphor of the art-world-as-gentlemen's-club-*pissoir*? I blame it on keyboards. They let you tap in anything, and then freeze your finger when it hovers above *delete*.)

But the point holds. In the WC of the Clarendon Club I knew how subject I was to power. Indeed, this evening, if it was nothing else, was an exercise in class terrorism clearly aimed at intimidating the art-world underclass and showing them (us) plainly to whom they (we) are beholden. Henry Troy is beefy, benevolent power, a force so magnificent that it persuades even Sir Simon McKenna to keep his counsel.

And, Christ, what an evening. I have to confess that this was my very first invitation to a gentlemen's club. It was an undertaking that I could only survive by adopting the participant-observer stance of an anthropologist in the Malinowski mould. I might as well have been observing the exchange of gifts among the Trobriand Islanders in the earlier twentieth century as participating in social life somewhere in the West End of London in 1993. This was the exotic Other all right, and it was frankly terrifying. The upper class with the upper hand.

The exterior of the place is utterly mute. Its perfectly proportioned late-eighteenth-century fenestration, the dull politeness of its brickwork, the discretion of its unexpectedly small-scale and impenetrably closed door on to the pavement, all declare grand exclusivity. Many, many more of us are to be kept out to wonder at its mystery than let in to participate. As I approached it, I found myself slowing to a sidle. I waited and watched until at last somebody did demonstrate that the door could be opened and walked through. So I did it. I crossed the threshold. Entered.

A narrow airlock of a lobby with a cubbyhole to one side occupied by a dignified character in a dark funereal suit. A sparkling hall, the floor marble, out of which a sweeping stair rises, the whole lit by a great chandelier. A squeaky, unctuous 'Can I help you, sir?' spoken out of the recesses of the cubbyhole. My voice sounding the words: 'Lord Troy's party.' 'Upstairs and on your left, sir.' The ascent of the stairs strangely breathless, as if after intense exercise. The gaining of the summit. The vision through open double doors of men in smooth, pressed casings of black cloth, throats jammed into stiff white collars fastened shut by their bow ties. Of women, ludicrously ornate, their hair piled or puffed out to form what the French call *chevelures*, great manes about which decadent poetry could be written (among them Miranda with her excess of brunette riches making a particularly Muse-worthy showing; I found her ultra desirable, perhaps because, for once, she was untouchable). The polite noises of society, broken by the surprising loudness of (usually male) laughter. Only here have I heard laughter come in *peals*.

Entering. Being there. Being (almost) one of them. Just for this evening.

Eating was not consuming this evening. It was allowing small fragments of slivered food to touch one's palette and slide down one's gullet as if digestion were a magical not a bodily function. We sat in little islands, confronted by clusters of silver: forks and knives which buckled and bulged at their throats with Rococo curlicues. Between us was a vast expanse of highly polished Regency table occupied by two flower displays like exuberant coral islands. Now and again a discreet nudge signalled the arrival of one of the team of deferential flunkies to serve still more 'beautifully presented' delicacies, or to administer the 'unobtainable' claret.

Opposite me, only just visible somehow (once the lights were dimmed), was Merritt. He had a way of so disporting his elongated body that his head kept merging with the flickering light of the candelabra. He seemed to be gently dying away like the flames in front of me, though his voice got louder and louder through the evening and was more and more directed at me. It seemed not to be emitted by him at all, but to descend out of the darkness above the table, demanding to be heard like the voice of an increasingly mischievous divine force.

'Of course Breton's mistake was to dirty his mind with politics at all. There simply was no problem, my friend. One of Jack's failings, to my mind (and I say this without in any way denigrating his painting) . . . no, one of Jack's failings was to take the Breton of *Légitime Défense* and the second manifesto seriously. He actually believed that artists can act to change the behaviour of ordinary people, that art can *be* political. Silly stuff really.'

What can you say to that? The thing is, Roland, you agreed with him most of the time (except when he became silly and fantastic). He was booming things straight out of your own mind. It was just rather eerie to have your truths uttered as if divinely by a critic who seemed to be gently putrefying opposite you. Wasn't that the problem?

'Surrealism never was about politics. It was about the

image. Yes? The image, hence the imagination. And desire. I still feel the call. Miranda, my dear, what would you say if I informed you, indiscreetly of course, that you figured in my dreams?'

Miranda's suggestive little giggle at my shoulder.

'You're just an old flatterer, Brian. I'm rather pleased to hear it, but I suspect you of inventing things to ingratiate yourself.'

'You, Mr Matthias [why did he insist on calling no one but me 'Mr' all evening?], believe that old rakes like me are beyond the pleasures of priapic imaginings, eh? Miranda doesn't, do you, Miranda? Girls can see what they do to people with a little imagination, that's the thing.'

'Ignore him, Roland. He always gets himself invited by Henry because he likes winding the evening up. He's built his entire career on being naughty. It's all the fault of a neo-Dada youth spent behaving like Just William among people brought up on Bloomsbury.'

'Thank you, Miranda, dear. I flatter you and you flatter me. Except I don't flatter. It's not in my nature. It's simply a matter of fact that you cause serious disturbance in my loins. Desire. But to change the subject (regretfully), I assume, Mr Matthias, that politics are not your strong point, something, I must say, that commends you to an old atheist like me.'

'They're certainly not *mine*,' said Miranda, intervening suddenly in her business mode. 'Not Coverlie's style at all. Anyway, not where art and artists are concerned. I think the most important thing in this exhibition is to reclaim Driver's painting for painting. To take it back from Socialism. We're not thinking in terms of a political Driver at all. It's one of the things Henry really wants to underline this evening.'

'Well, I don't know what poor old Jack would make of that. But it's fine by me. I have only one political belief, you know. That psychoanalysis should take over from the Church of England as the state religion and the entire Royal Family should be analysed on television thrice weekly at peak viewing times. The soap operas couldn't compete, and people would start remembering their dreams again.'

Laughter. He could be very funny, something I have to say I've never noticed in his writing. But he is not a cynic. He has convictions, despite the games he plays, and he does let them show from time to time. Physically he is like Graham might become when he is in an advanced state of degradation. He too is almost inconceivably long. But there the resemblance ends.

Henry Troy and Sir Simon McKenna, fortunately, were so distant (at opposite ends of the table) that I could feel at least relatively out of their reach, even if this was so palpably their realm (or rather, Troy's realm). From Troy's end came his continual shuck-a-shuck-a-shuck, which sometimes mounted into a high-pitched peal, surprisingly thin for such a big man. Things were hearty. There was much carousing. From McKenna's end came an even hum. Voices were not raised. Things were important; issues were weighty. Graham was being conspicuously relaxed at the Troy end. His behaviour was that of an habitué in such places as the Clarendon (I seem to remember a biographical note somewhere that recorded his attendance at one of the smartest public schools, though I'm not sure which).

The speeches came when I was trying to decide whether Merritt had dropped off to sleep and whether I liked the sticky, resonant taste of very good port. There was one from McKenna and one from Troy. McKenna came first. He said a few elegantly phrased things and nothing. He was cool and careful. He was more careful about avoiding commitment of any kind than anything else, and, when he smiled, it was with the thinnest of lips and from deep behind the slightly tinted glass of his Christian Dior (?) spectacles. He was the refined Bloomsbury aesthete and the aloof mandarin in one. This is a man who leaves nothing to chance, who never loses in public life, because he never throws the dice.

Troy was injudicious, indelicate, funny and outrageously charming. He breathed generosity of spirit. Even when he insulted people (and he made a point of insulting powerful people), he did so with affection. His body language was all expansive gestures. He helped us laugh at his jokes (which were good) by laughing at them himself, first and loudest. And yet I like him for it. He spoke to us 'off the record' as if we were all in his confidence, and by trusting us, he made it easy for us to trust him.

Only at the end did he become serious; it was then that he talked about his painting, and it was then that he talked, very briefly, about Driver and politics. It's worth getting down. It went something like this.

'I'm a painter. You all know that. But no one here has ever seen my work. I don't think I dare show it to the curators of the Tate. Certainly not the director. Shall I tell you about Henry Troy the painter? He was very talented indeed, but not very good. Yet the thing is to have *been* a painter, to have *experienced* the unfolding of the relationship with the canvas, and to have cared about it. I say I *am* a painter, in the present tense, because to have been a painter is always to be a painter. Now I run a business, but I look at pictures as a painter. It's a matter of passion. Nothing has made me more a painter in my looking at pictures than seeing the work of Jack Driver. I don't believe he was an intellectual painter (as some say he was); I believe he was a painter's painter. We have all seen now the first ten of the lost early pictures. Could anyone disagree with me after that?'

Then came the political addendum. It left a hushed silence behind it, which was only broken by Merritt waking up and beginning to clap. After a bad start, the applause could only be called warm, distinctly warm.

'Driver's politics weren't mine. He was a Socialist,

and for him his Socialism was a matter of passion. I understand that. Those were other times, when even I would allow there were good Socialists. Of course. But surely it's now clear that his work was *not* about Socialism. *Pace*, Jack; *pace*. We only have to show the paintings for that to become the plainest of truths; they can still move us, even now, when we're so many worlds away from that world. They can still work without the Socialism. There was something deeper, more timeless in Driver than politics. We all know it. Of course we do. Jack would too. Of course he would. This exhibition is not for us; it's for him, for Jack Driver the great artist. And we shall see him right . . . we shall see him right.'

I wonder what Felicity would have said if she'd had to reply to that. Troy doesn't know much about Driver. But Miranda does, and these are her sentiments too. I don't know whether they're right. Driver *was* a political artist, whatever Merritt says and they say. But I have to be honest: I like him better without the politics too. Politics gets in the way of so much, unless it's just something contextual. The fact is, Troy's good for Driver, even if his plain truth isn't everyone's. He cares about Driver. He has feeling. And he has the power to make things happen.

I need to add a postscript to my interlude among the famous in the WC. The immediate sequel to it was deeply significant. I was taught another lesson. Nearly as important as Troy's speech.

'Let me show you something,' said Troy as we appeared decorously at *piano nobile* level in close proximity to the chandelier that lit the entrance hall. 'I suppose you know the group portraits we have here, Simon?'

McKenna nodded.

'They're in there, I seem to remember,' he said, indicating closed double doors. 'But I always take the chance to look at paintings.'

'Good, good. Come along in. You too, Matthias, come along.' And Troy led us both through the double doors into a spacious room, whose tall windows looked out over the lights and noise of St James's Street. It was empty. Indeed, it felt as if it had been left empty solely so that Troy could have it to himself and us. On one wall was a pair of eighteenth-century group portraits. Looking out of one of them was a more rubicund, bewigged version of Troy himself.

We stood contemplating the pictures in silence for a long time. I have to say I found them dull. I cannot pretend otherwise, I just find portraits of powerful and self-important eighteenth-century gentlemen dull. But, obviously, I had to seem earnestly involved in coming to terms with pictures of immense interest.

After a while I said: 'Who are we looking at?'

And McKenna turned to Troy and said: 'You and your friends, isn't that so, Henry? You've been here for a very long time.'

'Me and my friends. Well, a fairly distant relative of mine, in fact, Simon. But tell me, what do you think of the pictures?'

'It's odd to me,' said McKenna, 'to see a group of *bon viveurs* painted following the conventional format and poses of *The Supper at Emaus*. [A brief shuck-a-shuck-a-shuck came from Troy.] I'm not quite sure we can talk here of the taking of a religious sacrament. But stylishly done. Elegant in the Italianate way that Reynolds made us all accept as English.'

'Always the diplomat,' said Troy and then winked at me. 'My ancestor, Matthias, was described as a dilettante. Still applies to an old amateur like me, eh?'

I laughed noncommittally, and added a shrug so as to underline that I was ready to go along with anything at all he might suggest.

Troy had made his point. He was part of something that could be called 'Tradition', something whose inert force was immovable, something that transcended class and, most of all, transcended mere professional status. I knew where I stood in the hierarchy of things. And I knew where Sir Simon McKenna stood too. Power like that is like Fate. One can only succumb. And anyway, Troy *is* a good thing. I don't have any doubts. Why should I?

Looking at pictures has always taught lessons.

If there is a war, Troy and Coverlie's will win. I'm sure of that now. And I'm sure too that I want them to win. I shall be with them when they do.

As you will have noticed, Troy's speech mentioned the fact that by that dinner on the 28 July 1993, all of us in that room had seen, not five, but ten of the lost Drivers. The second trip to number 2 Orlando Street had taken place, followed in the next couple of days by further trips for McKenna, Troy and others (Graham, of course, included).

I am in serious danger of being forced into yet further temporal confusion at this point in the manner of 'ambitious fiction'. But, in fact, there is no need for me to take you for very long all that way back to the date of the second trip to the Orlando Street studio (which was, incidentally, 24 July). After all, what's required in giving you the facts is not an indiscriminate everything but a properly sifted and weighed selection. *Relevance* is the criterion to be applied. What matters for the scrupulous historian may be, as I've repeatedly maintained, to give you *all* the evidence, but only all the evidence that applies to the *relevant* facts. Of course, the *oeuvre* catalogues (like mine of 2005) give you all the works; but this is a history, even if it is written by a cataloguer. And I'm beginning to enjoy all these decisions about what to have in and what to leave out. After all, it's another kind of power. You can even control the facts in the end.

Bearing the above in mind, there really is not a lot to dwell on when it comes to the visit, because it was very much a repeat of the first, except in two particulars: Felicity was not so much serene as businesslike, and the fabulous Fabritius (who turned out to be Dutch, despite his Etonian vowels and his liking for tartans) brought us coffee to help us 'concentrate'. Otherwise, all you need to know is what we saw stacked against the walls of the studio at the top of the shaky wooden stairs. And, if *relevance* is the criterion for expending words, what I really need to give you, besides a list of what was there (looking from left to right, as before), is the extract from my jottings which deals with just one of the pictures on view.

It is a group portrait (in a sense) and so, oddly, made a connection in my mind when I looked at Troy's distant ancestor and his friends a few days later at the Clarendon Club. The relevance of this particular picture I do not have to explain here; it will be clear soon enough.

But before I give you the results (relevant, I promise) of my first, slow look at it, here is a list of the other four pictures that Felicity showed us on 24 July 1993. You can check it against the Tate/Coverlie's catalogue, where they are all included (the numbers from that catalogue are given in square brackets).

1. *Fight Fire with Fire*, 1960 [7]
2. *Trivialisation and its Discontents: 1) Sins of the Sons*, 1962 [29]
3. *Trivialisation and its Discontents: 2) Sins of the Fathers*, 1962 [30]
4. *[See below]*
5. *Darling,* 1967 [93]

The picture that is relevant (4, above) was the one on the furthest right of the three against the facing wall as one stepped off the stair into the studio. It is the one, ironically, that Troy bought direct from Felicity (and is still in his collection). Its title is *Jealousy/Jalousie.*

*   *   *

4. *Jealousy/Jalousie*, 1967 (unexhibited and unreproduced; date not a problem: consistent with *Desire/Désirée*, which also uses the motif of the Venetian blind shattered, as if by the sun, and which is reproduced in the French periodical *Matière*, (no.4, September–October 1967, p.117).

Three photographed heads transferred on to the canvas as if dissolving; one, Driver as younger man (student in the fifties?); one, Paul McCartney in Beatle haircut and Jimmy Nutter suit; the third, an individual whose identity has yet to be established (male, balding, hair straggling in the wind . . . anyone in particular? Should have asked Felicity, she might have been told). Driver's head is the most completely dissolved. It is almost erased by marks, part Cubist faceting (recognisably related to Picasso's faceted head of Ambroise Vollard), part by random squalls of paint (more sixties Picasso – the late nudes – than Pollock). This quoting of styles, especially Cubism and Picasso, is very out of tune with almost all the rest of British sixties painting; but it *is* characteristic, and it's just the kind of thing that gets Graham into a postmodernist stew, going on about heteroglossia and suchlike. Behind the heads, a Venetian blind, which appears most clearly behind the head of the unidentified man, where it is part of the original photograph. Above the three heads, a burst of sunlight that shatters the blind; it is positioned above the heads like a symbol of Divine revelation. Above that a postcard sky (California again). Across the bottom of the canvas, painted as if by a professional sign-painter, the legend: 'JE(A)LOUS(IE)Y' (the French word for sun-blind, *jalousie* combined with the English jealousy). Again that French aspect of Driver alongside the English and the American, so characteristic of him, and so unique.

Observations: Jealousy of success? Pop success? Picasso's success? Where's Freud and sex? Suc-sex (corny). Why sun-blinds? I don't see it (have another look at *The Interpretation of Dreams*). Light as Surrealist revelation means revelation through love – sex (light in Freud? In Jung?). The only self-portrait by Driver that I know from the period after his student days. Driver alongside an anonymous (?) stranger. Or a friend? Driver alongside Paul McCartney. Driver as jealous genius?

A pity always to end up in banality. Is this all?

Think about jealousy.

Think about *jalousie*.

7

JE(A)LOUS(IE)Y

You've guessed, of course. Of the five pictures we saw on 24 July 1993 the one that is *relevant* to this history is the one among them that Felicity chose to look at slowly with 'Jack'. *Jealousy/Jalousie* was, in fact, in the ninth of the twelve 'rooms' of the Tate/Coverlie's exhibition, but it was the first of the pictures that Felicity took Jack to see in her undated text.

This is something about which you will have to take my historian's word. I realise (and so must you) that, since Felicity's text has so far never been published in part let alone whole, you have no way of verifying that the sequence given here is the *correct* one (and in my capacity as one of the three trustees of her archive I shall continue to vote against the publication of anything but extracts).

You must, I think, be beginning to have suspicions. Could not a little fiction be entering in here? After all, the way one event slots into the next is becoming rather *smooth* for *real life*. It is so very convenient that *Jealousy/Jalousie* should be among the second batch of five to be shown us at the Orlando Street studio, and then reappear as the first picture to be responded to in Felicity's undated text. And it is equally convenient that the lesson of the Clarendon Club group portraits should have occurred in such close chronological proximity to the revelation of Driver's only group portrait.

You see, as an honest historian, who believes in setting

out the facts *as they happened*, I have to alert you to the
dangers of credulity. A *critical* reader will have to ask
him or herself whether I may or may not have tampered
at least with the sequence of things for *merely* fictional
reasons (i.e. for the sake of a good story).

Well, I'm tempted to say – I, Roland Matthias, the
last of the dedicated men of facts – I'm tempted to say:
so what.

You can take it or leave it. I'm sticking to my story line,
which is that *Jealousy/Jalousie* was the first of the pictures
that Felicity looked at with Jack. There are no two ways
about it. That is how it was. How it *really* was. OK?

Here you are, Jack, something difficult and uncomfortable
for us in Room 9, something that made me delay taking
the plastic off in the shack at Orlando Street, something
that bridges my time and your time, 1978 and 1967,
something that takes me back, something that reeks of
regret and loss: *JEALOUSY*.

Looking comes before thinking; then thinking and
looking come together, all at once. But the thoughts
are always in the images. There are no images without
thoughts. You again, Jack, speaking.

It's not a violent picture. The sunburst is just a detail
that threatens but does not take over the rest. The rest is
almost gentle. Such a soft picture to have so much in it,
so many difficult thoughts. The heads are not destroyed.
I see them as having been gently eroded or overlaid or
unfastened feature by feature. Even when you just took
the brush and loaded it and began to obliterate yourself
you seem (to me now) to have stroked the image, to
have begun no more than to coax it out of existence.
And the Picassian Cubism which you almost quote has
all the edges dulled. It does not cut or damage.

Why did you leave Selwyn so nearly untouched? Why
him, and not you?

He's dead, of course, now. I didn't tell you? Nor I

did. Ivor Selwyn died in '88, the year after you. An unlucky man, after all – at least, in the end. An early victim of the Aids epidemic. But that wasn't something you knew much about, was it?

I was invited to the memorial service. After all, he did have time to attend that secular function of yours before he made his exit – he was already known to have the virus – though he didn't make it to Gloucestershire for the funeral. I didn't go to his service. I preferred to think that finally he had been erased, obliterated, and I would never have to pretend to be polite to him again.

But there he is in that muted but definitive black and white of the snapshot beside your gently buckling, softly dissolving features. And yet it is still you that is most clearly there. Do you know something strange? Selwyn wasn't exactly unknown, but no one has seen him in this picture. No one at all. Somehow or other you've rendered him finally anonymous.

I think the sunburst works. Do you remember when you first showed it to me, I said that it didn't work? I said it insisted too much. OK, it isn't paint; it's paint photographed and then the image of the paint cut in pieces and screen-printed on and then, at the very end of the process, overlaid with just a little real paint but only a *very* little. Still the actual paint that was there for the photograph, in the beginning, such smudgings and knifings. My Christ, it made me think you liked that unctuous French high church stuff all along, you know, Rouault and all that. Well, now I like it being OTT (it means over-the-top, Jack – it's something they say nowadays). And it may be a detail, but it has enough punch. It really breaks open the rigid parallels of the blind. There is a challenge to the gentleness of the rest of the picture, and there needed to be.

Yes, it works.

But the letters, the title, I can't look at the title and make judgements like this about it. I can't stand back

and be discriminating, and ask: does it work? It's not
a question that matters when it comes to Selwyn. And
Louise. And you.

The title says too much. There is a whole past in
it. You knew it would hurt me to bring back Louise.
You did it to hurt me. And the anagram doesn't
work anyway; when you make the 'Louise' there's a
redundant 'e'. But you knew I would see it. And I still
do: JE(A)LOUS(IE)Y: JALOUSIE: JEALOUSY: JAY
LOUISE: LOUISE JAY.

It doesn't hurt me now. It saddens me. Negative
feelings again, Jack. I know I shouldn't. Negative
feelings mean negative outcomes.

But I think of the time. I think of the time just before
the diagnosis. When the mischief began in you.

I simply have to interject here. It's the cataloguer in
me. You do see the significance of all this, I hope.
The conclusion to be drawn is quite clear. And I don't
merely mean that Felicity has, finally, told me who the
unidentified intruder is (she did not tell me it was Ivor
Selwyn when I asked her), nor that *Jealousy*/*Jalousie* has
a third level of reference, namely to Driver's first and,
some say, most influential mistress, Louise Jay. No, what
is especially exciting is that it is already perfectly clear
that this work was not wholly executed in 1967, and that,
despite the closeness in type of the title to the 1967 title
Desire/*Désirée*, its title (which is an integral part of the
work) was certainly added later, in fact just before the
diagnosis of Driver's MS. And one can be more accurate
than that, because Felicity's passing reference to 1978
in her opening passage establishes reasonably precisely
a double date for the work: 1967/1978.

This is the only documented case in my experience
(and no one knows more about this than me) of a new
title being added to a painting by Jack Driver. Indeed,
it is at least possible that this is a work which was

shown earlier, in the late sixties or early seventies, under another title.

Whatever the case, *Jealousy/Jalousie* became *Jealousy/ Jalousie* only in 1978, with Felicity a witness, and the onset of Driver's illness coupled with his relationship with her were factors in the transformation.

Fascinating. Don't you think?

You see what you did by putting Louise into it? You saw it well enough then, I know. It's very simple. Louise was before. She was before me. Before rejection. Before disappointment. She went with having ideas, having excitement, having travel, having a future. Having health. I went with decline, disappearance (even gentle, *slow* disappearance). Illness.

I see Louise's name everywhere. It always was everywhere. I suppose that was embittering for you. To pick up the paper and see her name below another feature on the disappearance of neo-Dada or the return of 'punk'. We're on to the 'post-managerial woman' nowadays; decision-maker clothes. She keeps the copy coming. And she keeps the success going. She is the doyenne, it is said, of British fashion writing. She is to the fashion page what Elizabeth David was to the cookbook. And she's everywhere. But she's never at your openings. I made sure she was invited both to the Whitechapel and to the Tate. She never comes.

I suppose I have her invited because I know she never comes. I hate her. Jealousy: she's growing old and grand so beautifully. Perfect bones, perfect skin, wit, style, age without loss.

One thing you never told me: besides pleasure, did this woman ever *feel* anything? When she left, I know how deeply you felt it, but what about her? Has she ever *lost* anything?

I hate her.

And she's always there with me. Not just when I

open the papers, but here in the exhibition. Not just because you put her into this picture, but because she was with you for those seven years before 1966 when so much that's here was painted, because she comes into everything from the wall placards, to the guides, to the BBC2 film, to Roland's catalogue entries and biography and even Graham's essay (even Graham who usually leaves biography out has to find room for Louise).

Fig.7: 'Driver's beautiful companion at a party in the Los Angeles beach house of Myra Briganti is Louise Jay, who had already been described as "the one we all follow".'

Fig.31: 'Seen here sharing a joke with an extrovert Driver at the opening of his first Mackray show in New York is Louise Jay.'

Fig.46: 'Driver was caught here by the photographer leaving the London night club, Fortunato's. His arm is around his companion of the early sixties, Louise Jay.'

p.213: '*Star in a Sunny Sky* can be read, too, on a private level, as, not merely in some general sense a painting about desire, but in a very specific sense a painting about Driver's desire for Louise Jay. The discarded, yet heraldically placed pair of nylon stockings are now securely identifiable as Louise's. Driver adapted them from a photograph he took of her (with flash) in their Camden Town flat in 1960 (the year after their meeting), where they can be clearly discerned draped over the bed. The tie cannot be specifically associated with Driver himself, who rarely wore them. But its significance as a symbol of the masculine and of desire is not at issue.'

You see what I mean? You can hardly turn a page in the catalogue without Louise making an appearance. But I have to be fair, Jack. The one thing she will never do is be interviewed about you. Long before we opened she put out a public statement.

'I answer no questions about Jack Driver or about me

and Jack Driver or even about the person I was when
I was with Jack Driver. Jack Driver has nothing to do
with me. Period.'

And she's kept to it. 1966 she left you. 3 November
1966. You made me feel what it was like for you. The
desperation of phoning all those people, of going and
banging on doors and ringing bells, asking and asking,
and no one saying anything. The completeness with
which she went. The efficiency with which she planned
it. No note, no sign, nothing. Just gone. I'm sorry,
hearing about it didn't make me feel much for you, poor
deserted Jack, all I felt was admiration for her. I confess
it. This is a woman who makes decisions and acts.
Formidable. Enviable.

And I remember what you said: 'I've had two
Françoise Gilots in my life. I suppose I should count
myself lucky. Two formidable and desirable women.
Louise was the one who went. You're the one who
stays. I know the one I want most. Don't look at me like
that. It won't change anything. It's the way it is.'

You can still make me cry, Jack. You always could
and you always will.

The third of November 1966. How many months
before you finished the picture? You have to have
finished it *early* in 1967, because it was before the
bust-up with Ivor. Your friendship is in the painting,
so it has to have been before. You were working on
it when she went, weren't you, Jack? You never said
so. But I think you were. I *know* you were. That's
why you put her in it. Because she *was* in it. With you
and Ivor.

And so am I. You wrote my jealousy into the
painting. You wrote my jealousy with yours into the
painting, both together.

Hypotheses. Feelings. You need some facts. What follows
is a section of the *Biography* I put together for the gallery

guide that came free with the exhibition. Those not in the know about Driver, unlike Felicity, could take it from room to room with them.

A quick word about gallery guide biographies. Do not expect too much from them. They are not biographies. They do no more than list events and name places and people. They are datelines, lists, graphs in prose. They are not a challenge to the profession of Giorgio Vasari, Michael Holroyd and their successors. They suit people like me. They are chronological sequences which cannot be manipulated just to tell a good story.

1965

Driver takes part in the group show, 'Ivor's Choice', at the Berkeley Gallery in Clifford Street (April) and is given a third New York show at the Mackray Gallery (September/October). *The New York Times* hails the Mackray show as a 'serious challenge to Lichtenstein, but especially to Rauschenberg and even to Johns'. Driver is found by Burgoyne Miles in *Artforum* to have a 'complexity and sophistication that places him in that rare category of artists comparable with Johns'. An important article on 'Driver in America' appears in *Studio International*; it is unsigned but is known to have been written by Brian Merritt.

1966

Driver is given his second and final Berkeley Gallery show. Both the Tate Gallery (*First and Last*) and the Arts Council (*Homage to Fame*) are buyers. The American collector of 'Pop', Maurice Gelber, buys three pictures for previously unequalled prices. The French periodical, *Matière*, publishes its first article on Driver (by the noted follower of Barthes, Jean-Paul Matthieu). *Catch Me* appears on the cover of the leading American periodical *World Art*, which contains another article by Burgoyne Miles. 'The rough and ready surfaces; the merger of a collage imagery and a post-Abstract Expressionist handling call to mind Rauschenberg at his best,' Miles opines. November: Louise Jay, Driver's constant companion since 1959, leaves him without warning, initiating a deepening crisis in his life.

1967
Some time before May, Driver decides not to show for two years. His reasons are, as he puts it in an open letter to Ivor Selwyn (dated 21 May), 'over exposure', 'the need to think', and 'the imperative need to sever all contact with art dealers for as long as it takes to do some real work'. 'Art dealers are a pernicious excess in any painter's life,' he adds gratuitously, 'an excess to be excised if at all possible.' Selwyn releases him from his contract and attempts to prevent publication of Driver's 'open letter'. It appears in the *Guardian* (3 June). Driver refuses co-operation for a planned BBC film, but allows another article by Matthieu to appear in *Matière*, because it includes the full text of his letter.

1968
Driver finds and rents a studio at 2 Orlando Street, which he uses to facilitate what later he will call his 'disappearance'. With the May events in Paris, he travels there and stays throughout the summer. He plays an active role (which is noticed by the British press) and returns to become one of the leading voices in the wave of protests and sit-ins that hit British art schools. A Hornsey figure.

1969
Publishes 'Getting On Without Them' (*Art Data*, June), a plea for painters to return to the art schools and to 'say no' to the dealers. Argues that the artists should be in education (where radicalism is possible) not in commerce (where 'only collusion with Capitalism at its most rapacious is possible'). Takes a job two days a

week at Camberwell School of Art. Does not exhibit, but begins to work intensively again at 2 Orlando Street. The painting of 1961, *Connie* (now recognised as a celebration of the sexual revolution consequent upon the winning of the *Lady Chatterley* case), is bought in at Sotheby's Parke-Bernet in New York. Ivor Selwyn publicly regrets his 'mistake' in backing the work of a '*petit maître*'. He will be one of the very first dealers in London to look seriously at the still hardly known Conceptualists.

1970
Does not exhibit. Publishes a bitter attack on 'new tendencies' that have diverted attention away from 'the power of the image and of imagination'. *World Art* prints a diatribe by the emerging anti-formalist American critic, Bernard Kachnur, against Driver's work of the early sixties. He describes it as 'indecisively placed between the force of popular imagery and the idealised discreetness of the art of painting'. *The New York Times* features an article, 'The Disappearance of Driver', which ends with the observation: 'This is a loss which the art community has found easy to afford.'

1971
The first year since 1958 without any bibliographical entry on Driver. He approaches Ivor Selwyn for discussions on the possibility of showing once again. Selwyn refers him to the article of June 1969, 'Getting On Without Them', and none too politely declines to be involved. Continues to teach two days a week at Camberwell. Meets a final-year student there, Felicity Ryan, with whom he develops a close relationship. They begin to work together in the studio at 2 Orlando Street (probably by the end of the year). Felicity Ryan graduates with a first-class degree.

If gallery guide biographies are graphs in prose (a rather functional kind of prose), then this, of course, is the graph of Driver's descent from success to failure, a failure which he seems plainly to have chosen. One cannot, surely, blame Ivor Selwyn, who was the butt of Driver's savage attack on the 'dealer system' and the 'supine acquiescence of the sixties generation' (Driver's own generation).

The Conceptualists and installation artists of the seventies attacked the dealer system, of course, but their solution, the production of unexhibitable or ephemeral work, ironically found them a place *in* the system, since they kept the highest of public profiles (helped by such dealers as the shrewd Selwyn) and made sure the museums and the critics never lost sight of them. They always provided something for the great institutions to collect and exhibit. Here I go along with the 'New Millennium Criticism' of the Tory 'moral intellectuals' of this new century of ours: these 'third-area activists' are to be dismissed as much for their hypocrisy as for their denial of the traditional arts of image-making. Driver's was a *real* rejection of the system. He actually went 'out of sight' and therefore 'out of mind'. He followed Rimbaud as few have had the courage to do. And then when he wanted to 're-emerge', the moment had gone.

He succeeded in failing too well.

The role of Louise Jay in all this is unclear. But I would still speculate (as I did with the support of Felicity in the Tate/Coverlie's catalogue) that the coincidence of her departure and Driver's decision to turn against the market is meaningful. After all, as he chose failure, she unequivocally chose the highest-profile success in the one world that combines commerce and cultural élitism without shame: fashion.

But it was Selwyn who became Driver's public hate-object, not Louise.

'Jalousie' came before 'jealousy'. The sun-blind came first. The sun-blind – I'm remembering what you said – the sun-blind is Selwyn's 'attribute'.

'Dealers were once painted by their painters as studious connoisseurs. Sober people looking earnestly at art. The attribute of the dealer was the work of art. Not money. His virtue was cultivated intelligence, not business acumen.'

Remember looking at the Renoir portrait of Vollard in the Courtauld Institute Galleries? The plushly garbed but sombre dealer turning that little figurine over and over in his hand. Devouring it with such dour intensity. No, you could never associate Ivor Selwyn with earnestness, or even much with art. Nor much with money, I suppose. Just the *idea* of money. Money with him was all figures with lots of noughts. It was as abstract as a Mondrian.

I'm listening to what you said again.

'Ivor goes in my mind with hedonism in sunny places. That house of his in Marbella. You never saw it. Wouldn't ask me there now, eh? All glass and Venetian blinds; built to be open and closed at once. You see, that's it. Ivor liked the sun to be there, as long as it was outside. The sun meant pleasure and luxury. But he wasn't a broad daylight person. He liked to be cool, inside, with his current boyfriend and the blinds down, not sweating too much. He was always comfortable when he took his delights.'

So there he is, Ivor with his attribute, the sun-blind, and the sun nearly but not quite shut out. But Ivor as a friend. Because he was still a friend right up to the spring of 1967. He was (your words) 'suddenly and for a very few months' the only friend you trusted. The one you talked things out with, listening hour after hour to Beatles records in his bachelor house behind the Brompton Oratory. Your words again: Paul McCartney is there between you as the attribute of your friendship.

Yes, it is just what you said it was: a bad painting that works. Too much this-equals-that. The sun-blind equals Selwyn. Paul McCartney and the Beatles equal friendship. Closes everything down to you in your little world of success, and nothing else. And that anagram closes everything down even more. To you and your bitterness. Against me and against the past.

'JE(A)LOUS(IE)Y'

It only works because nobody else knows what's in it of you and me. It works for them. It stays open. It cannot work for me.

For you and me, Jack, it's just a bad painting that stirs bad feelings.

And the worst memories.

I'm sorry. Again, I simply have to interject. I cannot accept what Felicity says here. This is not a bad painting. My opinion remains what it was in 1994 when I wrote my entry for the catalogue.

'*Jealousy/Jalousie*, despite the mystery of one of the companions with whom Driver painted himself and of the anagram beneath them, is perhaps the most important of his works from the period just before the break with Ivor Selwyn and the Berkeley Gallery.'

I commented then that its images were like the elements of a rebus waiting to be decoded. Well, Felicity has decoded them for us. She has shown us what was actually in it, not just in 1967 but when that anagram was added in 1978. She's allowed us to see her and Driver in the painting in a way we could never have imagined. She's made it part of a story.

But the image hasn't changed. The facts cannot change it. They certainly can't turn it from being good to being bad.

Facts surely cannot be *in* a painting. They can only be *around about* a painting. Of that I have always been convinced. How can they take over from Genius?

The worst memories.

Wednesday, 3 May 1978. A clean, bright morning. Waking and seeing the sun in the moving leaves against

the window. And feeling that you were not there.
Reaching for the clock. Before 7.00. Before 7.00 and
you not there. Shuffling down the stairs feeling the sleep
come with me. Edgy. Anxious.

You naked on the boards where they emerge from
under the carpet in front of the glass door out into the
garden. Crouched and very still. Your voice level,
but weary.

'Been up a long time. Watching the sun come in
through the leaves. Waiting for it to touch my body.
Feeling the air. The warmth in the air.'

'Why did you get up?'

'The strange sensations came again. Like before.
Except stranger.'

'How?'

'My whole leg. Heaviness. Dullness. I think that if
I were to raise myself, I would have to use my arms.
Otherwise I couldn't. I just couldn't.'

'It's weakness?'

'And the feeling . . . It's as if parts of me aren't
completely there. Touch me. Touch my left thigh.
There. Yes, like that . . . Almost nothing. I'm not there
to feel you.'

'Like before . . . No pain?'

'No pain.'

'Anything else?'

'This morning when I opened my eyes. Yes. The
world seemed to split in two. It came apart in my eyes.
And for a moment, it wouldn't come back together
again. Then it did. I have the feeling it might happen
again. Any time. And if it did, I wouldn't have the
power . . . I wouldn't have the power to close things up
again, to mend them.'

You were deadpan. There was no fear in your eyes
or your voice. Just a matter-of-fact determination to say
what needed to be said.

It was when you stood that I knew something was

really wrong. I can remember exactly how you did
it. Such a complex series of manoeuvres. First you
stretched out your legs carefully, resting your weight on
your arms behind you. Then you sank down on to your
right elbow and swivelled on to your side. Then you
bent your right leg and pushed up with your right arm so
that you were in a half-kneeling position. Then, trying
to keep all the weight off your left leg, you got yourself
up on to your feet. You stood as if it was an unnatural
posture to take up, with your left leg rather stiff and
slightly at an angle to the vertical. Rather still to begin
with, and exhibiting great concentration.

And then you began to laugh. You stood naked
shaking with helpless laughter in the morning sun. It
seemed as if you must have been laughing with the
sheer relief of having done it.

When you stopped you said you were frightened.

That was the beginning of the mischief, Jack. Unless
there were other signs and you never said. That was the
beginning.

You must have been angry. Someone like you is
angry when they are frightened. Because you hate
yourself for negative feelings, especially fear. But for
a very long time – right through the weeks before they
told us, and for months after that – you showed no
anger at all. And though I knew you were afraid and
sometimes it showed, there was rarely a sign of fear
either. People in danger are said to make a lot of jokes.
You made a lot of jokes. Dirty jokes. You seemed to
have adopted the posture of someone waiting. Jokily and
patiently.

Why did you write that clever-clever, hurtful word
on the picture? Just for something angry to do, when
the anger wouldn't come out any other way? Something
against me? There seemed no sense in it. And there
seems none now. A whole morning in the studio to write
with all your sign-painter's skill 'JE(A)LOUS(IE)Y' on

a dead canvas about a dead friendship and a dead past. So meticulously. And then the little fixed smile that went with showing it to me.

I saw it immediately, Jack. I understood. But I wasn't going to let you know. Why should I have let you know how you hurt me? I wasn't going to give you that.

But you saw through my special little smile and my shrug, didn't you?

I always was transparent to you.

Especially my pain.

For me, as a professional historian, I have to say that the most satisfying part of all in Felicity's piece about *Jealousy/Jalousie* came last. You see, I got it right in my jottings about the sun breaking through the blind. I was right about revelation. There's nothing more satisfying than having that kind of insight confirmed by absolutely unimpeachable evidence of this kind, even if it does come so many years later. To see it become a fact *in* the painting (and I mean not just round about, but *in* the painting). To see that it was really there all the time.

Watching the sun come through the leaves. Looking at your OTT sunburst threaten the parallels of the blind behind you and Selwyn.

At first, when they put you in your chair, you loved to lecture, didn't you, Jack? You had your own little mobile platform for performing. You didn't have to give up teaching for a year or two still; and you loved teaching.

You sitting in the middle of the studio, surrounded by rags and cans, swivelling in that chair, lecturing me.

'Light has always been revelation. Though, like knowledge, it often blinds. Chartres, Monet, André Breton. Light dazzles, but it's inside. Something that suddenly bursts out when one penetrates inside a closed and a very protected space. It's what's called "truth" in the Divine, in Nature, in sexuality. We need to protect ourselves from it. Louise wore sunglasses even in January. It needed just a glimmer of sunshine and she "protected herself". Long before all this talk about ultraviolet. Selwyn pulled down his blinds so that he could have his delights without seeing too much. He never saw much in pictures either. I never remember him looking at one for longer than ten seconds.'

But you said of me – and I shall not forget it – that I was not one of the 'light-hating species', that I was like you.

And you are in the anagram, aren't you?

'Je'– 'Io' – 'Jo' – 'I': they're all there.

But I don't know how to be sure. They're in a lot of other words too.

That would be, of course, the best place to end this chapter. And I would end it here if I preferred dramatic effect over the obligation to be honest. You see, I think I owe you something. You need to know the next picture that Felicity looked at with Jack. Otherwise I shall be under suspicion of manipulating the sequence again.

The next picture that Felicity picked out was not one of the lost pictures. Indeed, she did not pick out for her tour with Jack any of the eight (rather than five) lost pictures that were revealed on the third and final visit to the Orlando Street studio (which took place at the beginning of autumn 1993, in early October – a great pity, since there are three I would particularly like to know about, pictures which have no previous history of exhibition or publication). The next picture she chose did have a previous history; it was one of those against which critics liked to write in the late seventies, one of the forest pictures, *Ecce Homo* (the title alone was enough to invite charges of melodramatic pretentiousness).

It hung in the next room, Room 10, on the wall that faced you as you entered, inviting you into the last two rooms of the exhibition. She would have turned away from *Jealousy/Jalousie*, which hung in the middle of the long left-hand wall in Room 9, walked past the row of collaged works on paper beside it and through into Room 10 and there she would have been confronted at the far end by the dark enclosure of conifers that hems in rather grandly the images of *Ecce Homo*. Then she could have approached it slowly down the length of the space as if down the length of a clearing, because on either side of her would have been rows of forest pictures, all from the seventies. There were no works on paper in this room.

I shall leave you with a little of the necessary data to be getting on with.

Ecce Homo, 1975. Mixed media on panel, 8' × 7'8" (243.9 x 233.7cm).

First shown in 1977 at the small exhibition of Driver's forest pictures put on by Felix Snow in Tottenham Mews, one of four attempts towards the end of the decade and then at the outset of the eighties to revive interest in his work.

There is a strong sense of conifers forming, as it were, a wall above and around the central group of images. But the conifers are in no sense described. They are made up of densely streaked and swirled and spattered acrylic, the colour ranging between deep greens and blues with, here and there, edgings of yellow and orange burning through the interstices between the marks. This mass of paint frames an equally expansive area of paler grey and off-white (the work is one of the larger pictures Driver made in his career, almost eight foot by eight foot, though not quite a square). The paler grey and off-white area reads as a plastered wall, which is covered in cracks and graffiti. This area is, in fact, worked across a ground of plaster built up on the wood panel. It has been scratched and cut with sharp tools (the graffiti); and some of the surface is actually made up of photographs of the *same* surface, stuck on to it. In one corner of the 'wall', relatively small, but impossible to ignore, is a roughly yet deftly drawn insignia among the graffiti marks, a sun with stylised rays around which is wrapped a snake. The same motif, this time painted in yellow and gold, glows like a star among the conifer shadows. Both treatments of the motif combine a distinctly naïve, even childlike air with the sense of something sophisticated and mysterious. Otherwise the plastered 'wall' has been scored savagely with vertical cuts as if with a knife, leaving an image of rhythmic destruction, and the scoring crosses and seems indeed to cut up the more gently scratched outlines of a female torso, the drawing of which is distinctly gauche. Most surprising of all, the whole of the lower area of the work is a photomontage of various images of the sea apparently transferred from sunny tourist posters. Across it are the words: 'Tranquil seas'. The letters making up the words are put together from reproductions of different typefaces from some kind of printer's primer.

The picture has great force, but for me it used to raise more questions than it allowed me to answer. They are questions that Felicity will help us address. But not yet.

8

Neurotic Obsessive Behaviour

I can remember too. Felicity isn't the only one. I can remember the twenty-four years back to 1993 and 1994, to the days and days I spent tapping at my keyboard, putting together the facts.

I would arrive at the office presided over by Miranda by 8.15 a.m. No one else arrived at that sort of time in the offices at Coverlie's. I was the only person who could have recognised a single one of the army of cleaners which started off there before dawn. I would always follow the same routine. I would flick the firm padded seat of my swivelling chair (modelled on Kit Moss's famous swivelling chair) with my right forefinger, before lowering myself between the arms. I would swivel twice, first left, then right. I would stretch out my arms and sigh (pleasurably). Then I would switch on and listen to the desktop computer squeak and hum into being. Such an efficient, 100 per cent reliable sound. Then I would tap in my programme, and access the right file, and watch the data in question appear, eep, ep, swoosh: white on blue across the screen. And I would be in it. Adding, subtracting, checking the facts.

After about an hour (I would look at the time), the muted whinnying of phones and the pounding and racketing on the staircase outside would have begun to tell me that the days of others were beginning too. And I would resolve that another two lists had to be completed, or another set of correlations had to be checked out, before I would allow myself to stand up and look out of the window, and think of coffee. And before I thought of coffee, I would restrict myself to no more than two swivels every five minutes, plus one minute of comfortable reverie. My morning, in sum, would be spent imposing on myself and then surviving petty restrictions and deprivations, all in the interests of facts.

Unless Miranda came in.

I only ever spent afternoons and evenings, never mornings, in Felicity's living room beside the Mies van der Rohe Barcelona chairs, and Driver's chair. And in my corner of Felicity's living room *my* chair was not a swivel chair. It was very solid, with elaborately turned legs and upright back. Heavy and static. I rocked unsteadily on to its back legs instead of swivelling. I kicked back. But whatever the time – 2.00 in the afternoon, 6.15 in the evening – I stretched out my arms and sighed (pleasurably). And there too I spent the hours that I dedicated to the gathering of the facts about Driver subject to my own satisfyingly severe restrictions and deprivations. Not drinking coffee, not eating those irresistible truffle biscuits Felicity kept in the cupboard with the wooden slats, not stretching or kicking back or sighing.

Unless Felicity came in.

I have been rereading Freud. I know he isn't fashionable nowadays. I know he goes with that other dubious five-letter word which is hardly ever uttered: Lacan; quite apart from that four-letter word which is *never ever* uttered: Marx. But then, in the nineties, intelligent adults, even from the academic establishment in the humanities, were proud to litter their footnotes, and indeed their texts, with Freud, and, as you will have noticed from my jottings already, so was I. Thinking of then got me thinking of Freud.

And Freud has got me thinking 'analytically' of the Roland Matthias who so happily lived under all those self-imposed restrictions and deprivations to make the catalogue of '94. There simply can be no doubt about it: I was the victim of neurotic obsessive behaviour. I lived under the most exacting and ridiculous of taboos. What could it have been but the erection of a defence, the most elaborate and effective of defences? And taboos – how could it be otherwise? – are, of course, the outcome of ambivalent emotional attitudes. Towards what or whom or who? Towards Driver? Perhaps or perhaps not. But most of all towards Miranda and Felicity.

The logic is simple. I really was such a fool not to see it at the time. I played at love (of a kind) with Miranda, and *consciously* she was the object of my bewildered, deferential, fearful admiration. I knew that I could not even play at love (of any kind) with Felicity, and *consciously too* she was the object of my admiration, though it was marvelling and certainly neither fearful nor even deferential. But *unconsciously* (and not all that unconsciously either) I despised Miranda, who *wanted* me to touch her on a regular basis, while I loved Felicity, who I would never have dreamed of touching (outside my fantasies). You can laugh. Freud wouldn't have (you can check out ambivalent emotions and obsessive neurosis in the 'Rat Man' case and *Totem and Taboo* if you like): I really did despise Miranda and I know now I loved Felicity. It's just that I have no gift for writing about undeclared love and repressed hate. It requires the gifts of a *writer*.

That Miranda was despised and Felicity loved were both truths I had to avoid. Hence the neurotic obsessional behaviour. All those austere routines which I suffered with such self-righteous satisfaction. I suppose it could be said that the meticulous noting down of every detail, the insistence on consistency of punctuation, in the use of italics, of capitals, of single inverted commas, the absolute need to corroborate and then to corroborate again, the very process of building the catalogue measurement by measurement, ibid by ibid, dotted 'i' by dotted 'i', was neurotic obsessional behaviour. (Miranda used to treat as a matter worthy of wonder my 'unbelievably anal dedication to detail'.)

And I suppose that the catalogue was my defence against . . . What? My love and my hate of Jack Driver? Hate? Not possible. Driver was my real obsession. Driver was my insurance *against* neurosis. He made me sane. How could I believe that I ever hated him? At all.

Either I have misunderstood my Freud, or Freud is – to put no finer point on it – wrong. There was no ambivalence in my feelings for Driver. My catalogue was built on solid certainty.

But my relations with Miranda and Felicity, they *were* built on ambivalence. An ambivalence which I controlled when living my careful life of taboos on the screens of my VDUs, but which threatened to get out of control when either of them were with me. Then, I swivelled and stretched and made coffee and ate truffle biscuits and broke every one of my precious taboos. My entire defensive system of carefully structured obsessive activity dissolved, and I knew that 'anything could happen'. Especially where Miranda was concerned.

(Notice how I put the 'anything could happen' in inverted commas. Inverted commas are just one defence against words. They place them at a distance. They take away their immediacy. They weaken their power.)

Perhaps I should be honest. I knew that anything could happen, there and then, immediately, *without inverted commas*. And in italics.

8 November 1993
Miranda is a phenomenon. She is so healthy. If you scan her carefully from top to bottom in movement (it is necessary that she be in movement, because she never stops), you read a litany of signs declaring health. Thick, abundant brown hair, which seems not to have had to derive its glossiness from hair conditioner. A complexion as clear

of blotches and pimples and stray hairs as possible in a functioning human being under urban conditions. Limbs that move with total ease and flexibility. Irrepressible energy. A BMW of a woman running on some special kind of four-star for super-dynamic bodies.

She never has viruses. Even colds. I don't think she can ever have experienced what I know as an ache or a pain. She describes people as 'pains', but she never seems to have them. Except that is when the time comes for her monthly 'decline', which lasts for precisely three days, is announced by sudden, unexpected withdrawal and mostly takes the form of total withdrawal to her office and her male secretary/assistant, Gerry. Times of blessed release from the dangerous obligations to be ruthless, efficient and yet delightful and pleasure-loving *at the same time*.

Her extraordinary demands increase day by day otherwise. Coverlie's might be paying it, but I'm only on a postgraduate scholarship, and I'm beginning to be the classic executive stress victim. I'm becoming the very paradigm of unhealthiness. There's no justice.

The most recent of her 'declines' was last week, and it's only Monday. Such a lot was expected of me today. Thank God I've been able to rejig things to bring my Barnes timetable forward. I can't continue like this. And anyway, there's the job to consider. She seems to think that the job will 'get done' and all the time I'm getting behind. I'm way behind target: three entries behind target. She comes in and everything comes apart. The catalogue becomes an irrelevance. Quiet is simply inconceivable. There are phone calls to make, details to get straight, instant decisions to be made, and then comes the inevitable switch into the titillating mode . . . The caricature comes back full of sexual promise, and threatens to turn everything into the most dangerous kind of indulgence possible.

It's delicious. OK, it's delicious. So why are you complaining, Roland? There's *lots* of pleasure. So what can be wrong with that? You *want* pleasure. Of course you do. You may be experiencing a little stress, but you're normal. For Christ's sake, she's like a living, breathing wish-fulfilment in her very person. You know very well that you've always hoped that you could be the kind of man who qualifies for executive stress on account of too much unhealthily dynamic behaviour in work and play. Shouldn't you be *grateful*?

But even the play can be problematic. There's the question of role-play. Why does she insist on me being dominant? I like *her* to be dominant. And she is, really. But she insists more and more that I be the big, fatherly, *older* male ('Henry' in disguise, obviously). I'm not very good at it (I'm simply not 'Henry', and never will be). She goes all small and cuddly and I'm supposed to be strong and protective and then I'm supposed to abuse her with 'regal indifference'. How can I seriously abuse anyone – even Miranda – with regal indifference? She becomes daily more absurd. Besides which she becomes daily more unacceptable. Where's all the caring-and-relating sexual stuff I've been so conscientious about all these years? This is primal. She wants me to be a *gorilla*. In Miranda old-fashionedness is something visceral.

And there have been one or two moments of worrying seriousness. I couldn't even hint that I might be thinking of going serious. But she does. And I can't really tell if she's seriously being serious or just enjoying the discomfort she can cause by threatening to. I have a nagging (but incredulous) suspicion that there actually is an element of seriousness in it. There was yesterday.

'What would you say, Roland, if I said that I'm beginning to need you around me?'

'I would say . . . I would say . . . Well, you wouldn't.'

'But I might. You're evading the question.'

'It isn't really a question. I'm not going to answer a question that isn't actually being asked.'

'OK.' And then with audible pique, 'No one's asking, as you say. Not actually asking quite that question.

Not of this moment. So you can keep avoiding things as usual.'

Then silence and her dark chestnut eyes on me, before she picks up the phone and switches modes abruptly.

Avoiding things? How am I avoiding things? And what about that long look she gave me? Am I to read messages there? No, that's going too far. I don't think I could survive it.

But what tests me the most is the way that she won't slow down, not when she's in those immensely long periods between declines (twenty-five, twenty-six whole days). It's that indefatigable health and energy. I wish her declines could last just a little longer. Four days, say. Or five. Or a week. Or two. *A whole month*.

I get so tired.

See what I mean? I was wishing 'decline' on Miranda. In my dreams (the kind you have at night) I'm quite sure Freud would have found all the evidence he needed to diagnose in me the strongest of desires for her end – *murder*. Indeed, he would probably have been able to make the diagnosis from my diary entries.

I suppose he would have said that Miranda had become (by projection) my substitute sibling, with whom I was deep in an incestuous guilt-ridden affair, and with whom I was caught in the most savage rivalry for the affections of (you've guessed it) my (our) substitute mother, Felicity.

Ambivalent emotional attitudes or not, the fact of the matter was that by the autumn, even without any further crisis at the Tate (yet), I had become a cataloguer under mounting stress. I became unaccountably rude. I had intemperate outbursts (never, significantly you will say, with either Felicity or Miranda). I became difficult to work with (for everyone else). And there were times, in that office with its crammed filing cabinets and its shelves of tidily arranged secondary sources converging from all sides, there were times when every part of my body seemed suddenly, intolerably sensitive, the sum of accumulated irritations for which there was only one remedy: to sink deeper into the facts that flashed up white on blue on the VDU.

8 November 1993 (continued)
This evening I could hardly raise my fingers to the keyboard. My whole body aches. All the smooth parts and the edges, even the insides, behind my eyes, deep in my temples, everywhere aches. I can feel the various channels of my head and throat contracting to the tiniest diameters, and filling with the thickest asthmatic mucus. I think I am forgetting how to breathe. Miranda has wrung me out to dry. I am exhausted.

I got no more than an hour alone with the catalogue before she came on a 'flying visit' this morning.

'*Buon giorno, caro*. Have a *croissant*.'

(The italics are seriously necessary here. The thing is, she goes in for the language as she is spoken, Italian Italian and very French French; she especially likes showing off with the Gallic 'r' and 'u'.)

OK. I like cr-r-roissants. No danger. But croissants are *not* office food among professional cataloguers. They are crumbly and greasy and they stain everything they touch before depositing countless tiny fragments of themselves wherever they have been. These countless fragments then refuse to be picked up by any known cleaning device, scattering instead in ever more infinitesimal flakes over wider and wider areas. Most serious of all, *they get caught between the keys of keyboards*. They could remain there for *ever*.

Placed where they were, on top of the photographs which were at that moment the only visual data for the entry then in train, they instantly produced in me an intense desire to throw them out of the window. They, by their very presence, were a gross infringement of a whole range of prohibitions, including eating before elevenses. But, instead of doing my duty and ejecting them summarily, I found myself compounding all the problems by grabbing one (which literally burst in my fingers), breaking off one end (with still more crumblings) and stuffing it into my mouth, while enthusiastically thanking her.

It's called positive reinforcement. She'll be doing it every morning now.

'Delicious, don't you think? I pick them up from the most divine *patisserie* called Claude's just opposite my flat. Shall we make a regular *rendezvous* to wolf them together when I get in?'

'Oh, there's no need. Really. Fabulous. But no need to put yourself out, really.'

'Well, I think there's a *desperate* need. I really enjoy eating with you. And I especially love seeing you with all that flaky crust just covering your chin. You look really sinful, Roland.'

This is the kind of Miranda line in conversation with which I know now I cannot deal. I capitulate, and she doesn't even realise she's won a victory.

This time the switch of mode from indulgence to ruthless MBA efficiency was even more difficult to cope with than usual. And what she did then makes me anxious still now. I think she's busy manufacturing a crisis with June and the Tate. She and Troy. And I'm implicated. I'm right in it. What it's really about isn't at all clear, but the problem that came up today is one that's been threatening to cause a crisis for some time (my first note about it in these jottings was nearly two months ago): the question of what we're to do about June's list of works for the show when it's so far from ours. Miranda's put it on one side for the last few weeks. She obviously had her reasons for waiting. But no longer.

She began as if we'd been discussing it regularly for days, and as if I should have come up with a solution myself by now.

'Have you had any ideas about June's list?'

'June's list? I'd forgotten . . .'

'Well, I haven't. Action is needed, now. Problems like this have to be resolved. You should have been giving it some thought. She's your friend.'

'I'm sorry. I thought . . . Well, I just thought that since selection was your province, it wasn't really up to me.'

'It isn't up to you. It's up to me. But you should still have an opinion. Do you?'

'Uh . . . We should talk to her.'

'Arrive at a compromise?'

'Yes. There are some things that can only be resolved by compromise.'

'Well, I could have predicted you would have said that. Being chummy with people always gets in the way of clear thought. I sometimes despair of you, Roland. Surely you know me well enough by now to realise that I'm never going to agree with compromise. Feeble stuff. Not my style at all.'

(She's so clever at manoeuvring me into displays of weakness. This time she did it in order to accentuate her decisiveness. Hers and 'Henry's'.)

'There's no need to compromise with anyone,' she said. 'June's list isn't to be taken seriously. Anyone who wants to include the trio of *Labour Wins* pictures has no judgement. There simply isn't any mileage any more in those *political* pictures. It's Driver at his most banal. Why should we give her the compliment of even considering such an idea? No, I talked to Henry and he agreed with me. We just proceed as if she hasn't made a list at all. It's an irrelevance. But, tactically, it's necessary to play her along a little longer. So would you drop her a hint when you next see her in the Tate?'

(More unsavoury clandestine duties to perform. The anxiety intensifies.) 'How do you mean, drop her a hint?'

'Make her think there's no problem. Things are just delayed a little at our end. You know, say something about the time it takes to clarify the whereabouts of pictures, that sort of thing; the importance of being as up-to-date as possible with our information before finalising things. No need to say much at all. Just let her think we're working on it, and she's not been forgotten. Reassure any doubts she must have. Be your honest, dependable self. She trusts you. There's a little more of the game to play, you see. It isn't the moment to bring things to a head quite yet.'

In that bubbly, sociable little person there are such chilling reserves. She's begun to use her temper on June too. Just once in a while. As a diversionary tactic or to keep her at a distance or just to render her dysfunctional for a little while. She relishes the chance when it comes, especially because June becomes so catastrophically dysfunctional. The poor girl has no experience at all in how to survive such outbursts of venomous ranting.

Miranda and Troy *are* playing a game. And I'm playing a game too, because they make me play it for them. I'm not sure why. What it's about. How can she and Troy ignore everything that June says? And how can they seem to care so little what McKenna might think? McKenna never gets a mention.

And yet, the thing is that when it comes to the issue – the works to be selected, in this instance – Miranda's always right. She's wrong about the politics, but she's right about the works: the *Labour Wins* pictures *are* banal. It's not just that she has June beaten tactically (as far as I can see); she's just better at the job. Nothing's fair. Why should someone so lacking in what everyone calls 'depth' be so bloody good at making an exhibition? Still, she couldn't *begin* to put a catalogue together; hasn't the staying power. We can be thankful for that, *n'est-ce pas*?

So there you are. That was your morning, Roland. The croissant disaster followed by conspiracy and deceit. In the afternoon came sex. Things were lifted on to a new plane, grotesque even by Miranda's standards. She seems, temporarily at least, to be shelving role-playing for the 'advancement of skills'. Efficiency is taking over from everything else. The Coverlie's management ethos is to penetrate even our interpersonal relations in the field of sex.

She started by introducing the element of surprise. Certainly I should have been expecting it; I should not have been at all surprised. After all, it's not the first time.

She'd been with me for half an hour, keeping unusually quiet, because she was checking valuations – one of the few things with the power to keep her off the phone. I was contentedly tapping in footnotes. Doesn't sound much when I put it down, what happened to puncture the calm.

She kissed my right ear. I'll say it again: she kissed my right ear. But the thing is, when you're not expecting it, a kiss on the right ear *is* quite a shock. The noise of lips imparting suction, however sveltly, right up against one's auditory aperture is only rivalled by a heavy lorry starting up on the car deck of a cross-channel ferry.

'There, you do like it when I take a little nibble. The ear is such a sensitive place, *n'est-ce pas*? I've been thinking, Roland *chéri*, that we need to develop the athletic side of our lovemaking. Seriously, I saw a really interesting video the other night. It did occur to me that we could have rather an exciting time watching it together. Especially if you buy us some of that massage oil. But the thing was, they went about it so *vigorously* and *athletically*. I don't think we're ambitious enough.'

I made a pathetic attempt to return to a sense of moderation.

'Isn't it better to leave these things to instinct, Miranda?'

'No, no, no, instinct was never enough. We have to develop our *skills*. Pleasure can be taken on to a quite different plane with just the minimum of instruction. That's what the commentary said. Quite right too, always do things as well as possible. Don't you agree? [It has to be agreed, she's the highest possible achiever in everything.] I was going to suggest that we watched it this evening, before I go off to that cocktail party of Marcus

Warburton's. I've asked Gerry to set up the video in my office.'

I couldn't have been expected to conceal my horror entirely at that point. Gerry Dworkin was now, it seemed, openly aiding and abetting.

'Gerry's setting it up in your office!?'

'Yes, he thinks we're going to be watching sixties and seventies footage on the art world and so on. You know, David Sylvester interviews and *Monitor* films. Did you think I'd gone off my head or something?'

'Well, you never know with you, Miranda.' (My relief was palpable, I'm sure.)

'You're on then. Five forty-five on the dot this evening. We'll have precisely seventy-five minutes, so don't be late.'

There was no plausible reason for not being 'on'. So just before 5.45, I was rather sheepishly announcing my arrival to Gerry with the massage oil safely concealed among my correspondence and three-and-a-half-inch disks in my briefcase.

Well, wasn't it *any* fun at all? Yes, of course it was, even though the video turned out to be full of extremely thin men and women with quantifiable ribs and astonishing stamina. They gave the impression of being a cast of specially selected cross-country runners. The very thought of them *vigorously* rising and falling in interlocked postures of Laocoon-like complexity still tires me out. But at least we weren't role-playing. I'm not sure how the extremely thin males in the cast could have served as role models for abusing anyone with 'regal indifference'. In my opinion, they were utterly without dignity let alone regality. But then, that's what I am when Miranda makes me do things with her: utterly without dignity.

'We've got so much to learn,' she said brightly. 'I really can't wait.'

And then she capped it all by threatening to get serious again. I can't read her at all. She's a completely fictional creature – someone invented her and it wasn't me – but she's not sure which kind of fiction to stick to. Quite apart from the fatigue, she's getting me into a very complicated kind of anxiety state too; there are whole new dimensions of anxiety involved.

'You know, Roland, I can enjoy things with you such a lot.'

'Can you? I'm glad.'

'I would never have imagined it. I just thought it might make things less boring to begin with. You come across as solid and dependable at first, not exciting at all. But you've almost become a lover, you know. It's so delicious the way you go along with my little *faiblesses*. You understand my *petites faiblesses, n'est-ce pas*?'

'What do you mean, a lover?'

'Does it matter?'

'I'm not supposed to mention love.'

'Oh, that. No, but being a lover isn't quite the same thing at all. It doesn't mean being in love. Lovers have mistresses. I'm beginning to like feeling that I'm your mistress. It fits. You can be really quite exciting, after all.'

'You're not going to say you need me?'

'Why would I say that? But I like you being my lover. *Compris?*'

She wouldn't say she needed anyone, apparently. Except perhaps if Henry . . . If Henry what? But no doubt Henry doesn't associate love with lovers either, even if he was taking on the role (a heavy responsibility, I would tell him – if he asked me).

Thank God, I could end it all after our seventy-five minutes of hot and cold video-watching by saying with irreversible decisiveness that I wouldn't be in tomorrow afternoon.

'Not my fault,' I said. 'Felicity has summoned me.'

'But I really can't spare you.'

'Sorry. Can't say no to Felicity.'

'Damn Felicity! Why should she always win?'

And I suppose it has to be said. Felicity always does.

Things were blessedly much quieter at Felicity's. I could almost pretend to myself sometimes that they were monastic in the most austere sense. I had my own key. So, as long as I warned her beforehand, I could work there when she was away on her days teaching at Chelsea. I often timetabled my Felicity afternoons with that in mind, and also of course with the absence of Brenda in mind too, because Brenda seemed unaware that the Hoover made a noise.

I would give Felicity a call, ask if she could leave out such and such a batch of archival material for me (press cuttings, photographs, etc.), and then bask in anticipation of self-denying peace. The possibility would open up of hours and hours of uninterrupted cataloguing under the severest repressive conditions. No stretching, no kicking back, no coffee, no biscuits, no *mention* of sex. It was my way, of course, of expiating my constant breach of taboo after taboo under the infuriating autocracy of Miranda.

But as time went on between autumn 1993 and the beginning of 1994, my tappings reveal a gradual change in the situation at Felicity's. The single long extract I've given you from 8 November 1993 can stand for all of those days when things went a bit far with Miranda (about once every two or three weeks). The routine of indulgence, doing business, and early evening 'games' followed by speechless exhaustion (on my part) was an established one.

I should add that the moments of seriousness were not serious. Or so it seems now. Nothing came of them. I suppose you would have guessed as much. You will have realised, as I did, that Miranda simply wasn't capable of depth. She can't have actually wanted me (or anyone?) as a lover in the full sense. It's not credible, is it? I'm sure you agree. I never really knew, though, whether her moments of seriousness were anything as calculated as a tactic. Perhaps it was just a way of binding me in tighter, so I could be better counted on when the crisis came. Miranda – Lady Roache – never has gone in for love, after all. 'Relationships' wouldn't get a mention in any obituary, and that includes her single, expertly judged marriage (to which she has stuck, no doubt since it was not too confining and since she is, after all, an 'old-fashioned girl' at heart). When I read about her now – and she's everywhere in the deeper reaches of the broadsheets still – I feel that, for all her hyperactivity, she's lived nearly as barren a life as me. Don't you think?

Conveying the way things developed at Felicity's is more difficult. I can only do it by giving you a carefully chosen sequence of shorter extracts. I've selected a first extract from November (the same week as the 8 November entry), a second from early January 1994, a third from late February and a fourth from early March (the following week, in fact).

What I find here unmistakably is growing *tension*. A transition from blessed peace to nameless apprehension.

Of course, I know what happened next. I had every reason, as you will see, to be apprehensive.

10 November 1993

My nerves are mercifully in a state of serene deadness. I've laid them to rest. I've finally (for the moment) killed off the over-excitement induced by over-exposure to Miranda, and I sit here untouched by aches and pains, ready and willing to tap. Such perfect days of productivity in the interests of Genius should be preserved in one's memory so that one can just step back into them when the hyperactive threaten one's sanity.

To walk into Felicity's house when it is empty. The silence is so warm. There is not just stillness but profound comfort: the sense that nothing will ever move again in this place. A stable, harmonious indoor world, behind the little porch with its sloping roof.

It is not a sad house. It possesses Felicity's serenity. I have never felt Driver's absence, because, I suppose, she does not relate to him as a person she has really lost. She treats him as if he's around. When I ask her about him, and she has to remember, she's pleased with him or angry with him, or regretful of something said between them. It's as if the things she remembers have just happened.

'Why did he have to say something like that? It really didn't make the situation easier with Ivor.'

'Oh God, trust Jack! He hasn't left a single note about it. His records always were a mess.'

I have never sensed that this is a house of mourning, or ever was, even though the chair stays there, her *memento mori*. True she remembers *how* he died (though she never mentions it now), but sometimes I think that she does not remember that he is, in fact, dead. It's as if the illness and dying were just a passing phase, and he's now well out of it. She talks about him as if his feelings are still to be taken into account: as if he's there to be consulted.

This afternoon I started at 2.00 on the dot. I knew when it had turned 3.35 because that was the time today when the sun was due to hit my screen (it is a few minutes earlier every day) and the words and figures were due to disappear in haze. The sun stayed on my screen for just five minutes, before it slid below the hedge and suddenly the garden and the living room had become cool, shadowy places.

While the sun was there I could not work, without taking a lot of trouble to shift the screen. So I took my first break and reflected on the luxury of two and a half hours of unbroken discipline, bent over my keyboard, shuffling papers, turning pages, sorting photographs, getting things right once and for all. There was the time now to make an instant coffee, to eat three chocolate truffle biscuits and to walk up and down the carpet as well as rock and kick back on my chair. And I could do it with that lovely sense of deserving virtue. Haven't I been a good boy?

Then, the instant the sun had moved off my screen, and

the white on blue was there for me to read and to add to again, I was back in the calm of total absorption, expiating still more of my guilt under my severest self-denying regime. Satisfaction.

When I am working there on her teaching days, I've noticed how Felicity always makes her entrance in precisely the same way. It is invariably between 6.00 and 6.30, well after I've lit the lights and after the darkness has closed right in outside the windows. There is nothing more perfect than the expected happening just as it should. I don't think I can remember her ever breaking her routine.

I hear the latch click. I hear her in the hall. I hear just how elaborately she tries *not to make a noise*. She takes her shoes off the moment she crosses the threshold. She does not step down the hall, she slips along it. A kind of shushing sound, which edges quietly into the living room, just enough to tell me she's on the move. It makes me smile. Once in the kitchen, she pours her *pastis*. I know it is her *pastis*, because I know it is never anything else. I hear the gentle rasping of the bottle top being unscrewed. I hear the trickle of the liquid, and then the shoosh of the water that turns it white. I hear the muffled thud of the heel of the glass on the wooden kitchen table. I hear the chair eased back.

There is quiet. She waits for me to break it, because she knows and I know, although a closed door separates us, that it is for me to break it.

'How was your day?' I say, and I might as well be the son of the house. It's such a very comfortable feeling and I know she feels it too.

'Fine,' she says. 'Just fine.'

Today was exactly like that.

May tomorrow be. And the next day.

4 January 1994

Something happened today that was strange. It was a small thing in itself. I wonder if it is significant.

I've recorded before somewhere in these jottings Felicity's routine on entering after her days at Chelsea. It is, after all, still more evidence of her special qualities of tact and sensitivity. She is one of the few who understand that when one is right inside one's work, one cannot interrupt it just like that, so she has always left it to me to be the one who breaks my silence. Today was different.

I heard the door. I heard her quiet motion along the hallway. I heard the pouring of the *pastis* and of the water to turn it white. And then, extraordinarily, she opened the door of the kitchen into the living room and spoke.

And she didn't just say 'Hello, what sort of a day have you had?' She spoke intrusively.

'Goodness, Roland, why isn't the light on in here? You're sitting nearly in darkness, you'll damage your eyes.'

I was sitting perfectly happily at my table with the little table light on the Arts and Crafts chest of drawers giving quite adequate light. And anyway the screen was more than adequately lit. I nearly said that it was none of her business. Probably just as well I didn't. But the fact is that her breaking our routine like that, and *intruding*, disturbed me. It still annoys me to think of it.

That's all there was to it. Nothing more. After that the pattern reverted to the old routine exchange about uneventful days, and as usual I told her one or two of the more interesting things that had emerged. I told her, of course, about the complete set of the screen prints Driver made for Selwyn on the theme of *Catch Me* turning up at the Hobbes Gallery.

So normality did return. And I made my last cup of instant for the day as she sipped her *pastis*.

But I didn't feel so comfortable. The expected didn't happen quite as it should.

Why should it disturb me so much? It was such a little thing to happen.

25 February 1994

What is it about Felicity at the moment? She's started making a new kind of conversation with me. She's started *getting at me*. Not very aggressively. There's a word that might apply: 'joshing'. She joshes me. She gently, humorously, but in the end extremely unsettlingly *winds me up*. She seems to be looking for some sort of reaction. I wish I knew what it was. It may be that she wants me to josh her. But she must know I can't. It's not in my nature. At least, not with special people like her. Or perhaps she wants me to be angry. Except it's so gentle that you couldn't call it provocative. That's why the word josh seems just about to sum it up. It does disturb me though.

Perhaps it would help to try to reconstruct the conversation as it was today. Perhaps I will be able to see what was *behind* it happening in *how* it happened. After all, you often see the why in the how in history. So here are the facts of the matter.

It started the minute she came through the door from the kitchen with her glass of *pastis* in her hand. She didn't open with any of the routine greetings.

'You're such an orderly person, Roland,' she said. It was as if she was making an accusation, and not an accusation about some minor domestic omission (which does sometimes happen), but an accusation about me, my ways, my *character*. Though there was nothing aggressive on the face of it. She said it quietly, with that little smile of hers.

'Ah, Felicity, you took me by surprise.'

She had.

She was totally at ease sipping her *pastis*. She was across the room leaning up against the Edwardian mantelpiece with her colourfully braceleted arm stretched out along it. Her elegance can sometimes make me feel a lump. And there was such an amused look in her eye.

'All those papers and books. So many to have out at once. And all so absolutely orthogonally placed, so tidy.

Unbelievably De Stijl. How is it you always manage to open your books so neatly, everything smoothed down and at a right angle to everything else? It beats me. I'm sure Jack would never comprehend that his chaos has led to such order.'

'It's the way I do things. I want to get them right.'

And that's it: how else are things to be got right? If she wants the job done, she has to expect an orderly sort of person in her house, for God's sake.

'Do you know what I think? I think it would do you a lot of good to be *dis*orderly sometimes. Perhaps you are . . . in very private places, late at night. Is there another *dis*orderly Roland, who emerges like Mr Hyde, and flings his papers all over the room and becomes passionately self-indulgent?'

'But I *like* order, Felicity. It's the way I am.'

She shook her head and mock tut-tutted.

'So it's a great deal more serious than I thought. It's the way you *are*, Roland. You're simply too good for your own good. I bet Miranda tells you that, doesn't she? She tells me that you can be quite a ball of fun when she gets under your skin.'

'She tells you what?'

'You heard. That you can be quite a ball of fun. No need to be ashamed, love. It's a great relief to hear. I worry about you, Roland. You mustn't blame me. It's just that I'm quite fond of you. And I can't help feeling that you're in danger of becoming boring.'

Now the trouble, as you know, Roland, is that you yourself are worried about the danger of becoming boring. It is a danger, as you have often told yourself, in someone who is so passionately dedicated to getting the facts right. And to be a man of order in one's work does *not* necessarily mean being boring in person, does it? No wonder I was taken aback. She must have seen she had, as it were, touched something vulnerable in me.

'Don't take offence, Roland, I don't mean you're boring

now. I just worry about all this head-down perfectionism of yours. I'm terribly grateful really. You're such a love.'

So there you are. Nothing more than a little joshing. All right, the bit about being boring got close to being insulting, but she retracted instantly, and you couldn't call any of it hostile, or even unkind. There was very little in it at all. So there really can't be much behind it either. And yet . . . and yet, it disturbs me. There *is*, after all, something new in it. As if she wants something to *happen*.

And there's another thing I've noticed. She's started calling me 'love' and even 'Roland, my love'. Just as a matter of course.

I suppose it's no more than my being around so much. I'm part of the household. Like Brenda (though she doesn't call Brenda 'my love').

And it has to be said: there's still nothing more peaceful than an afternoon at Felicity's.

4 March 1994

For a moment this evening, just before I left Horley Road, I had the impression, very vague but still distinct, that my fantasies about Felicity are not perhaps so fantastic.

She touches me a lot. She has always touched me a lot. A slight pat, a hand on the shoulder, lightly, even once in a while a sort of hug she has for communicating pleasure in seeing me. It's a kind of hug she gives all her friends (I've seen), so it's not a special hug, and it is certainly not a sexualised hug. This evening there was a moment when she touched me and it was different. It was sexual. Not much about it said so. But enough. I know it was sexual.

It's difficult to describe. There was so little to it. The place was the kitchen. The situation was mildly amusing conversation about nothing in particular over a bottle of red *Pays de* somewhere. I was standing against the kitchen unit. She was just to my right, sitting up on the unit. She was therefore above me, with me facing her, looking up. If there had been something I or she said – a joke or a remark about her or about me – it could have been normal (just about). But it happened when there was a pause. We were both momentarily silent.

I should not, perhaps, have continued looking up at her. There was, it is true, a slight awkwardness in that. But it doesn't explain what happened. Not the way she looked at me, and the way she put her hand against the side of my cheek. And then down on to my shoulder. And not the way that she rested it there with the index finger still touching just where one is so sensitive, close to the lobe of the ear.

I was careful not to return any sign. Not to seem either to encourage or discourage it. And there was nothing else.

Her hand dropped on to the surface of the unit, and she said rather brusquely, 'Well, that's enough for today. It's time to leave me to myself. Drink up if you want to finish the bottle. Otherwise you'll leave me to drink it alone, which isn't very healthy at all.'

That's the way she talks when she's being bright and breezy, which isn't the way she really is.

I wonder what I would do if anything else happened. I don't think I dare think about it. The fantasies are much safer.

Perhaps I exaggerate. It was only the briefest and lightest of touches. Not much to get so fussed about.

She wouldn't.

So here I am, the obsessional neurotic, trying to keep my head down under as many taboos as possible, harassed on the outside by Miranda and Felicity, and on the inside by ambivalent emotions. Conflict. Tension. Apprehension. What *would* I do if Felicity *really* did something? My fantasies told me in lurid detail what I should do. But they were only thoughts.

If truth be told, not much happened of any moment between the midsummer of 1993 and May 1994 when the controversy at the Tate finally broke. But if one wants to see a couple more straws twitching in the wind (the wind around and within the Tate), there are two letters from McKenna to 'Rag', which are worth bringing to your attention.

28 February 1994

Dear Rag,

Had June in my office today, June Sutcliffe. She has a way of being firm and angry which is distinctly impressive. She came with a dossier. She is the kind of person who keeps records meticulously and can support a case. She is the best kind of bureaucrat. And as you know I respect good bureaucrats; the ones who make things run as they should. This is a person who cares passionately about what is going on. She cares passionately about Jack's show.

In her dossier was her correspondence over the last two months with Miranda Browne plus supporting material: the minutes she has kept of meetings (sometimes involving Matthias and sometimes involving both Matthias and Felicity), notes taken after telephone calls, selection lists and so on. The story it all tells worries me, and I'm not sure I know what to do about it.

Sometime in November, just after the last of the visits to see the lost pictures at 2 Orlando Street, both June and Miranda made selections. There were significant differences. June, as curator of the show, insisted that all of the works on her list should be included, and accepted all the works on Miranda's. This resulted in an expanded selection, but an acceptable one (145-odd pictures), especially since the space allocated to the show was enlarged from ten to twelve rooms. June heard nothing for a very long time (two months) and assumed that it was all so routine that no official agreement had been considered necessary on the Coverlie's side. Meantime everything was proceeding by telephone calls and meetings 'satisfactorily'. Though June does note a certain 'impatience' on Miranda's part about the 'speed and efficiency' with which arrangements were being made. Then, towards the end of January, out of the blue, Miranda sent June an 'approved final list' (approved, that is, by Troy and Miranda). Coverlie's had simply ignored all the works on June's list that had not been on Miranda's. June wrote a polite but determined reply reinstating them. Miranda became unobtainable on the phone, until a curt and definitive note arrived from her, announcing that there was 'no room for compromise on this', and that Coverlie's was 'adamant from the chairman down'. She followed this up with a phone call in which she ranted at June about 'the IRRELEVANCE of the *Labour Wins* pictures', told her she had the 'brain of a *petit pois*', and warned her to 'KEEP OUT OF THE WAY'. One has to conclude that ranting has become a normal part of Miranda's telephone manner lately. So here I am with June in my office.

I shall, of course, make a couple of phone calls, not to rant, but to use my famous diplomatic talents. There is, however, something about the tenor of the exchanges that leaves one doubtful about the outcome. Miranda's treatment of June is nothing better than rude. Quite apart from the delays and evasions, there is hardly a vestige of courtesy in her letters, and one can only say that the tone, in places, nears contempt, while her outbursts on the phone are simply unacceptable. Now, Miranda is shrewd. She may appear an empty socialite, but one knows well enough that she plays her cards with care. If she treats June and the Tate in this cavalier way, it means she thinks that she can get away with it.

The question, Rag (and I know you cannot answer it for me), is not whether she will get away with it, but *why she thinks she will*.

There are very few possible answers, and each of them worries me.

Coverlie's sees no need to treat us with respect any more. That's what's new.

Tell me I'm merely paranoid.
Yours,
Simon

9 March 1994

Dear Rag,

One has to confess it, old friend, my famous diplomatic talents are not what they were. Or we live in a world where diplomacy has no place.

Miranda has her way. June is even more angry and determined than she was; she is muttering now about resignation. Troy is affable but immovable. My trustees are committed to Coverlie's and will not allow any talk of pulling out of the sponsorship deal. Felicity seems unmoved by it all, and will not see that there is an issue of principle. She talks rather bewilderingly about 'the new world order'. I am nonplussed.

I have the feeling that a war has been declared, but that no one has thought to tell me about it.

Say I'm wrong.
In haste,
Simon

9

Ecce Homo

Nineteen seventy-five was our Nietzsche summer. That was a dangerous and wonderful time.

I walked up Room 10 and I singled out the six summer 1975 pictures, the Nietzsche pictures. Miranda has hung them all in a cluster around *Ecce Homo*, which she has given pride of place on the end wall. Alone. She doesn't know that they're the Nietzsche pictures – no one does except us – but she has sensed the danger that is in all of them as in none of the other forest pictures. She knows they cannot be separated. She has that kind of sixth sense.

They all still feel dangerous to me: dangerous like the funny and thrilling and crazy wisdom of those texts we spent the summer reading. You knew it all already. You always did. And it gave you such pleasure, didn't it, to watch me go through the learning process, to see me switching from laughter to anger to elation and back again.

Miranda is right. *Ecce Homo* has to be shown alone. It's the most dangerous of them all.

Why did you bury us and Nietzsche so deep? The title never helped. No one has ever seen Nietzsche in it. Not even the dogged Roland. The clues are too obscure, and the title is too easily read as you-as-Christ presented by Pilate to the people. The way it was read at Felix's exhibition in Tottenham Mews.

'What are we to make of the "suffering artist" taken to this extreme of self-pity? How are we to feel more than a slightly uncomfortable sadness? Jack Driver has finally dissolved into a rather heavy kind of hot air.'

Well, what the hell did you expect, Jack? It was bound to come over as posturing. They all had such a good time ridiculing the idea of God-in-Man-in-Jack-Driver.

And even that word 'tranquil' sounded like posturing: tranquil = lyrical/poetic = absurd anachronism. No one talks about 'tranquil seas' now. And they didn't then. And no one reads Nietzsche *that* carefully, so who was ever going to see how the phrase connects?

But none of that matters now. And I mean it. No one calls it posturing now. It's not like the 1977 show. I don't quite understand how it's happened. People come *determined* to take you positively. Even *Ecce Homo*, the title. They allow the image to hit them. I've seen it. I've seen the way they turn and walk out of Room 9 and into Room 10 and just stop. And then I've listened to the way they talk about it. They don't find the title inflated at all now, and they find the phrase 'tranquil seas' 'rather suggestive' or 'interestingly archaic' or 'haunting'.

They talk about the *contrasts*:

'Fantastic. The contrasts between the great, wild swirls of paint in the trees (don't you see? You have to see them as trees all around), and the calm seas in the collaged fragments below (don't you see? There, below, it's sea, the writing tells you: "tranquil seas"). It's almost as if the forest grows right out of the sea. Great.'

And they talk about 'ecological cleanliness'. That's a phrase of Graham's. He's dedicated a whole section of his catalogue essay to turning your forests (and especially *Ecce Homo*) into 'a series of telling statements that prefigure the environmentalism of the 1980s and beyond'. So they've become your 'Green Paintings', and (you'll never believe this) they 'are to be read as a late-twentieth-century echo of the nature-worship of Ruskin'.

You painting 'Green Paintings'! Fake radicals, you used to call them. Well now you're one of them. You and the Nietzsche paintings are 'Green'. And they're not far from bringing Caspar David Friedrich into it, and turning you into a fully fledged Romantic with a capital 'R'. They've very nearly rumbled your pantheism – though for all the wrong reasons.

Can't you see how they would do it? I mean turn you Green. Not at all difficult. Those battered plaster walls in *Ecce Homo*, cut to pieces with your Stanley knife, signify 'the degeneration of the inner city' and 'they are set against the dark majesty of the forest and the unpolluted purity of tranquil seas'. And, of course, 'Ecce Homo' is a reference to 'original humanity', to the 'natural' against the 'civilised'. So (it's only logical) the graffiti and the mark-making on the plaster – that sign of the sun with the coiled serpent, that cutting up of the surface and the outline of my body you drew into it – they are 'the signifiers of the regressive degeneracy of the civilised condition'. And when the 'tranquil seas' aren't signifying purity, they're signifying 'the complacency of Establishment values before the environmental holocaust'. Graham's even developed an elaborate psychoanalytic/anthropological theory about the clean and the unclean and the formation of the ego.

If you were really here, Jack, you would have to write your own *Ecce Homo*, like Nietzsche did, to tell everyone how badly they've all got you wrong.

And I'm sorry, but I can't stop myself from saying it: I told you so. I said you *have* to put Nietzsche in – the head or the figure or the name of Nietzsche in. And I got the worst flak for it.

'Here, read. Look what he says. He understands: "I am one thing, my writings are another." You have to see. It's like that with my paintings. I am one thing, they are another. They make their own meanings. I won't *put* meanings into them for people just to read them off the surface.'

OK, you can quote Nietzsche like that, but he wrote *Ecce Homo* to be *understood*. How can you deny it? You don't. You just ignore it.

'What do you want me to do? Twit! (I hate you calling me twit; why do you do that? It patronises me.) I suppose I could graffiti his head and his walrus moustache on to the plaster, eh? Well, Christ! *Everyone* would recognise the profile of the great Friedrich instantly, wouldn't they? After all, his moustache is engraved in every mind's eye, like Richard Nixon's nose. You can be really banal, do you know that?'

I know I can be banal. But so can you, Jack. Especially when you're being sarcastic and angry. You were wrong. The fact is that what people find in *Ecce Homo* when they can't find Nietzsche is worse than banality. And the fact is that the title, the words, the marks, the sun and the coiled serpent, they were and *are* attached to things, to things we experienced, we lived. To the danger.

People *do* feel the danger. I've heard it in the way they talk about what they're seeing. They can't *read* the marks on the wall and they can't read the forest and the 'tranquil seas', but they can feel the wildness against the calmness; they can feel the tension. The impact is real.

And I feel the danger still too. Do you remember that strange passage from *Ecce Homo*? You must do. It was you who quoted it to me.

'To *communicate* a state, an inner tension of pathos through signs, including the tempo of signs – that is the meaning of every style.'

The tempo of signs. Your forest takes me up and spins me round. And I can see you in the *baraque*, with the canvas stretched out in front of you like Pollock, moving so fast and so deftly around it to work the green and the blue out of the cans across the surface, sweeping and swirling and scouring the paint. I still feel the forest as paint moving. A dance. Like it was. Like the making of all your forests. Dionysus.

And even the making of the sea was like that. The cutting up of the images, the fixing of them to the canvas. Tempo.

Do you remember deciding that there must be sea, 'tranquil seas'? If the forest is danger, we are solitary in it. We together.

It was a way of giving yourself courage again. Nietzsche on solitude and the dangers of glory. He made your isolation something strong.

'The inventors of new values have always lived away from glory and the marketplace.'

'You go above and beyond them: but the higher you climb, the smaller you appear to the eye of envy. And he who flies is hated most of all.'

And then, the very best, the passage Nietzsche wrote specially for us.

'The earth remains free for great souls. Many places – the odour of tranquil seas blowing about them – are still empty for solitaries and solitary couples.'

Tranquil seas and the dance of the forest.

For fuck's sake, Jack, I can't take you seriously sometimes. You and I know that we were not 'solitaries' at all. OK, we could sit outside in the sun devouring (that really is the word) *Thus Spake Zarathustra* and *The Birth of Tragedy* and *The Gay Science* and *Ecce Homo* (in between the other paperbacks we filled the back of the Cortina with), and we could look up at the forest all around us and think we really were on some kind of solitary retreat from the world, like Nietzsche on his 'piece of high land' at Sils-Maria. But we weren't really. You know it and I know it.

We spent a hell of a lot of time 'coming down from the mountain', I mean going into the village and 'having a drink', and you spent a hell of a lot of time being charming with the locals, the way you always did. I don't remember much fearless yes-saying and no-saying. You were far too busy being the irresistible Jack. The Nietzsche summer was the least solitary of all, wasn't it? And the best.

When I think of that time – or at least when I think of that time without thinking of sex – I don't think of us alone in the forest and working in the *baraque*. I think of the little bar at the Hôtel Moderne, with the football pennants all around it, and the team photographs of the sporting youth of Saint Genès-aux-Bois. Strangely out of place, you said, that iconography of competition and health, when you take a real look at the Hôtel Moderne's clientele.

You being their bit of exotica and loving it: '*le peintre anglais*', a bit mysterious, even '*bizarre*', but '*très sympa*'.

Sitting there as well in the Café Bosquet, three to the table: you, me and Monsieur Carron, with Madame Carron drying glasses behind the bar, and Jean-Paul and Hélène and Hélène's baby, the little François, all there. The heaviness of the stone all around; the heaviness of the wooden furniture, all posing there as 'natural', apparently hewn and sliced out of whole trees from the forest, yet covered in plastic varnish and warm and waxy to the touch. The strange farming implements suspended against the stone walls: wood and metal shaped like extinct creatures. The bright yellow ashtrays saying 'RICARD' loudly. Me with my *pastis*, white and milky. You with your hyper-gaseous beer. Monsieur Carron quietly emptying glass after glass of *vin de table*.

The conversation like an extremely uncoordinated collage, full of strong statements buried under *non sequiturs*. Monsieur Carron's French descending with his wine into deeper and deeper obscurity, the words running incomprehensibly into each other. My French coming regularly to the end of its tether and turning into nonsense with a good accent (they always said how French my accent was). You nodding vigorously when you hadn't understood a thing.

The man was a '*brave type*', yes, but he hated Socialism, Jack. He was at his most comprehensible when he was insulting everything *gauche*. And all you did was nod convivially as if he was a soul mate. I can't do the French, but I can remember the sense of it:

'Giscard d'Estaing is a great man. He's an educated man. He speaks English like the English. Isn't that right? You've seen, eh? And he knows the French. He cares about the French who do some work. Not the lazy ones. He cares about business. Mitterand, he's nothing. He'd have the Communists in government tomorrow. The Socialists are just for their civil-servant friends: all those schoolteachers and time servers. And all those spongers who pick up their hand-outs just for being alive. I pay taxes. I pay taxes to keep up the hand-outs and the pensions. And I know you're an artist, and you're not like that, but the arts are the worst. They spend millions on things no one understands. Did you know that? Millions of francs. They'd put me out of business tomorrow. Monsieur Boileau, you know the *maçon* from Condat, the son of the farmer at Les Carrières, he's still paying off their fines. They ruined him. Said his accounts weren't up to scratch. The Socialists are tyranny, my friend.'

And you were his friend. And Madame's friend. And Jean-Paul's and Hélène's and little François's friend. You got right into their family life: where '*la petite* Bernadette' was now with her husband who refused to settle down and was (the worst insult of all) '*pas sérieux*'; how Bruno, '*le neveu*', was doing at the construction course near Brive; whether Hélène should worry about the '*petit* François's' gargantuan appetite (it was congenital as far as I was concerned).

And you got right into it, because you love being
friends with people, when they're 'ordinary people',
even when you violently disagree with everything they
say. You laugh and nod and buy them drinks and relax
into the warm feeling of being accepted such a long way
outside 'your world'. It's one of your contradictions,
Jack: how you cultivate that *extraordinary* air, being
so very special everywhere you go, but how you
romanticise the ordinary in ordinary places. The Café
Bosquet was a very ordinary place.

Makes me smile to think of it. You nodding, so
'*sympa*', so understanding, at the growling pugnacity
of a fervent anti-Socialist, and going home to the latest
phase of your unrelenting assault on 'capitalist values'.
You aren't so far above me, you know – I mean above
the me who is charmingly grateful to the likes of Troy
and Duncan.

Remember Nietzsche on 'the many too many', 'the
superfluous'? Christ, he could make you angry.

'Your neighbours will always be poisonous flies: that
about you which is great, that itself must make them
more poisonous and ever more fly-like.'

'Flee, my friend, into your solitude: I see you stung by
poisonous flies.'

Do you know what I think? I think that the Carrons
didn't really count for you. Not in the end. They made
you feel good. Their warmth made you feel good.
They accepted you and me without questions. Not like
London. They were necessary. Like our bottle of red
wine in the evening. But *really* they didn't matter. They
were from 'the many too many'. So it made no odds
what Monsieur Carron said about Socialism, or Giscard,
or the state. Those were the things you thought about
with *your* kind of people. Your equals. Not with them.

Nietzsche's danger wasn't for everyone, was it? It
was only for 'you men of knowledge'. I've got *The Gay
Science* beside me, and the great passage you loved

to declaim, exclamation marks and all. I can hear you speak it.

'For believe me! – the secret of realising the greatest fruitfulness and the greatest enjoyment of existence is: to *live dangerously*! Build your cities on the slopes of Vesuvius! Send your ships out into uncharted seas! Live in conflict with your equals and with yourselves! Be robbers and ravagers as long as you cannot be rulers and owners, you men of knowledge.'

He didn't write it for the Carrons, did he, not for 'the poisonous flies'.

But I don't care. I want to feel our danger. I want that summer back.

And it's there in the forest, in the way the moving of the colours, deep on deep greens and blues, spins inside me. It's not in my eyes and my head. It's in the body. I stand motionless and look, but I am moving, whirling.

We laughed when you read out that passage from *The Twilight of the Idols* about 'the condition of inspiration'.

'The man can be hilarious,' you said. 'So funny.'

OK, we'd call it OTT now. And most of the great Friedrich is OTT now. But I wonder.

'In this condition one enriches everything out of one's own abundance: what one sees, what one desires, one sees swollen, pressing strong, overladen with energy. The man in this condition transforms things until they mirror his power – until they are reflections of his own perfection.'

There. Reflections of your perfection. Why OTT? That's what the forests are.

The thing is, Jack. That summer I desired you more than any other time. Christ, what sex we had. The images in my mind are of your body. Not the whole of it. Not you naked in the heat, moving and painting. Parts of you. The weight of you. The strength. The warmth.

Why should I feel guilty to think of it? Don't laugh, it's cruel. You never used to laugh at desire. I want you

now. It gets inside me and works at me. I want you now.
I want to go to the garage where the smell of painting
is and give myself orgasms. Not one. I mean one after
another. Don't laugh at me.

'You say "I" and you are proud of this word. But
greater than this – although you will not believe in it – is
your body and its great intelligence, which does not say
"I" but performs "I".'

Your strong hand and forearm. The way it cuts with
the Stanley knife into the paint-soaked plaster after
you've built it up on the board. The force of each cut.
Felt. The clean line of the cut in the blotched white.
Then the next and the next. The abandon of it. The
abandon of destroying the plaster and making something
with each cutting blow. Another mark. And with each
one another sign that holds in itself the force of the
cutting that made it. The tempo of signs. The fall of your
hand and forearm, the swing of your naked shoulder, the
swivel of your upper body above the waist. The dance of
your body. Sweating. Sweating. The smell of the dance.

I think of the parts of your body, and I think of you
cutting the plaster. We made love like that. We fought.
I bruised you and cut you with my nails. It was a
wonderful madness.

'Where is the lightning to lick you with its tongue?
Where is the madness, with which you should be
cleansed?

'Behold, I teach you the Superman: he is the lightning,
he is the madness!'

No one can write with exclamation marks any more.
Even I can't do it, thinking of you, speaking to you,
seeing you, feeling you.

There was a way you had of riding up over me and
going deeper and deeper. And then I am on you. I am
riding you. With your hands on my breasts. I am all
sensation.

You scratched my body into the plaster after you

made those deep cuts. But not last of all. Last of all
came the sign of the sun and the coiled serpent. You
cut that too, deftly, precisely, but the way you traced
the lines of my body was different. You drew with the
knife as if you were drawing with a pencil. Gently.
Ruminatively. So my body was hardly there in the
plaster. Just a faint suggestion traced on to the surface.
They see it now as a body cut to pieces. A simple act of
destruction. But the body came afterwards. It came out
of, against the cuts in the plaster. It was the last thing
you did.

You loved to stroke me afterwards. To stroke the
whole of me. Odd, not to lie still when it was finished.
But the stroking was so gentle.

Me stroking you. That morning in the living room at
Horley Road. You standing naked in the early sunlight,
with your poor useless leg held in that odd, stiff way.
You frightened. I stroked you then. And your hard body
seemed suddenly brittle. All the toughness was gone out
of it. I stood naked against you, and felt your warmth. I
can feel it now, how we were. My hands on your tight
buttocks and your waist between my arms. You sank
against me. A weak, vulnerable body. You seemed
without sexuality. As if I had taken it all. As if I were
you, as if I had all of your old power as well as mine.

At that moment I was masculine as well as feminine. I
was you and I was me.

'But equally hateful to the fighter as to the victor is
your grinning death, which comes creeping up like a
thief – and yet comes as master.'

I felt it with you. Your death creeping into you. I took
your power. I still have it.

In the painting, in *Ecce Homo*, the graffiti sign in the
plaster is not there to be felt on the surface, as it was
when you made it in the paint on the plaster ground;
it's a photographic image. It's at one remove. But I can
still see in it the deftness of your cutting. It was the last

element to be added. First the cutting of it in the plaster, then the photographing of it, with the lights placed just right to make the lines sharp and clear, and then the developing and fixing of the photographic image exactly where it had been on the plaster.

It is the sign of power and of knowledge. The blazing sun is power – the will – the coiling serpent is knowledge. It is the device on the golden haft of the staff which Zarathustra's disciples gave him when he went back to the forest. It means everything.

'When you are exalted above praise and blame, and your will wants to command all things as the will of a lover: that is when your virtue has its origin and beginning . . .'

'Truly, it is a new good and evil! Truly, a new roaring in the depths and the voice of a new fountain!

'It is power, this new virtue; it is a ruling idea, and around it a subtle soul: a golden sun, and around it the serpent of knowledge.'

You died nearly ten years ago, Jack. I took the sun and the serpent.

There was no one else to take it.

Nietzsche after all. Not Freud, not Jung. At least Nietzsche for the forests. Well, there's a nine-letter word that's not at all unfashionable. In fact, of course, it's all the rage, and has been since the beginning of this twenty-first century. Our way of reinstating Genius with the right kind of thrilling intellectual credentials (*pace* Copley). Very reassuring to find that Driver is even more up-to-date than I thought. You could actually call him trendy now, couldn't you?

And yet, I couldn't read that long, rambling piece of writing by Felicity with unmitigated pleasure. I still find myself shifting between a great sadness for her and an uncomfortable kind of embarrassment. She's right about being OTT. It's most of it Over the Top, and with the biggest possible capital letters, as well as exclamation marks. Who says no one can write with exclamation marks any more. She can. She just doesn't put them in.

But the evidence is there. Creativity *is* sexuality. Don't laugh; it's not funny; it's dead serious: Jack Driver is Nietzsche's Superman. Got it? Not Clark Kent's Superman, Nietzsche's Superman. I'm not sure whether to find that more or less of a claim than Jack-Driver-as-God-in-Man. There's nothing really to say. You either take it or leave it. And I suppose you'll take it, that nine-letter word being what it is nowadays. We're all looking for super*men*.

But the really satisfying thing is the way it dishes Graham and the Copley view of Driver. Felicity has finally and comprehensively killed off the postmodern, death-of-the-author Driver. It gives me the greatest pleasure to include a (blessedly, you will say) brief extract of Copley on the forest paintings of the mid-seventies from his essay in the Tate/Coverlie's catalogue. Fortunately, he wrote it in a less obscure style than usual. Miranda (the determinedly populist editor) could even force Graham into submission.

My pleasure, you must understand, is the greater, because of the way the press hardly mentioned my catalogue when the reviews came out, and made a point of going on and on about the importance – *importance*! – of Copley's six thousand words. 'A major contribution'; 'penetrating'; 'an extraordinary demonstration of interpretative *élan*.'

And so much of it nonsense:

Ecce Homo is the most unsettling of the forest paintings. It is also the greenest and the most veiled.

At first sight it offers a deep, dark tangle of paint in which is embedded a heart of dirty white and grey, a large area scored with savage markings, a wall surface apparently lifted directly out of an area of dereliction in the most deprived of our inner-city neighbourhoods. The working of the paint and the sheer violence of the scoring of the wall-like surface is perhaps the closest Driver comes to leaving the illusion that he has placed himself in the picture. But the instant any reader/ spectator begins to look with any attention, Driver-as-Driver disappears. The image becomes a *text* without an author, a forest of *signs* suspended in front of the gallery wall.

Nothing on this wooden surface (for the support is wood, broad planks of wood joined together), nothing is whole or immediate or transparent. Everything is at one remove. The forest is paint, obviously worked with tools by a hand: brushes, knives, sticks, rags, everything has been used and used with astonishing energy and decision. But, if that hand leaves a signature, it is not the same signature as the hand that has cut into the plaster surfaces that the forest encloses.

Like an actual graffitied wall, this one is the work of many hands. That is how I read it. That is how it has to be read. The hand that suggestively outlined the contour of a woman's body might be the same that cut it to pieces. But might not be. The hand that carved the little insignia of sun and coiled serpent is certainly another.

And the wall is not a wall. It is sometimes a plastered and painted surface whose marking is actually there directly to be seen; and it is sometimes a wall photographed dingily in some dingy place. While the sea below it is not at all the sea, but only the sea represented for the consumers of the ideal, of 'tranquil seas', the sea represented for tourism.

In the end, Driver cuts himself off from the image he has made. He is not his painting. He leaves it to us to create its meanings. It is the closeness that he comes in the working of the forest enclosure and in the scoring of the wall surfaces to the look of expression, *self-expression*, that gives these images their power. But it is a power, in the end, that comes of disavowal. A presence is offered – a momentary sense of Driver as the essence of meaning – and then it is taken away.

The result is vertigo.

The final touch is the painting of the insignia of sun and coiled serpent in yellow and gold in the forest itself. The intrusion of that graffiti hand, which has the feel here of another hand altogether, into that area of apparently self-expressive rhetoric is enough finally to take all the bombast away.

Does the insignia have one meaning? Perhaps. But nothing can be more certain than the fact that it has many, even if it has one.

Felicity ended her piece on the picture with the yellow and gold insignia. She added her own final touch.

You may find it puzzling.

The last thing of all was the blazing sun and the coiled serpent in the forest.

It was right to make it yellow and gold, like a sun-star in the forest. To paint it so intensely. So small and so visible.

'I love him whose soul is lavish, who neither wants nor returns thanks: for he always gives and will not preserve himself.

'Gold-like gleams the glance of the giver. Gold-lustre makes peace between moon and sun.'

I gave it. But it came from you. When you could hardly see and the drugs had taken you away.

It was my gift.

10

Two Endings

When it came, Sir Simon McKenna's resignation was not a surprise. His letter was dated 18 June 1994. Its measured tone concealed the bitterness that was the inevitable consequence of the severity of the battle, however brief it had been. My view then, however, was that his demise was inevitable and the last essential ingredient needed to ensure the success of the exhibition. I was, you will realise, extremely good at seeing the best in the worst; and I wasn't alone.

It was easy to make it seem to be the right thing. My priority, with Felicity, was the making of the best possible exhibition for Driver. However much I might have respected McKenna, however sad it was to see him go, if that was the price to be paid for Driver's restoration to the head of the British canon, then it was a *necessity* that it should be paid. The culture sections of the broadsheets represented McKenna as a 'blood sacrifice' to the political and corporate Establishment. The *Guardian* bemoaned 'the final extinction of all but commercial values in the culture of Britain'. But, for me, the question was: how far did he bring his resignation on himself? How far did his refusal to accept the realities of Britain in the mid-1990s amount to the wilful offering up of himself as sacrificial victim? The option presented him was, after all, not at all unacceptable.

I've still got the press statement that announced

Coverlie's takeover of the exhibition on 24 May 1994. The terms were extraordinarily generous. They accepted 'full curatorial responsibility for the exhibition' 'in return for the transfer to the Tate Gallery of a six-figure sum', and they secured an agreement with Sir Gordon Creasey and the Tate trustees that the sum paid should be earmarked for contemporary purchases alone, known to be a McKenna priority. A contribution was also to be made to the special price agreed for the Tate's purchase of one of the most significant of the lost pictures: *Six-six Vision on the Big Screen* (1963). This last stipulation was particularly generous on the part of Troy. For him, *Six-six Vision* was the ultimate Jack Driver. 'The quintessence,' as I remember him putting it, 'of Jack's art.' It was almost as if he had made a personal gift of the painting to the Tate, because he would certainly have bought it for himself otherwise.

The press statement ended characteristically: 'Coverlie's is, therefore, both to take over the heavy cost of organising this major exhibition and to make possible a significant enhancement of the Tate Gallery's purchase grant in the area of the living visual arts. Our hope is that this will ease the Gallery's burden at a time of continuing stringent financial controls in the public sector.' It all seemed the greatest common sense at the time. Real magnanimity on the part of a great private concern which had the public interest at heart.

I could not have known that an integral part of Troy's and Duncan's strategy was to force McKenna out, that their object was not merely to implement Duncan's preferred policy of partial privatisation of the museums but to create a crisis to which only one outcome was possible. When certain commentators suggested that McKenna's job was in danger, to me it seemed like the worst sort of conspiracy theory, collective paranoia in the service of liberal prejudice. McKenna, I thought, should have been making friends not searching for enemies. He should have been looking to the future. He should have heeded the advice given him by Creasey's predecessor, Sir Gerald Cuffley, when he first accepted the directorship of the Tate: 'Never look back.'

Characteristically acknowledging the precedent, Creasey himself was to repeat the same advice when he announced the appointment of Lester Howell as McKenna's successor: 'Never look back.' Good advice for an entrepreneur or perhaps an artist or even for aspiring public servants. Not very good advice for an historian. I've spent my life 'looking back', professionally. It's what we do. Looking back now, today, is not very comfortable, but I shall do it, scrupulously, as I always have.

The best way to tell the story of those few weeks is to edit into something approaching a chronological sequence a selection of my dated jottings and (fairly complete) of McKenna's letters to Peter Frew.

Characteristically, despite his combative appearance and style, 'Rag' kept his distance in Dorset throughout (except for one visit to attend the Tate 'friendly demonstration' on 11 June), pleading the need 'to paint hard' for his next New York show. There must have been phone calls too, but even in this period of crisis after crisis for him, McKenna preferred to write letters so as not to intrude too much on his friend's work.

For my part, there were times when my jottings became an almost nightly practice, so febrile was the atmosphere.

And it was not Coverlie's takeover of the show and McKenna's 'fight to the end' that alone left me feverish and disoriented. Fantasy was finally overtaken by reality at Horley Road.

25 May 1994

Dear Rag,

You will have seen Coverlie's press statement. I have no resources to fight it. I shall have resigned within a month. One has to confront the reality of the situation: there is not very long in which to be heard.

They have been cunning and ruthless; I have been credulous and a fool. One should have been able to read the entrails when Jason Furnival's report was published a year ago. This was the obvious guinea-pig exhibition. Coverlie's, one knew well enough, had it virtually under their control already. Miranda had already manoeuvred June on to the peripheries. Remember that business about her list? June could see what was happening. I sat on my hands and waited.

Shall I tell you how they let me know? It was like a Mafia execution. Give the victim a good meal in a restaurant of his choice, and machine-gun him over his favourite spaghetti carbonara.

Two weeks ago Gordon gave me a ring and asked me to make sure I had the evening of the 23rd clear. Please would I ask Penny [McKenna's secretary] to book for four at Mario's in Covent Garden. It was to be a 'working supper' to discuss major changes in funding policies for the museums. Duncan and Creasey were to be there. I was not told that Troy would be there too, though one did wonder about the fourth person. My heart sank, but I did not guess.

Well, it wasn't over spaghetti carbonara that they let me have it, it was over *rognoncini in padella con funghi e spinaci*. But (I hope you approve) I didn't fall down and die; I got up and left. There was nothing to discuss. They had already discussed it all between themselves and arrived at their conclusion. I was/am superfluous. I have become a kind of caretaker-manager, as they say in football. Or at least, that is what they want me to become: the one who can make it happen with dignity and restraint, and then who can ensure the smooth running of everything until someone 'more like us' can be eased into the post. Well, I hope all three of them choked on their *pernice al forno* (that was what I left them eating). I have only one regret: I couldn't finish my *rognoncini*. It's the *funghi* I love. I can't resist wild mushrooms. Like Jack.

I am going to behave without any restraint and with absolutely no dignity whatsoever. As from today I have given up the management of change for the Tories and their sidekicks once and for all. It's such a relief. I might have had to leave my *rognoncini* but my digestion is better already.

Duncan was at his most articulate. He always thinks advocacy will change minds. And he has such confidence in his advocacy. But all those words of his were wasted on me. My greatest pleasure was to leave him in mid-sentence. I actually witnessed a moment of hesitation. Nothing he can say, one feels, was ever worth hearing.

They gunned me down. But I'm not dead yet. If I can't stop this from within, I shall make myself the leader of the opposition from without. I need the artists and the academics and the press. I've made a few calls already. Gabby Cabe was her no-nonsense, energetic self. One has confidence in her. She will come in with us. So will Henty on the *Guardian*. We're not alone.

And I need you back in London, Rag. I need you to mobilise in the schools and the East End. I know you have pictures to make, but things are desperate here.

The greatest loss for me is Jack. They've stolen his work and his reputation. It's to become a form of 'revenue generation' and a 'money spinner'. It's to be 'the way forward to a fully market-directed cultural policy of the Right'. And the deepest sadness of all, if June's worst fears are to be realised: they are intent on emasculating the Socialist Driver. That mindless declaration I told you about, at the end of Troy's speech last year, was actually a statement of policy for the exhibition. Not just bluster at all. It's hard to believe. Jack pressed into service for market forces, and then disarmed: depoliticised.

I need to hear from you. I know that your work is what still must count, but give me a call if you can.

I need you.

Yours,

Simon

25 May 1994

I tried to be ready for it today. Miranda said not to go into the department in Queen's. Stay at Coverlie's. Keep your head down.

You're an idiot, Roland. Why can't you ever keep your head down? You get nervous; you get distinctly apprehensive; and yet you still go into the place where most of the grief is to be found.

The thing is, it's much more difficult to stay away and imagine what they *might* be saying. I used not to be, but now I'm so good at imagining the worst. I knew well enough that if I stayed in the office I'd kick back more and more so that I could think the worst; and that if I stayed here in my room, I'd get the tin down from on top of the imitation Art Deco wardrobe and binge and make the worst seem even worse. But the question is: was it better to know that Cabe and Waldeau and the rest of them really *are* thinking what you were terrified they were thinking? Miranda was right. Ignorance *is* bliss.

I've never said a thing against Gabby. And even at the time of the letter to the *Guardian*, she was always very nice face to face. She always said these were bigger things than I could handle by myself, and she understood the pressures. She had nothing against me as an individual; she just felt she had to act.

'This is a matter of principle. It has nothing to do with personalities.'

She was really quite cuddly and big-sisterly when she talked about my 'weakness'. She put her hand on my shoulder and said I had to learn to stand up for myself.

But she wasn't at all cuddly today. She was an angry, very uncuddly person today.

Why did I freeze? Do you know something, Roland, you nearly *cried*.

And yet, you are right and she is wrong. She *is* wrong.

Why did it have to happen in the cafeteria queue? Everyone saw the way I froze. And they all heard what she said. There was lots of noise. There always is. But they all stopped nattering when she was in full flow. Everyone froze, and they either pretended not to look or they bloody stared.

She was in front of me in the queue. She only saw me when she turned towards the counter and began to order her baked potato and Cheddar. She actually stopped at that point and swung right round and those first years in between me and her retreated closer to the counter to be out of the line of fire. Because everyone could see who her eyes were fixed on.

It wasn't very subtle or at all informed, what she said. It was just an outburst. Fury. She doesn't have a proper argument. All she can bloody do is appeal to things like loyalty and values by telling me I haven't got them. And she isn't supposed to believe in values. She's the ultimate relativist, for Christ's sake. It's threadbare stuff, but it still tears me apart.

'You have no business in Queen's, Roland Matthias. You may not have made it happen, but you've stood by and let it happen. You're an opportunist, and I personally shall see to it that your opportunities become rather limited. You don't bring this department into disrepute with impunity. I shall have to see what can be done about revoking your registration. I'll take it to college council; I'll take it to the university academic board if need be. Don't count too much on your precious Kit Moss. No one listens to him any more. You'd better start thinking of a permanent future with Coverlie's, if anything with Coverlie's *could* be permanent. No self-respecting university department is going to have you now even if you do end up with a Queen's Ph.D. I shall get on the phone especially to see that they don't.'

Did she really say that? She couldn't have said that. No, that was what was there between the lines, when you worked out what she really meant by phrases like 'scholarship and commerce don't mix' and 'sitting by, hoping Kit will make everything all right, doesn't let you off the hook'. No, she didn't actually curse me for the rest of my days in so many words. But she did in so many inferences. No one could miss the inferences. I didn't.

And Kit isn't around. He's lecturing in Cologne. Not back till next Monday.

The worst thing was that I was a stranger in the department today. I go in too little. There isn't anybody left to talk to. I didn't know anyone in the library or the canteen at all. I just know faces now. They were all strangers except Gabby. And they were all on her side. None of them knew any better. There was no one to commiserate. Just speechless, staring hostility.

Thank God I'm going to Felicity's tomorrow afternoon.

2 June 1994

Dear Rag,

I don't know why I'm not devastated or at least mildly depressed. My career seems to be at an end. Everything one has worked for is on the point of becoming obsolete. And all I feel is exhilaration.

There is a complete disjunction between the events in which I am plunged and my feelings. There can be only one conclusion. The large canvas, the great principles on which I have always thought I have based my life matter far less than one's freedom of action – one's *personal* freedom of action. Me. Simon. I have never been allowed to be an individual before: someone whose words are his thoughts. And now, suddenly, I have been released. I can say *anything* to anyone. I can write anything and the newspapers will publish it – at least the *Guardian* will for the moment. Henty has done his stuff. God, Rag, it's fucking wonderful, and I'm going to start swearing in my fucking letters just like fucking you.

Now and again, when I think about it, I feel guilty. Stupid, but I do. Why am I incapable of the dignity of great and dark feelings about the tragedy of lost, of destroyed principles? One has to confess it: in the end, the collapse of my career has shown me that I am quite a small man. And yet perhaps I shall be happier if I am allowed to be quite a small man who makes quite a lot of noise. My very own noise, made because I *want* to make it.

Did you see the centre-page feature they gave me in the *Guardian* today? I have spelled out their manoeuvres and retold their lies and named their names, and this is just the beginning. First, I expose their dishonesty and their disrespect for those they have exploited and then discarded, June Sutcliffe above all. Next, I shall expose the slipshod frailty of their arguments. They will continue regardless, of course, but I shall make them cringe and bluster before I go, even the extrovert Henry Troy and the socialite Miranda, neither of whom has ever shown before that they are capable of shame.

Don't worry about me, Rag, I'm proving more resilient than I ever expected.

I never thought I would enjoy failure.

Yours,
Simon

5 June 1994

Dear Rag,

I have been working on a major piece for the *Guardian*, which I intend to launch on Thursday evening in a way that should cause maximum embarrassment for Gordon and the rest of his trustees. I want to try a passage on you. Here it is:

'The distance between the makers of visual art and the makers of exhibitions is not so great. Exhibition-making is a creative activity. It does not take place in isolation, in a very private place, like so much of the image-making we call art. It takes place in a flow of telephone calls and faxes and meetings, and it culminates in the control of increasingly uncontrollable pressures as the difficulties of transport, finance and publishing deadlines mount. But in the end, the exhibition-maker works from initial conception, through multiple resistances of a material kind, to the putting together of an image. That image is memorable only if it has emerged from a deep, even an inexpressible sense of connection with the artist or the theme that is the exhibition's topic. If there is something we can call art, the best exhibitions are works of art about works of art.

'Between the museums and galleries and the BBC there is a telling parallel. The opening up of the museums and galleries to a genuinely large-scale (if still too restricted) public has paralleled the development in this country of public service broadcasting. At the same time, a cadre of curators with a sense at once of commitment to the work in their charge and to its public has been formed, a cadre whose skills and experience have been allowed to grow and flourish in institutions which have encouraged knowledge and critical awareness as well as innovation. The BBC similarly developed such a cadre of producer/directors, who were properly trained and allowed to grow in the job.

'The BBC is now, of course, finished as an integrated organisation with a framework in which talent can develop into genuine effectiveness. That is what is about to happen to the museums and galleries. We shall be left with a dispersed community (if that word is at all applicable) of freelances living hand-to-mouth, sponging up whatever knowledge they have the time for. Some will, of course, be talented, even genuinely creative, but their talent will be far too easily wasted or ignored; it will certainly not be nurtured and developed.'

What do you think? Is one claiming too much for my 'exhibition-makers'? I used to do rather a lot of it myself, of course. One can't deny that there's a strong element of special pleading.

Anyway, in my (for the moment) continuing role at the Gallery as high priest at all our group rituals, I have to give 'a little speech' to mark the retirement of Mark Brodel on Thursday. Now there, certainly, was an exhibition-maker who one can say came close to being a creative artist. Creasey will, of course, be present in his presiding role as household god, and at least a few of his fellow trustees will be present too in their roles as lesser gods. I shall use the more embarrassing parts of my article for my little speech, and there's going to be a great deal more in it that's embarrassing, you can be sure of that. It's due to appear in the *Guardian* the next morning (Friday). Mark approves 100 per cent.

I told you I was beginning to enjoy myself. Too fucking right.

Yours,
Simon

7 June 1994

Dear Rag,

Gordon tried to stop me speaking out today. He uttered threats. The charming, cheery Gordon became really quite nasty.

They get more and more like mafiosi. The techniques are hardly sophisticated. Hints of dreadful injuries that can be done to you alternate with offers you can't refuse. Today he started as so many liars start with the words: 'You can trust me', followed by the assurance that he was 'coming clean'. The 'coming clean' amounted to confessing that he knew as he was sure I knew that I would go before 'this affair was finished'.

'You know you're fighting a lost cause. The only way out in the end will be to resign.'

He was always good, one feels, at stating the obvious.

There followed an 'even-handed attempt to look at the options'. Did I want to go with honour and a sound financial position, or did I want to go 'messily' into penury (or some close equivalent)? If I wanted honour and security, it would be 'much better all round to prevent this thing getting out of hand in the public sphere'. After I had gone, of course, I would be free to say what I liked about government policy. I'm exaggerating, but in essence that's how he put it.

Well, I shrugged him off. And tomorrow night I shall deliver my little speech. I'm glad you approve of my creative curator passage. We really are worth preserving, don't you think? Of course we fucking well are.

Incidentally, thank you for ringing round the London art schools. I've had an awful lot of support on that front. There's even talk of some kind of demonstration next week, and that's despite the fact that they're all caught up in their degree shows at this moment. The university departments in London are beginning to organise too. That phone call to Gabby Cabe worked, as one knew it would.

I'll keep you posted.

Wish me luck for tomorrow.

Yours,

Simon

1 June 1994

I couldn't work at Horley Road this afternoon. I wanted Felicity to come.

Summer's here. I sat in the garden for half the time, not even pretending to work. I tried not to look at the silhouette of the desktop computer in the front window of the living room. For June it was really hot. When the sun was on me, I could feel the sweat coming out beneath my hair, wetting it, making it straggly and damp. I watched the leaves. They still have something of that piercing lemony green of spring; the green hasn't deepened yet. It's such a beautiful time.

I didn't get bored for an hour, maybe two. I think I slept, but mostly my mind was filling up with things. It took me through whole conversations with everyone from Kit Moss to Simon McKenna to Gabby Cabe to Felicity. Especially Felicity. I told her everything that had happened and then everything about me that she didn't know and then everything about my desires. Her eyes never left me; that's how I made it seem to myself.

And when I got bored, I binged. I went to the kitchen, and ate thick pieces of toast with butter and organic honey. The honey dripped all over my fingers and down my chin. And then I finished all of Felicity's inimitable truffle biscuits. The chocolate mixed with the honey on my fingers and around my mouth and on my chin. But the whole of me felt so densely packed with substance, so massive and incapable of action that I just stayed sticky.

I sat in front of my VDU for the longest time hoping I would get a little less massive. The screen was its reassuring blue and white, but there was nothing on it. Not a single fact. I just sat.

I heard her at 6.40. The digital clock on the Edwardian mantelpiece told me. The sun was still in the garden, but its light was softening a little in the room.

I wanted to look busy. I wanted to look like a professional obedient to the taboos, austere and honed.

But I knew I wouldn't. I knew I would look like someone who had sat in the sun and then binged hopelessly. I knew I would look like an overweight version of those dirty chocolate-covered little boys in commercials about cleanliness and loving mothers.

I heard the kicking off of her shoes. But before she could slip along to the kitchen to pour her inevitable *pastis*, I broke the routine: I called out.

'Bring your drink in, Felicity. I'm really on edge. I need to talk.'

She opened the door immediately. She didn't stop to pour her drink. She knew the way I was the moment she saw me. Not so much that I had 'let myself go', but that I had collapsed inside, that all my resolve had gone.

She came straight across the room to me, and standing over me, her eyes on mine, she took my hands. She seemed not to care that they were slightly tacky. For a very long time she just stroked my hands as she held them, her thumb lightly working over my fingers and my knuckles. The circling warmth of it seeped right into me. My whole body seemed to stretch out inside and wait. I was no longer massive.

Then she reached up behind my head and pulled me down against her breasts. There was no eroticism in it at all. Unless the maternal really is erotic. She was the understanding, the soothing mother. I loved her. I let myself love her in that mode. Vulnerable son to soothing mother. The way she touched me set the limits. They were clear. This was a very specific kind of contact. Intensely physical, but, if there was sex in it, on my side it was to be infantile. The comfort of childhood, nothing else was offered.

Then she patted me gently and stepped back.

I can't remember exactly what I said. Only that it rang false in every particular. I think I said that we could not let McKenna be sacrificed, that we were all guilty and that the exhibition could not be more important than an individual like that. It was what I thought should be said, but it had nothing to do with my sense of inadequacy and the panic in me. What I really should have said was that I was frightened of the passions that had been released all around us. Nothing else. It was the truth.

The change in her was remarkable. She went from soothing to punishing mother in a moment. It is the first time I have ever seen her lose control. She stood up very tall and straight, and her speech became almost guttural as she tried to hold the rage back, until in the end it broke right out, and she was shouting.

'Don't tell me about individuals. Don't tell me the exhibition is less important than McKenna. Less important than bloody McKenna! The exhibition *is* about an individual. The exhibition is about Jack. He will be there in the paintings. Just as much as you and I and bloody McKenna will be there to look at them. How dare you say McKenna is more important! McKenna isn't Jack. McKenna is much less. So much less! His bloody museum, his bloody people, that June Sutcliffe of his, none of them matter more than Jack. I'm glad they're going to force him out. He thinks too much of himself and his principles and his precious museum. Troy and Miranda have the bloody guts to do something. Miranda's got panache. I want him out! I've always wanted him out. You have to work with the ones who have the real power. He's just faffing around. He's got none.'

That was how it started. Something like that. Until she switched from McKenna to me. That was when the shouting really began. And in the end she actually took my shoulders and shook me. Like a child.

'You have no right. You have no right! Why are you so bloody feeble? I'm glad you don't have to deal with Jack. He doesn't tolerate the feeble, the unimaginative, the impressionable, the frightened, the bloody Rolands of this world. Do you hear, the BLOODY ROLANDS OF THIS WORLD! He doesn't give them the time of day. He wouldn't have them near him. Feeble-minded, feeble-spirited, gutless Roland. Don't you turn away like that! You need to listen for once. GUTLESS!'

Then it was gone, the fury. Hesitancy replaced the shouting and she stepped right away from me with that characteristic awkward grace of hers.

'I'm sorry. You don't deserve it. You have tried, I know. I'm fond of you, Roland. I hope Jack would have been too. You have to stand up to them. That's all. We have to have the exhibition. And it has to be the best. Promise me that you will stay with it now. Promise me that you will, whatever McKenna says, whatever the press say, whatever those others at your precious college say. Promise me.'

I did. And it is a promise I shall have to keep.

3 June 1994

Kit Moss has been named. Kit Moss is a name that is never named, except on the title pages of his books and articles of course, when he is J.M.C. Moss (the Christopher/Kit isn't even his first name). He is an anonymous force. Everyone knows that when a job is on offer he is called and his opinion registers. Everyone knows that he is there having quiet chats, listening, coaxing, saying wise, well-informed words that make things happen. But no one names his name.

Yesterday in the *Guardian* McKenna named him and had much more to say about his 'low profile' persuasive powers than about me. I was just a pawn, naturally. But Kit Moss was on a level with Troy and Creasey when it came to the manipulation of people and systems. His 'great talent', according to McKenna, 'is knowing what not to say and knowing who not to say it to. He seems to have no firm position on anything, but he is always identified with the "right" side when he needs to be. He takes no responsibility for anything but is responsible for too much. He has the highest visibility for a few, but to most he is invisible.'

The anonymous Kit Moss has been named as a 'great conspirator', no less. Words come to mind like 'unmasked'.

What will he do? Will this be deemed 'grave'? I can't help feeling apprehensive about it. And yet the thought of him in shock makes me giggle, ridiculously.

How can it have happened? Kit Moss named!

5 June 1994

I don't know what I should do. I *have* to keep my promise to Felicity. Where does that leave me with Kit?

Last night Kit rang me here and left a message on the machine. I was to be in his room at 10.00 this morning. Things could not go on as they were. Nowadays things never can. I was beyond bingeing. I lay down very still on my bed and felt the beat from the CDs next door vibrate softly through me, unable to move or think at all.

I was there right on time, and so was he. The situation was too 'grave' for delay to be possible. I went straight in without a single second on that chair in the corridor.

He started by trying to appear his old calm and collected self. In control enough to make self-deprecating jokes about McKenna's treatment of him in the *Guardian*.

'Ironic, don't you think? To be famous for *not* being famous. I suppose I should thank Simon for doing me a favour. Companies pay a lot of money to public relations people for name-recognition.'

McKenna alone was not enough to disturb his equilibrium, that was clear. But McKenna *plus* Gabby Cabe and Waldeau *plus* the hostility of growing numbers of students *plus* the targeting of him by known artists egged on by McKenna, all of this together was more than enough. I suppose I should have realised that he would desert me.

But I could have done without the man-of-conviction stuff. How did it go?

'In the end, though, I really do have to thank McKenna. I've been thinking of writing to the *Guardian* to say so. I want people to know that I *do* agree that one's position should be open. The imperatives of diplomacy are far less important than the imperatives of conviction. I've always and will always oppose the intrusion into scholarship and curatorship of merely commercial interests. Of course that's so. The alliance between the Tate and Coverlie's was a positive development so long as the Tate remained the more powerful or at least an equal partner. But this . . . this is going too far.

'Look, Roland, we shall have to admit it. This has been a mistake. No one's fault. *We* couldn't have known that Troy and Creasey would stitch up this sort of deal with the connivance of Duncan. I promise you I had no prior knowledge of their plans. None at all, whatever McKenna might insinuate. I've never let you down before, have I? Never left you in it. You have to trust me. And my judgement tells me now that you have to tell Coverlie's that the situation has changed so fundamentally that you cannot continue.

'After all, you took on the role of Coverlie's Visiting Fellow *at the Tate*. You owe some allegiance *to* the Tate. Clearly. Coverlie's have put you in an impossible position. We . . . you have to pull out, right now.'

I should have said something strong, but all I said was: 'Are you sure?'

And he was:

'Look, if you stay in now you can't continue here, because I can't continue to supervise you. Simple as that. If I withdraw, no one else is going to take you on. That much you can be one hundred per cent sure of.'

I should have said that I'm too far in, that Felicity and Driver matter too much to me, that it is simply not possible for me to pull out just because *he* has to.

But I said something indecisive which allowed him to believe that I *would* pull out.

I said it and yet I knew and I know that there really isn't any doubt in the end. I shall keep my promise to Felicity.

I *can't* pull out.

Christ, Roland, what do you do now?

Talk to Miranda.

7 June 1994

I talked to Miranda. She was shrewd, she was direct, and she was right. At her businesswoman best. She said talk to Felicity. She said Moss had to be converged on from at least two directions at once. She would talk to Troy who would converge on him from one direction, if I talked to Felicity who would converge on him from another. He would not take long to decide that life was easier on our side in the long run. No one, after all, knew that he had 'pulled out', so if he 'came back in' it would be as if nothing had happened. He would have no face to save.

She's a clever girl.

I talked to Felicity on the phone this afternoon. I talked long enough for my handset-holding wrist to go numb. She called me 'love' often and 'my love' more than once. I was 'not to worry'. I still 'have a career'. And she had no doubt that Moss would listen to her. She was thinking of making a public statement of thanks to those who had remained 'loyal' to her and to 'the memory of Jack', and she was thinking of featuring Moss as one who had left himself open to hurtful attacks for their sake. She was thinking, indeed, of allowing him 'to appear a little heroic', as she put it with something close to a giggle (Felicity doesn't usually giggle).

'Anyway,' she said before putting down the phone, 'I might even present Queen's with something to hang somewhere special. Who knows? In recognition of all you and Moss have done for Jack. Moss won't be able to resist that.'

And just an hour ago, Miranda rang me with the news

that Moss has caved in (again). He seems to be even better at caving in than me. He had been converged on, in fact, not only by Troy and Felicity uttering threats and bearing gifts, but by Creasey too (probably both uttering threats and bearing gifts or at least invitations to prop up yet more prestigious boards and committees).

I'm not alone. But I still feel exposed. I still feel frightened.

Things are going so fast. They're buzzing and buzzing; and they're buzzing so loudly.

11 June 1994

Dear Rag,

I'm glad you came up. I'm glad you were there. For me, it was the most important thing of all, that you were with them. One knows how much it costs you to lose a day's work when you're really going well.

What a sight! All of you sitting under the dome and right along the Duveen Gallery, in between the sculptures. Before I came down to make my little speech of thanks, I saw you from above. You know, from the gallery landing around the drum of the dome outside my office.

And before I came out on to the gallery landing, I watched you all streaming up the steps and listened to the noise growing. It was all around me. It came at me from outside – all those people on the steps – as well as from inside. It sounded, as they always say about the noise of crowds, like the sea. Except it had an excited, upbeat note. The sea, I always think, has a mournful, monotonous note. That regular beating of waves. This was without any regularity. Hubbub is the word. You made a wonderful hubbub of a noise.

And from above, you looked far too variegated and bustling and chaotic for the sea. All those colours. The movement of all those young people. Art students restore one's faith. You certainly did yesterday.

I begin to think that Creasey might back down. Maybe I

shan't be resigning after all. If I'm still here in two weeks' time, and the exhibition is finally rescued, it will be in no small measure because of you and the rest of you and all those wonderful students.

Thank you. I needed to be given hope.

Get back to work. It's still what really counts.

Gratefully,

Simon

14 June 1994

Dear Rag,

We've got them fucking on the run. You're an idiot, you know that? To be so pessimistic. One more push, as the Labour Party said in '92, and go on saying, but this time, unlike the last election, this little bunch of Tory stooges really will be pushed out.

Did you see Gabby Cabe's wonderful article on Jack and the ironies of his takeover by Coverlie's? In the *Independent* this morning. A half-page feature. One feels that it was time the case was made from something other than the point of view of us bureaucrats and the politicians. She writes with real *élan*. And it just can't be said enough: we're talking about a Socialist, for Christ's sake, an artist who lived and breathed Marx.

And now the media is really getting in on the act. There's to be an hour-long programme on Channel 4. The producer told me they're going to bring out all the double-dealing and double standards and then they're going to give us the air time we need to really say something. The other side apparently is shuffling and looking uncomfortable and mumbling it would rather not appear. But we'll all be there. I gather that they've even dug out crotchety old Brian Merritt, and he's going to speak up for Driver and us; he's another who's turned against his masters. So many are on our side.

I hoped you would come up for it. What are the chances? I didn't give Patti Crowther, the producer, your country number, because I didn't think you'd like to be interrupted. But you'd make a real difference. Please say yes.

I am beginning to hope with real conviction now. Maybe we're going to win.

At least it's getting exciting, as if the result is actually in doubt.

Yours,
Simon

16 June 1994

Dear Rag,

You're a great man, you know that? With you on the team, we'll fucking pulverise them.

If you're coming up in the afternoon on the 20th, come and have a drink beforehand. It will give me real strength to see you in person, my friend, and have you to myself.

There have been rumblings from the direction of Gordon and the lesser gods to the effect that employees of the Tate have 'a duty' not to speak against its policies publicly. Well, stuff them!

I'm really looking forward to setting eyes on you, old friend.

Yours,
Simon

15 June 1994

So it happened and it didn't happen. My fantasies about Felicity will have to end. They have ended. I can't summon them up any longer. They have been overtaken and left behind.

Why Felicity? Why did I have to start loving Felicity? And why does it go on, when it's finished?

This is another moment in my life when I have to be sober and get it all down. Everything that happened. Not for the pleasure of remembering. Just because I have to.

Trying to escape into work has almost come off the last week. I've been able to solve problems while obeying the most draconian regime of self-denial yet. I have been virtuous and productive and Miranda has been so distracted that I've even been left alone at Coverlie's. But the facts cannot keep out the anger. I don't mean mine. I've not been able to find any anger yet. I can only find uneasiness and apprehension when I let myself feel things. But the anger's all around me. I run between outbursts. I am talked at and shouted at.

The events of this evening started with my second experience of Felicity angry, though it was mild and unthreatening compared to the first.

The setting was the living room as usual. That space has seen more drama than the stage of the Olivier. I was just beginning to become comfortable, to think it had been a really good idea to call her and come round. She had done all the right things to keep the apprehensiveness at bay: opened a bottle of Bulgarian red, talked about the future when the exhibition can be all we talk about again, laughed at the slippings and slidings of 'the wretched Kit', as she calls him.

Bloody stupid of me to mention Gabby Cabe – to ask her what she thought of that article in the *Independent*. I knew it was stupid, the moment I said it. She didn't shout to begin with. She made points, forcefully.

'So he was a Socialist. I was a Socialist. I still am a Socialist, and so would he be. But that doesn't give everyone who calls themselves Socialist the right to take him over for their own devious purposes. To use him against me. Gabby Cabe doesn't understand him and she doesn't understand me. They're all the same. They only understand what *they* see in things. And they none of them bother to look for longer than a few seconds at anything.'

At first I argued. Sometimes I can't help myself.

'OK, she's against us, but she's not all wrong [God, I

can be nauseatingly fair-minded at the most inappropriate moments]. She was right to bring people back to the fact of his Socialism. It gets forgotten. And if we hope the work on its own will remind people when they see it in the show, it's a hell of a long shot.'

'You don't understand either, do you, Roland? The pictures don't work on people by teaching them how to think. They work by changing the way they think – directly. They get in under the skin.'

'And everyone wakes up and finds themselves Socialists?'

'They might not call themselves that, but their perspectives on things, their priorities shift. Just a little. It's enough to keep budging people a little. And what that self-righteous woman Cabe doesn't *see* is that to budge people a little, you have to get the right platforms for the pictures to do their speaking. You have to adapt. Jack has to adapt. Even Jack. He's a Socialist in a society that isn't Britain in the 1960s or '70s. I have to help him adapt. He can't do it without me. Not now.'

That was when the anger really came out. It wasn't against me.

'I hate this country. I hate this decade. I hate the Gabby Cabes. I hate the young who've given up on Socialism. But most of all, the ones who think they know what Socialism is! I hate them as much as the Troys and the Duncans. I don't give a toss for any of them!'

It was just a little rant. Not much. And it calmed her.

'The lovely irony is that Gabby Cabe's got it so completely wrong about Jack's Socialism.'

She was beginning almost to enjoy herself. A slightly superior little smile sketched itself at the corner of her mouth. She knew what none of us knew, and that was briefly a pleasure.

'It's all Graham's doing. People like him and Cabe actually think he cut the pictures adrift, separated himself from them, made his painting bigger than himself. You know, all that stuff about the work being bigger than the individual, being an invitation to the 'creative looking of others', a declaration of the 'equality of the gaze'. Christ, the nonsense they talk. And in all seriousness. Well, for him and me it was and is a celebration of his creativity: Jack's creativity. He is an individual in the pictures, but he's there for what he can *do* and *be*, not for what he possesses. He stands against the profit motive. He says that only what you can be matters, inside yourself.'

How were we sitting? I was in my heavy desk-chair, turned towards her, my back to the VDU. She was sitting forward in her old armchair with the printed material thrown over it. As she sat forward, she pulled the material with her, and it rucked up all around her in a mass of William Morris flowers and stems, hedging her in with soft luxuriance.

She went from anger through wicked amusement to superior knowingness to something close to the conspiratorial. All in no time at all. Her serenity has gone. She has become almost mercurial in her moods. Completely unpredictable.

'I want to tell you something. Something important about me and Jack. His painting is never separate from him. Nothing was ever further from the way it is than Graham's talk about the disappearance of the artist behind – how does he put it? – behind quotation and a plurality of idioms: that *special* word of his, the heterological. Is that how you say it? Graham's idiot words. No. Jack's always there. I can feel him. You can feel him, except you don't know it's him you're feeling. Graham can feel him, but he doesn't *want* to believe it. So he uses his words to hide it from himself. Jack is there. With all his masculine force he is there.'

'How is he there? It's oil and acrylic and mixed media on wood and canvas that's there. It's just substances fixed to a flat support. Images which have no sex.'

She was no longer conspiratorial. She had moved to

something like a confessional tone now. Slightly hesitant. Her eyes lowered; looking up at me shyly from time to time. Her sentences halting and then changing direction and halting again.

'You know we worked together in the same studio. I told you. We did it from the beginning. We did it in the shack in Orlando Street. But you don't know why. It wasn't just that the company helped. That we criticised each other's work, and said supportive things. It was because we made love there. It was for the daytime, never for the night. He used to say, love is for the light.'

The question for me to ask was obvious. I felt everything click finally into place. An absurd vignette was suddenly illuminated in some recess in my mind. There was a necktie and a palm tree in it, and also red balloons floating in Mediterranean/Californian skies. I saw how the unprovable would be proved, finally, conclusively.

'So for Jack [at that moment, I really did call him Jack] . . . so for Jack his sexuality and his creativity were in close proximity, perhaps even one and the same?'

And the answer came straight back, without the slightest hint of ambivalence.

'Oh yes. Of course, he never doubted they were linked. Nor do I. In him they were one and the same. Yes, that's how it was. It's true, at times there was something almost detached, calculating in the way he put ideas together . . . in his head. But when he really worked his sexuality was *in* his creativity. That was how he wanted it.'

I asked her about the end, when they worked together at the end, when he had in a very literal sense lost his sexuality – lost it as power.

She said nothing for a second. Then she rocked forward, closer to me, and in a clumsy, self-protective movement, just for an instant she lowered her head still further and clasped her elegant hands around the back of her neck as if to stop herself from looking up, as if to keep something as deep as possible inside her and away from me.

When she next spoke, she was still close, and now she was looking straight at me.

'At the beginning of his time in the chair I came to him in the chair. The movement . . . the movement . . .'

She left the words suspended.

I was frightened when she asked me. I felt no anticipation. It frightened me to think what might follow.

'I want you to do something for me. I want you to get the chair out. I want you to wheel it over, beside me. I want you to sit in it. Will you do this for me? Please.'

She spoke in a cool, even way. There was no urgency.

I did what she asked, I sat in Driver's chair, out in the space of the room. On the *Yomut*.

She slid slowly forward from the armchair and knelt on the carpet in front of me. Very close. She put her hands on my thighs. They were motionless there. But for me, all sensation was concentrated in them. Everything.

She spoke now as if we were having the kind of conversation we often have about the matters that arise from my work, as if she was explaining something to me, answering some question that had come up, being a source of information, a teacher.

'You must have read André Breton.'

'Not everything.'

'Perhaps you've read *L'Amour fou*. Have you?'

I had to say no.

'Jack read it often. He had an original 1937 edition with Brassaï's and Man Ray's photographs. It's about the necessity of abandon.'

Her fingers were moving on my thighs. I stayed still. Agonisingly still.

'*Amour fou*. Mad love. Dionysus in us. Breton believed . . . Jack believed that through desire and through the act of love he could, we could find a kind of revelation. Light. Everything, even the tiniest things in the world, could be marvellous, could be infused with desire.'

I closed my eyes. There was only the sensation of her hands. Nothing else in the whole of existence.

I touched her hands. I think I would have kissed her. There was nothing else to do.

But the hands went. They left me. And the anger was back when she spoke. Except it was cold.

I don't want to remember. Please don't let me remember.

She said it slowly, and she meant every syllable.

'You have no passion.'

I was full of passion. I *know* I was full of passion. I desire her now. I desired her then.

'You have no passion. None.'

I can remember. That was what she said.

And it was finished.

Why do I have to love her still? It should all be finished. Not just the fantasies. The desire should have gone too.

18 June 1994

Dear Rag,

I know you didn't believe me on the phone. I could hear it. You really thought I could use my diplomatic talents, or at least reconsider my position, and everything would be all right after all. That was what you thought, didn't you?

I'm writing to spell it out. I shall resign tomorrow. That is, Creasey will receive my letter of resignation tomorrow. It's finished.

He left us with no option. He realised well enough that he couldn't summarily dismiss me, but, once the warning was given, he could have dismissed both June and Peter (Peter's always remained loyal to her; he was her mentor). They resigned without hesitation and so, therefore, have I. On the 20th we shall all be in front of the cameras speaking our minds. That's all there is to it. We have to be free to speak our minds.

At last it's over.

My only regret is that I let you all down. You all came and stood up for me and gave me hope, and I have let you down.

You will be here on the 20th, won't you?

Simon

11

On a Trip

The next picture Felicity picked out in her undated text should be familiar to you. That's why I didn't consider it necessary to prepare you by giving you some introductory data earlier. You've had the basic facts.

It was among the first batch of the lost pictures to be shown to us. It was the picture that caused McKenna a moment of doubt, because of the red balloon in the sky. Perhaps you should know that, before he left, his conservation people confirmed his suspicion that it was a late addition, and noted that it was the only passage of later overpainting to be found on the entire canvas. It looked as if one day Driver had just thought he'd put a red balloon in. McKenna is reported to have shrugged and said, 'Well, Jack never did make things easy for us.'

I am referring, of course, to *On a Trip*, the 1963 painting shown at Mackray's in New York that year and illustrated in the catalogue without the balloon.

So we turn back. Back through the rooms, past the forests, past *Jealousy/Jalousie*. All the way back to Room 3. On our way out (eventually), reviewing all we've seen. For the last time.

You first showed me *On a Trip* one winter afternoon in Orlando Street. You said, 'I'm going to do some teaching, and I'm going to be the topic. Me in 1963.'

You did your usual thing when you talked about the

sixties, you talked about fame and the fall, about how
no one took an interest any more, because of Selwyn;
and I did my usual thing and said I took an interest and I
wasn't alone; you weren't to be so self-pitying, it never
did you any good. Do you know? There was always too
much routine about the mourning of your past, and I
was always too soft on you. I'm not so soft now. I'm not
going to take any more of your self-pity. It was always
much worse than my nostalgia.

You in 1963. Finding fame easy and hard at the same
time. Taking your pleasures with Louise. She always
gave and took her pleasures freely. But she 'never
listened'. The other women in your life 'never listen'.
Is that always the case with the other women men
talk about to their current women? It always sounded
too familiar to me to be true. How could a talker like
you have gone seven years with a woman who never
listened? But I did believe you when you said she never
listened to you on the danger of success; she's never
found success at all dangerous.

It was an illuminating seminar for me, student
Felicity. You see, I don't think that I had realised before
then how much the paintings of the sixties came into
being as you were making them, how far they were not
juxtapositional ideas that you cooked up calculatingly
beforehand. It's not the way the pictures look.

The moment I started to work with you at Orlando
Street, I knew you were something different when you
were putting images together than I had ever imagined.
The speed, the impetus of it was the thing: the physical
mobility of you working, even when you were scissoring
out press items, or taking and developing photographs,
or making that meticulous lettering of yours, even when
you were in those *mechanistic* procedures. Everything
about you was alive when you worked, not just your
mind and your hand, your entire body. Tempo. The
tempo of signs.

But it's especially when you paint. You're at the canvas, around it. It's on the floor, propped up, back on the floor. That's why you don't work like most who work on the floor, with the canvas unstretched: that's why you work with it stretched, so you can keep it moving. You're bending, pacing. Only drawing is something that *looks* controlled when you're doing it, and even that's physical – a highly controlled *physical* act.

'I know joy in *destruction* to a degree corresponding to my *strength* for destruction – in both I obey my Dionysian nature, which does not know how to separate No-doing from Yes-saying. I am the first *immoralist*: I am therewith the *destroyer par excellence.*'

Nietzsche from *Ecce Homo*. You loved to quote it in the *baraque* during the Nietzsche summer. But at the beginning, before I knew Nietzsche, it surprised me, all your talk about destruction in creation. 'Vandalising the canvas', that's how you put it. In the end it went as far as those experiments burning areas of paint laced with spirit. Burning with acid too. Failed experiments, but necessary, you said, even when you recognised the failure. You wanted everything to be destructive. I saw you before as the 'intelligent artist', the one who remains detached, who thinks and controls the thoughts as they are represented. And instead you talked about the Dionysian, and about a destructiveness that could leave nothing alone.

But to talk about destruction, about losing control, in the same breath as *On a Trip*, that really was a surprise. It's the *most* 'calculated' of all the pictures of the sixties; or that was the way it looked to me. You know how Graham Copley puts it now? He talks about 'the idioms of idealism and expressionism directed by remote control', though I haven't heard him say it about *On a Trip*. They can't see anything of *you* in any of your work now; and above all not in the work of the early sixties.

But, when I listen to the way you took me through the making of *On a Trip*, I can see you working; I see you there in any studio space, it doesn't matter where, I see you in a shack, surrounded by debris, making images happen.

First, there was the grey of the concrete toy-town blocks of Parkhill housing estate, all those slab-blocks and elevated walkways screen-printed on to the surface and then roughly worked over with oil like the *béton brut* of their walls and ramparts. I never understood how you could call seeing those photographs in the *Architectural Review* a seduction. But when you're speaking, your voice convinces me, leaves not a shadow of doubt.

'Such a slick and glossy grey. Made things so strong and confident; built out of such definite light and shadow; but all silvery greys, all nuances spread so subtly across the shiny page. I just couldn't resist greys like that, sensuous greys, yet *constructed* like that.'

Oh yes, but the pleasure of 'roughing it all up', of attacking the nuances and the gloss, that I can understand all right. And I can understand how the blue of the Mediterranean/Californian sky had to come next, and the pleasure of laying on all that brightness. And then I can understand the pleasure of cutting it to pieces with paint. And I can feel the energy of laying those tracks of pigment over it, again and again; crossing it right out like the rain does. You make something, then you destroy it; you make something else, then you destroy it. And each time the making and the destruction are acts, positive acts positively felt. Yes-saying in No-doing.

Of course it's so. I know that Pollock's dripped and spattered paint is there because you *felt* what the paint did to the sky. The way the paint falls has your action in it. But no one else sees it: they all see 'irony'. Jack Driver's notorious 'ironic relationship' with one of the masters of Modernism, Pollock; you must have heard them going on about that by now. Anything that's any good now is 'ironic'; no one ever sees directness as a quality. I remember you on 'being direct'. None of them can see how you were *in* the moving of the paint, in the act. Yes, this picture has destruction in it. And no one will see it, even if I tell them. They don't *want* to.

You said it was a picture you could still take seriously. You said you could still feed off it.

I look at it now, Jack, and my first impression is that you were not so strong in the early sixties. You were not so strong with Louise. You need my strength. You know it really. This was one of the fashionable paintings. One of the paintings that made your name. It's still the early sixties they look at now. The press has hardly mentioned the forests. The forests are 'the later work', 'interesting' but not 'seminal'. All we get is just a few perfunctory words repeating Graham's nonsense about Green-ness. They dwell on the pictures in the rooms through to 5 and 6, but especially in this one, Room 3. And so will the film the BBC is making for next year.

Miranda has hung *On a Trip* on the left wall as you enter from the second room. Opposite is *Six-six Vision on the Big Screen*. Our picture. That's a strong one. There are three strong ones in Room 3. But that's the one that's caused the most stir of all. And it wasn't one of the old fashionable pictures. It's like the other strong ones. Nobody knew them then, in the early sixties. Of course not. We'll look at *Six-six Vision* too. We have no choice. But first I want to look a bit more at *On a Trip*.

Why don't I feel it's so strong? I think I know what you're saying. You're saying that I can't see the fashionable sixties paintings, because Louise is all around them, because I'm not in them at all. But you know it's not true. I could be in them. I *can* feel my way into them, even the ones with Louise all around them. And I did feel my way into this picture. Certainly I did. None of the sixties painting is alien in that sense. No,

Louise might be a factor, that much I accept, but she is too easy a reason to be *the* reason.

The reason is not that I can't feel myself in *On a Trip*; it's that I can't feel *you* in it. Not enough. And I can't feel you in too much of the sixties work. It doesn't come at me; it's not direct. Whatever you said about the making of it, the destructiveness, the immediacy of it, the picture comes over cold, detached, far, far distant. That sense of the calculated I talked about just now. Graham is right; it *is* remote-controlled. And even he has doubts about some of the fashionable paintings, including *On a Trip*. He's written hundreds of words on *Six-six Vision*; he's hardly mentioned *On a Trip*.

It was a slow afternoon, the afternoon you showed it to me and I heard your seminar. It was one of those days like the grey in the Parkhill part of the picture. Steady grey. My system was in slow motion. I had the energy for looking and listening, but no more. I didn't even have the energy for desire. This is a picture that blunts my desire, lowers my libido, switches me off. All I can get from it is the memory of you in motion, working with passion, a passion that was never translated from the motion on to the surface of this canvas. Except in those trails of paint across the sky, and then only in vestiges, traces. I stand in front of it, and nothing about it explains how it could ever have been fashionable. How did such a dead thing acquire such a life for people?

There is only one small glint of vitality in it. Real vitality. Life I can feel. It's in the sky. It isn't hidden by the dripped and spattered trails of paint.

I'm there in the Orlando Street shack in '85. The last time I took out the sixties pictures to show you. I'm looking at *On a Trip*. We're looking at the picture together. It's one of your bad days. We shall never be able to come to Orlando Street again. Fabritius and I have had to carry you in the chair all the way up that collapsing staircase outside, and we shall have to carry you down again. You are so light now that I can carry you from your chair to your bed without help. Why don't you eat? You get lighter and lighter, smaller and smaller. You are a child.

'The child is innocence and forgetfulness, a new beginning, a sport, a self-propelling wheel, a first motion, a sacred Yes.'

But you are a child without innocence and forgetfulness. At the end. And in the chair on the rotten wooden stairs you are suddenly heavy and dangerously unwieldy. A complaining old man full of hate.

The day is bright, not grey. The light in the shack is perfect. It hangs in the dust, as it hangs in the buzzing insects of the forest at Saint Genès. It soaks into the greys of the Parkhill flats and into the crossed-out blue of the sky. I can see your contentment to be back with the success. I can see your contentment to be back with Louise. You are dumb with the beauty of the past. There is an impotent sadness in it. But it is in me, not you. You are dying and your power *is* destructive. I have to resist it. My strength has to resist it, because you want me to come with you. You think of Louise and you want me to come.

You look at me silently. The contentment in your eyes is joined by the smallest of smiles. And you say one word.

'Viva.'

Then you say it again.

'Viva.'

On the table against the wall to the left of the picture is the usual mess of jars and cans and brushes. There are three slender-handled brushes standing together in a jar of white spirit. I used them last time I was here to finish something small. Something beneath your notice. But something I like. I come without you sometimes. You didn't know that, did you?

I take the brush I know to have the fewest hairs. I am wiping it clean. I open a can of vermilion and dip it in. I am writing very carefully – as you always wrote on the canvas, but I am writing small, not big. I am writing on the wall. The letters are very red against the grey. They leap in the dusty light.

'Viva.'

I write it and I look back to you. You are not there. Your eyes are on the picture. You are in 1963, moving, Yes-saying.

You don't care that I care. That I am dying with you. You haven't seen.

I feel something new. I feel aggression. I want to hurt you. I have never wanted to hurt you so powerfully, so irresistibly. My strength can be cruel too.

I want to destroy like you destroy when you make images.

I am very deliberate in my actions. I take the chair and I reverse it so that it is well back from the canvas, so that you can see what I shall do but have no chance of intervention.

I approach the canvas. There is a small, intense rage in me, but it diffuses and softens in front of the sky and the trails of paint. It becomes a small hope.

Slowly and with a delicacy I have learned in the small paintings, I paint in the balloon, floating up and away in the sky. Montgolfier. I paint it with the red of my 'Viva'.

I turn. I expect your eyes to be full of anger. They are not. You are looking at the red balloon with wonder. It is a pleasure to you.

Your eyes flick across to me, and your small smile returns. You nod.

'Yes.'

It was all you said.

So there it is: a small glint of life. And your 'yes' makes it yours as well as mine. But this is much more than the things I did for you, when I worked to make the

pictures you had got too weak to make, when I became
the hand you directed. Because this was something from
your time without me, from your time with Louise. This
was something absolutely your own. To have been able
to enter it was much more. So much more. And you
let me in.

Why the balloon? Was it the title that gave me the
balloon – *On a Trip*? Was it the conjunction of redness
and 'Viva' and the sense of staying still in a space that
was steadily closing down, from which there had to be
release? It just came and painted itself into the sky. An
image that came.

It's your balloon as much as my balloon. Perhaps you
know why it came.

It doesn't matter.

I am working again. My strength is with me. I go
through phases. There have been periods of more than
a year, even two, when I have not worked. Since your
exhibition opened, I have been working. All of a sudden,
I had to start again. It wasn't quite the day after, but it
was very soon after. There was a change in me, you see.
I needed to. As if I needed to test myself, to see if the
strength was still there. It is. But there's no destruction
in it. Not in mine.

I don't go to the garage. I can't work in the garage
any more. It's too close. That's where the illness and the
death really are. I go to Orlando Street as I always have
since you went. I've been making my small pictures.
Like the small pictures I made in the eighties. I've been
thinking how harsh you were about them.

'Felicity's cottage industry. Sometimes I think
Nietzsche was bloody right about women.'

You're wrong, Jack. They kept me alive, and they are
alive. Much more alive than your remote-control things.

When I hear your cruelty, I hate you. I think that
you didn't teach me, that you gave me nothing, that
you squeezed me, that you drained the strength from

me, that you made me give only for you. Not just in
the illness time, but all the time from the moment I met
you. Thinking about you is dangerous. It doesn't allow
me to live.

I shall keep making my small paintings in Orlando
Street. I shall still talk to you sometimes. But there are
things I shall forget.

I shall forget your cruelty.

Viva.

12

Opening

27 September 1994

The really strange thing about yesterday was McKenna. It surprised me that he came. But I suppose he had to. The really, really strange thing, though, was the way he behaved. He laughed a lot.

Everywhere he went in the galleries there were people around him. And mostly the people around him were not the museum people, but artists and writers. He caused more of a respectful ripple of expectation when he entered a room than our Royal. His hand was shaken, his shoulder was patted, he kissed fond and admiring women (on both cheeks in a distinctly expansive version of the French manner), he was the star in triumph. And he enjoyed every moment of it. Wherever he was there was laughter.

How can it have been McKenna's day? Or how can he have had the buoyancy to act as if it was his day? He was in some indefinable way more regal than the Royal, yet without reserve. He seemed to have outgrown his mandarin persona, to have become a man of relaxed and generous charm with a sense of humour (even if it was still tinged, now attractively, by reserve), a man who had learned to laugh.

It should have been *my* triumph. Everything went so well. Miranda has done a stunning job. Simply stunning. I have to admit, she can put together an exhibition. I've said it before: she has flair as well as an MBA. The show looks perfect. It's still broadly chronological in layout, as it was originally conceived, but she's not been rigid about chronology, she's gone for telling juxtapositions. And they are telling. There's drama too. She's brought out the drama in the painting. Everyone said so. And I didn't disabuse them when they thought I might have had something to do with it. Why should I? It's my show too.

The only thing that didn't go well was Lester Howell's speech as new Director, a speech which required something special and just didn't deliver. Coverlie's 'Great Occasion' specialists (who handled the public relations side of everything) put him on a platform in a corner by one of those columns in the Duveen Gallery. For some reason they had hemmed the platform in with palm trees, as if it was a pretend desert island. Howell certainly gave a convincing impression of being shipwrecked on it. He has neither the funny bluster of Troy nor the effortless superiority of McKenna. And his knowledge of Driver is so lightweight that it continually seemed to float away from him.

His speech was like a rather feeble cry to be rescued. It contained many such phrases as 'I cannot pretend to have known Jack Driver', and 'others are better qualified than I', and 'I am sure the experts would be able to put it better', as if he hoped someone would arrive in a helicopter, sweep him off his island and leave a more expert replacement to complete the job.

The most embarrassing part was the climax, when he went into an extended peroration on Genius. Even Miranda, who has always been politically incorrect, shuffled uncomfortably next to me when he started to talk about 'the rough masculine quality of Jack's work' (adding, 'I feel now I can call him Jack'), 'the strong sense of a free, questing spirit' dedicated to leaving the mark of 'an individual, a powerful, a potent male presence'. Someone laughed out loud at that point, and no one came to the rescue. He ended with the claim: 'If ever an exhibition conveyed the sense of a single, strong, integrated identity, a Great Man, this is it. Let us raise our glasses to Jack Driver, a Briton who confirms the Genius of Britain.'

But everything else about the day was a success. And the success that has given me more pleasure than any other is the catalogue. It is thick and heavy and very smart. They've put *Catch Me* on the front. Appropriate. It's had a lot to do with the Driver revival, and the words, of course, echo what we've all been trying to do: catch him (the 'Great Man').

I pick the catalogue up and feel the smooth weight of it. I flick through the pages, and see all that grey of the columns of print, and know that the words and the facts they spell out and the accounts they develop are mine. They all stand for my work, my resolve, my refusal of everything from the over-consumption of instant coffee to jaffa cakes and chocolate digestives and truffle biscuits. They stand for keeping going even under the severest pressures from Miranda. I know the sheer richness of the knowledge that's packed into that greyness. All that exacting care. All the days in front of the white on blue on the VDU. I love just feeling it and seeing it. And sometimes I read a passage – any passage – just to remind myself that I wrote it and it's in print.

Now and again, though, I spot an error. There are a few. Why can I never get anything completely right? But nobody else seems to see them. I think.

You shouldn't dwell on errors, Roland. It's a sign of weakness. Don't. You should think about the glorious fact that it's you topping the bill on the title page. You've done something, my friend. Roland Matthias is the lead name all right, there's no doubt about that:

'By Roland Matthias,' it says, 'with a contribution by Graham Copley.'

'Roland Matthias' in the heavier print; 'Graham Copley' added like an afterthought.

That's what he was, an afterthought. But it still makes

me feel uncomfortable, Graham being there. It gave me an uneasy feeling all of yesterday.

Everyone was very nice and generous about my catalogue, and they did refer to it as *my* catalogue. Kit called it 'the most significant contribution to the history of British art in the sixties and seventies for some years', and told me he could not have been 'more pleased'. It knocked Graham, he said, 'into a cocked hat' (what a strange phrase from a modernist). Even Brad Kronsky from MOMA (Brad Kronsky!) made a point of 'engineering an introduction' to me so that he could shake my hand ('Take it from me, this is the way into Jack Driver for all of us on either side of the Atlantic from now on'). The vibes were all so positive for the catalogue – for my catalogue. Just as positive as they were for the show.

But still I had the feeling that everyone really wanted to talk about Graham's little piece.

It's nothing. He's said it all before, and yet they want to talk about his bloody afterthought and they can't be bothered with my facts.

For Christ's sake, it's the facts that take the hard work, and that have something to say, not Graham with his bloody heterological this and heterological that and precursors of postmodernism and post-postmodern moments. There's no bloody justice in this world.

I have to wait for the reviews, especially the serious reviews. They'll see the *weight* of my catalogue and the *lightness* of the Copley afterthought. Then it will all come right. Someone who's put together the facts the way they should be always gets the right kind of respect in the end, at least from the real professionals.

But I didn't like the feeling I got yesterday: the feeling that they were, most of them, only impressed by the Graham-speak, that all they wanted was some kind of intellectuals' sandpit (without much sand in it) to play in for ten minutes (about the time it takes to read his piece). I even saw Kit in his 'I'm-a-freebooting-intellectual' denim jacket and open-necked shirt talking animatedly with Graham. I saw him take him by the shoulder in that way he does (with the little pat and squeeze to offer bodily assurance), and I saw him utter praise. Even Kit. How can I believe what he said to me, when I see that?

And yet there wasn't a lot in what anyone said that actually, in so many words, told me face to face my facts were boring and Graham's sandcastles were not. It was just that I got this uneasy feeling, strongly.

And then there was the exhaustion. I just didn't have the *energy* to be triumphant like McKenna. I hoped there might be at least a booster injection of adrenaline to get me through all the champagne-drinking and the glamorous socialising, but there wasn't anything. I started the day drained and I ended it dropping.

Why the hell did Miranda want to go through the office routine the evening before? We needed to take time off. We needed to prepare ourselves for the rigours of yesterday. But that's not the way she is. She never needs any preparation. There are no rigours in her life. Occasions like yesterday are simple pleasures. She could sail through them on a daily basis.

I thought it had finally ended, she'd had her fill and was off in search of something else or had actually found it. But no. The phone goes. The first shipment of catalogues has arrived without any problems. That's the very last possible disaster averted. Everything is finally done. And she decides to spend the entire day chattering along with me, driving me wild, and then, to 'mark a job really well done', having a 'celebratory fling' with her 'lover Roland'. And I still had the proofs of the exhibition guide to check.

Well, Roland *caro* has really had it.

And I'd had it long before the opening actually opened at six yesterday, let alone when it all was finally over at one in the morning.

That was after the dinner at Le Moulin Vert. I had had

it long before the word came that the taxis were outside and we were all to assemble to be ferried to yet more heady pleasures. But, even slumped nearly senseless with fatigue in the back of the taxi and desperately trying to give a semblance of animation at table, I was struck by one thing: the apotheosis of Felicity.

Yesterday Felicity ascended into the Heavenly Kingdom, where there are no Royals or McKennas or Troys or government ministers (we hope), though there may be (I suppose) artists, including, of course, the Blessed Jack. She was in a state of bliss. One cannot talk of the return of the old serenity. It was too high-spirited for that. There was something childlike about it. So much wonder and excitement. At least at the beginning of the evening, before we looked at the dessert menu.

Coverlie's had booked the whole of Le Moulin Vert, all eight tables with their sylvan surroundings of potted trees (deciduous but apparently incapable of losing their leaves – the theme of the evening seemed to be trees, but not the coniferous ones that Driver painted). I was with Felicity and Miranda and the minister (Duncan) and Lester Howell (who was a man still obviously under stress; he spent the entire evening nervously ticking beside me, seemingly on the point of rushing away to send faxes or answer urgent phone calls at any given moment). McKenna, of course, was not invited.

Felicity kept exclaiming about the absurdity of the menu and becoming mirthful.

'Come on, Roland, with your cosmopolitan experience of the world you must be able to tell me what "*avec son coulis*" means.'

'"*Avec son coulis*" . . . with its . . . "*coulis*". Sorry, can't help you.'

'Sounds as if there's more than one of them. And why are they *its* "*coulis*"? Do you think that "*coulis*" are what "*Roquefort aux champignons*" produce if you leave them together overnight?'

'No, no, if there were more than one, they would be "*ses coulis*", wouldn't they? It's something singular.'

'It certainly is.'

Endless prattle like that, with me being patient and Miranda supplying the necessary answering giggles when Felicity felt she was being especially amusing. Duncan was a bore. He knew all the answers (' "*Coulis*" merely refers to sauce. The difference between "*coulis*" and other sauces . . .'). But generally everyone allowed Felicity to be blissful and refrained from bringing her down anywhere close to earth.

Then, at the end, when I was finally close to passing out, her bliss became quieter. She seemed to retreat into herself, but without either the signs of fatigue or of sadness. The glow of triumph was something we could all feel. It warmed everyone at the table.

I still love her.

I know she understands what I have done. The facts matter to her. She told me so. She's told me so ever since I began. The day before yesterday, after she had seen Miranda's hang for the first time, she came to the office, and she thanked us both. She hugged me tight with such warmth. I felt the gratitude. I know it's there. I still love her.

And yesterday evening when we left, I wasn't so drained that I did not see how she looked at me and hear what she said. That is a look and those are words that I shall never forget.

There was such deep pleasure in her eyes.

'You have made me very happy.'

That was what she said.

I think I love most only the things I cannot have. The past, Driver's friendship, Driver's work, Felicity.

But I was too tired to have thoughts like that at one in the morning. My Christ, I needed my bed.

All right, I'm sure you've got the message. I certainly get

it when I read through that entry now, and it wasn't, of course, a message I actually meant to give myself at the time – me writing on me for me.

I am paranoid. I've remarked on it before, and it's true. I always did read the worst between the lines and hear the worst in the pauses for breath. But my paranoia this time was dead accurate. As accurate as the Greenwich Observatory. The plaudits *were* for Graham, and my catalogue sank like a lead balloon (we might as well keep balloons in the picture) deep into the wastes of reference-book knowledge, hardly to be accessed except by the most self-denying of neurotic obsessives (although it has to be said that it *does* still have a solid scholarly reputation; it really does. Ask any serious academic in the field of twentieth-century British art).

And there is no doubt, if Miranda's and Copley's were the lesser triumphs of 26 September 1994, the great triumphs were Felicity's and, in an odd, unexpected fashion, McKenna's. The press, predictably, had a field day with 'in-depth interviews' giving the McKenna perspective on this and the McKenna perspective on that. And he was devastatingly generous with his opinions, acknowledging the skill of Miranda's 'hang' and even the 'usefulness' of my catalogue (as against 'the sparkle of Graham's lively intelligence'). He even had magnanimous things to say about Lester Howell. He triumphed as a man of moral integrity, even if immediately afterwards he was to become an irrelevance quickly dispatched to foreign parts.

Felicity, too, was ubiquitously interviewed and quoted. There was a great deal about money, naturally – all that stuff about 'the millionairess of Barnes' that she told Jack about at the beginning of her undated text, when she wrote her rather dismissive account of the opening. But what she did most of all was use the press to promote ATA (if you've forgotten, the Jack Driver Foundation for Action Through Art), which she talked 'up' whenever she could. Her refrain was: 'This is just the beginning, the beginning for a lot of young artists.'

But that was the public side. Felicity's triumph was really inside her; it was not a matter of public attention and celebration. After all, most of that went in the end to Driver and his work. Her triumph was something to be felt, unmistakably, in the way she looked: in her eyes, in the flush of her skin, in the way she held herself. We all felt it.

I had prepared myself for fame. I had really convinced myself that my moment would come too. Miranda and Felicity promised me it would. By the day after the opening, I knew – though all I would admit to was that 'uneasy feeling' – I knew that I would never be a Famous Art Historian and Scholar.

Such a small aspiration. But it seemed as if I had lost the world.

13

In My Flesh I Shall See Him

The last picture that Felicity took Jack to see was also the most significant. It was, as I've said, another of the lost pictures from the sixties and it hung opposite *On a Trip*. It was the second of the pictures which I considered securely datable to 1963 and which had a red balloon floating in a Mediterranean/Californian sky, this one with a ladder hanging down (I hope you remember). It was one of the half-dozen lost pictures that had never been shown before.

It was, of course, the 'strong' painting, so especially celebrated by those who wrote on the exhibition, Henry Troy's favourite, the painting whose purchase by the Tate was made possible by Troy's and Coverlie's beneficence, the painting with the unwieldy title: *Six-six Vision on the Big Screen*.

You can't look at *On a Trip* and *Six-six Vision on the Big Screen* both at once. You have to turn around from one to the other, holding the images in your head, if you're to think of them together. Miranda has hung them facing each other.

That's good. When *Six-six Vision* was made, something about *On a Trip* was there, all around it, but only in the mind. Miranda is right; they are not pendants.

Don't you see it, Jack? How *Six-six Vision* has the force. It isn't cold. It isn't all *calculated* force, pondered juxtapositions, remote-control painting. It's a sixties painting which has you in it more directly than almost any other. Not many people feel it. I listen and what I hear is surprise that you could have been looking at Raphael – the *Transfiguration* 'quotation' – and curiosity about the red balloon and the ladder. People find it an unusual painting, and I've even heard it said that it's not really 'like' you, Jack. Now, there's irony, don't you think? It's true that some remark on the *way* the grey of the Marbella villas and the bathers has actually been worked, and on 'the muscular drawing of the figures', however fragmentary they have become. But they don't *feel* it.

And it's there. *I* feel it. Because I can be inside it. With you. Nothing else in this show is our painting like this. None of the others are. Even the others that came after, and are perhaps as strong.

When I see it, I think of theft. I think of what Copley and Roland and Miranda and Troy and even McKenna have stolen from us.

The day I read Copley's essay for your catalogue, I rang him to thank him. But after I thanked him I said something you used to say: 'In the end the pictures stand and fall by themselves; they can make their point without you.' Do you know what he said? It took my breath away.

'They stand,' he said, 'because I built the conceptual scaffold that allows them to stand.' Then he added as if I was defective in some way, 'You do understand, Felicity?'

And that was not all.

'To build the scaffold for them,' he said, 'I had to break them free from Jack's grip. I had to break them free for us to take on our terms. You can look at the pictures your way. I can look at them my way. We don't have to look at them *through* Jack any more. I've opened his pictures

up again. They're not his any more. I've liberated
them.'

Liberated. Looted. Stolen. It's the effrontery of it that
startles me still. Without a moment's hesitation, cool as
you please, he BOASTED that he had taken your work
for himself. Theft.

And he's not alone. They've all stolen what you did.
Turned it into what they want. He's just the one who has
never bothered to pretend to anyone that he hasn't. He's
incapable of feeling guilt, let alone confessing error.

I wonder if they would have been so barefaced about
it if you had really been here to see the show.

I think of the funeral, Jack. I know I shouldn't think
of the funeral. It's another negative memory that drags
me into the nostalgia. That's what you would say. But
you would be wrong, Jack. The funeral wasn't at all
negative. Not at all.

You see, I could feel no grief. You were not that
shrunken, childlike body in the coffin at all. I could feel
nothing but relief to have lost that. You hadn't been
there for such a long time. All that day I knew you only
as you were back in the time before the mischief began.

Such surprising and difficult instructions you left.
You, an atheist, to be buried in a churchyard with a
Christian burial service and yet to be 'remembered' in
a memorial service that made no mention of God. But
your village churchyard was a lovely place, and I was
grateful to see the little West Country village which was
'the first home of Jack Driver in childhood'. You never
even mentioned it before.

A lovely place on the side of one of those bumpy
Cotswold hills. A tiny church, with the graves leaning
and tilting, some of them fallen, all of them slowly
crumbling around it. A couple of them bearing the name
of those small gentry forebears of yours you never talked
about. The yew trees shaggy and unclipped; dense,
confined patches of ancient darkness.

They dug the trench with a view out across the valley. When we stood to throw the clods into it, all I could feel was the spaciousness of the place, the clear blue air all around us, the sense of it going out and across and up and away. The balloon was in the sky. Viva.

I had words in my head. The priest's words from the Book of Job. They come back often.

'And in my flesh I shall see God.'

In my flesh.

My eyes gave me space. But you were in my body. You are in my body. In my flesh I see you.

Still.

The funeral, the blue air, those words were in my head when I took out the canvas in Orlando Street. Do you know something strange? I feel absolutely, entirely myself when I make my little paintings. They are mine. I have my strength. But I can only make them when you are strong in me. I can't find the urgency to go to Orlando Street without it. That's the way it has to be. That's the way it was then.

It isn't theft. I haven't stolen anything from you. You were there. You made it happen. It's you with me.

Do you want me to explain? I don't know if I can. It sounds half-cocked. I shall feel such a fool. I shall feel you telling me I'm weird, I need help, I shouldn't listen to voices, they aren't there, and they aren't anything to do with you. You were always so down-to-earth, so bloody materialist about people who said they had 'experiences'. But it's how it happened. So I shan't explain. I shall just tell you the way it was.

I never give myself a format bigger than 45 × 36 [centimetres] when I make my small pictures. 'What's 45 × 36? It's hardly *there*.' I can hear you say it. Orlando Street seems very big and dark when I have one of those little white spaces in front of me. I try to get inside them to escape the width and height of the darkness.

Well, you see, that day I couldn't get inside. The little canvas had a few marks on it and otherwise just stayed white and empty. The space was in my head. It would not come out.

I started to move around the shack. I was restless. I was scratchy with desire. It happens when I want to paint and I can't. Even back then, so soon after you went, I had times when I had to masturbate. Don't worry, it *was* you in my mind that I was having those kind of thoughts about. I promise.

Then the pictures started coming into my head and I thought of *On a Trip*, of the balloon you allowed into it and the blue sky. I decided to find it and take it out of its plastic covering and look at it. I began searching through the canvases in the rack beside the door. And then I saw the empty one. I slid it out and propped it against the rack. You see, I never did find and open up *On a Trip*, so it stayed no more than a thought. The thought that started me looking. Miranda is right, *On a Trip* and *Six-six Vision* were never pendants.

The canvas that I propped up against the stack was big and white, a big white wide-open space. The kind that you felt comfortable with. It was primed and you had begun to mark it. There were charcoal lines and smudged smearings of dark paint on it. They hung there like the echoes of hints, the very smallest of hints that would never become anything as definite as a suggestion.

I made no decision. The tools were there. The materials were there. I began to work. The sense of release was lovely. Wind, brightness, sunlight. For days and days, for weeks I was in such a big space again. Like the really big canvases and those great, rough pieces of wood we used to work on in the seventies before the diagnosis. When it began it was my work. *My* work. It was like an escape from the 45 × 36 format, all that littleness, into openness.

And the images came. They came fast. There was no work in it.

'All names of good and evil are images: they do not speak out, they only hint. He is a fool who seeks knowledge from them.

'Whenever your spirit wants to speak in images, pay heed; for that is when your virtue has its origin and its beginning.

'Then your body is elevated and risen up . . .'

The images began with banality. The first to come were your Marbella postcards, the ones with the little arrows you put in to indicate Selwyn's famous villa with the *jalousies*. Costa del Sol villas. Another kind of sixties space. The postcards were still in the drawer of the big table. Exactly where you left them.

The grey was something that seeped into the villas, something that came from the Parkhill blocks in *On a Trip*, something that came into me and then into the picture to destroy the villas, bury them in winter. And the bathers came with the grey. You came first. You standing naked in a body that still seemed healthy with your left leg stiff beside you.

Then the others came, figures out of those ridiculous old sixties news photographs of yours of running stars. Remember? Peter Radford . . . Herb Elliot . . . rangy athletic bodies. I stripped them and made them move. No one sees you among them now. There came a point when I had to change you. I didn't feel that you could still be fragile and frightened in this space any more. I made you strong like the athletes.

Then came the man pointing. They might all talk about Raphael now, the figure pointing to the Heavenly Kingdom from the earthly sphere. But he just came into the space. I promise you, there was no *Transfiguration* in my head when he came.

And then (it all took time – I wasn't hurrying) . . . then I changed the white space that was left above into the blue space of the sky. I painted the sky very calmly. I took it slowly across the white, feeling it destroy the white and open it up.

That was a good day. The day when I painted the sky. The best day. That was the day when I felt you were really there. That was the day when we really painted together again.

From the moment I started, when the canvas was empty, I knew it was your painting I was making. The images came from me. I saw them in *my* mind, and *my* hand formed them. But I knew they were yours. They are yours. I have kept your gift safe and it's still yours Jack, the blazing sun and the serpent. I have stolen nothing.

Only the balloon is really mine. I knew you would let me put it in. You let me before. You would let me this time too.

I could not leave the sky without the balloon. It wasn't possible. You knew it, didn't you? So I took the littlest brush I could find – a brush for my small pictures – and I dipped it in the vermilion, and with all the finesse I could summon, I painted in the red balloon.

Then the ladder came. The thinnest black lines for the rungs faintly but definitely against the blue.

At the end I felt as I feel now in front of it with you. It is your painting and it is my painting. Masculine and feminine. I have not stolen it from you, and you cannot steal it from me. It is our painting. And the others are our paintings too. The ones that came afterwards.

So I've told you how it was. And now I have, I can see there's nothing weird or foolish about it. There were no voices. I just did it. There was no need to hear voices. I am perfectly sane. I have not become feeble-minded, and I am not and have never been a paranoid schizophrenic. So you can take that quizzical expression off your face.

I felt you in me and I did it. Nothing could be simpler. I am strong and you are strong. You are still strong. I painted one of your paintings for you. And it's yours whatever you say, because I couldn't have done it without you. Like the others.

The words come back.

'And in my flesh I shall see you.'

Felicity's undated text ends here. There's little for me to add by way of historical commentary.

We can say with certainty – how, after all, can Felicity's text not be believed? – we can say with certainty that at least one of the lost paintings is not a Jack Driver at all. And not just any one of them: the most discussed, most celebrated, the very strongest of them. Perhaps the very strongest of all the sixties paintings. And if we can say that, as McKenna realised when he told Frew of his suspicions all those years ago, might there not be more? There *must* be more. Five of the lost paintings (besides *Jealousy/Jalousie* and *Six-six Vision*) were previously unexhibited and previously unpublished. They too arrived unheralded. And they are certainly among the strongest things Driver did in the sixties. Every one of them. Are all five of them actually not Jack Drivers at all, but Felicity's Jack Drivers? Or four of them? Or three of them? Or two? Or just the one? Could *Six-six Vision on the Big Screen* really have been the only early Driver that Felicity painted? If it was, what are 'the others' – 'the others' she refers to, including the three other 'strong' paintings she talks about in Room 3 – 'the ones that came afterwards'?

It is the final irony that Graham was right all along. But not in a way that he could ever have suspected. Driver did disappear from at least one and probably several of his paintings of the sixties. And his disappearance was real. Let me state the fact – and it is a fact – as baldly as possible: he did not paint . . . he did not paint . . . how many did *she* paint? There *is* no 'fact' to state.

For Felicity he never disappeared. He was always there. But there's no escaping what happened: it was she who imagined and made *Six-six Vision*. The Tate have a Felicity Driver. Maybe they have more than one. Just which are 'the others'? Was the strength that was found in some of the lost paintings not Jack Driver's strength at all?

And then as well, Felicity – I'm now convinced – was not just the 'executant' of the paintings of the last three or four years either. You've seen it now as plainly as I have. The evidence is there in her texts, implied if not stated. They came from her in the fullest sense. Driver was just a spectator in the end. As he was when she began to paint the early work too: the one or two or three or five early pictures that are hers.

I have known this too long. What price my catalogue? My catalogue of 'the work of Jack Driver'? I have known too long that all the '*raisonné*' good sense in the world cannot make sense of this kind of doubt. I am an historian who has always believed in facts and in Genius. My purpose has been the preservation of both. And the facts are not the facts. Such a small thing to ask: to be able to believe in the facts. Just a little peace and quiet to give contentment now and again in the centre of the world as I know it. Even that I cannot have.

Felicity was sometimes 'Jack'. No. Jack was sometimes Felicity.

· 14 ·

Curriculum Vitae

Professionals have to bring things to an end properly. That's something I told you at the beginning.

I shall end with comforting things even if they are the product of a life that is not comforting at all. I end with facts I cannot doubt, because they are my very own facts, the ones I have recorded about myself, my own life. I shall keep them to a minimum. There are many, many more that I have carefully chronicled in files that have been packed tighter and tighter into my hard and soft disks as their capacity for condensing data has increased.

Artists have 'biographies' written for them. Academics write down the facts of their careers in another form, which some consider an art, the 'curriculum vitae'. This is a very much reduced curriculum vitae, which incorporates some of the characteristics of a biography. It covers the years between the 1994 Tate/Coverlie's exhibition and this year – we are now in the New Year, 2019.

It is the twentieth year of a new century which is on the brink of maturity.

Curriculum Vitae

Dr Roland Matthias – 1995–2019

1995
Travels with the Driver exhibition to New York. Delivers special lecture in a series at the Museum of Modern Art opened by Graham Copley.

July – receives Ph.D. from Queen's College, University of London.

November – publishes important article on Jack and Felicity Driver's collaborative works.

1996
Starts work on the full *catalogue raisonné* of Driver's *oeuvre* financed by Coverlie's and by ATA (the Jack Driver Foundation for Action Through Art).

Unsuccessfully applies for three lecturing posts in British universities.

1998
Publishes important exploration of the forest paintings in their local French context.

Unsuccessfully applies for two lecturing posts in British universities.

2000
Invited to write catalogue essay for an exhibition of Felicity Driver's Small Paintings (1981–2000) at the Culver Gallery. Remarks on her use in one canvas of the cast shadow of a balloon, as if in response to Jack Driver. The exhibition is an unexpected success. For the first time, Felicity Driver is given a certain recognition, distinct from Jack Driver's.

2001
Accepts invitation to become full-time salaried secretary of ATA.

2001–2008
Works as secretary of ATA, in 2005 publishing the four volumes of the full Jack Driver *catalogue raisonné*.

2007
23 January: death of Felicity Driver (breast cancer first diagnosed two years earlier). Over the next two years ATA collapses as a result of the bequest of the remaining Jack Drivers in her collection to the Tate Gallery and of overborrowing to finance the expansion of bursary programmes. Even the sale of many of Felicity Driver's small paintings cannot save it.

2009
Appointed lecturer in history of twentieth- and twenty-first-century art and of Modern British Heritage Studies at the University of Yorkside.

Begins work on the official edition of Jack Driver's published and unpublished writings, a task made possible by role as trustee of the Driver archive, which also includes all Felicity Driver's papers.

2009–2016
Lecturer at University of Yorkside. Finds difficult the new rules for the academic game, according to which to be appointed to a post for scholarly distinction (Reader or Professor) the most important qualification is 'management and entrepreneurial skills' and the most serious impediment, scholarly distinction.

2016
After repeated delays caused by the weight of teaching and administrative responsibilities, publishes the two-

volume *Complete Writings of Jack Driver*. Promoted to Senior Lecturer, not, of course, on the strength of scholarly achievement (now aknowledged to be 'solid'), but above all in recognition of a five-year appointment as university timetabler and course quality controller in the School of Cultural and Leisure Studies (incorporating the Humanities).

2018

Accepts early retirement (perhaps hastened by the efficiency of quality control services rendered to the University).

What should I put down if I were to write the curriculum vitae of Driver's work after the great exhibition of 1994? It is, after all, a kind of 'life'. There would be my four volume *catalogue raisonné* in it, and my edition of the writings (with all its 2,773 footnotes), and there would be an endless list of exhibitions and critical books and articles, which no doubt I would take the greatest of pleasure in getting absolutely right down to the last semicolon. Graham would be there turning his coat year in and year out, ending up with his *Collected Essays on Jack Driver: Views from Another Century*, published last year. Graham would be there with many names you will have heard of, distinguished and sometimes spectacular names from across Europe and America.

But one thing would not be there: my view from 'another century'. My certain knowledge that my failure is not alone. That Driver's pictures – Felicity's and Jack's pictures – have ceased to act, have in the most important sense ceased to live. That they ceased to live long before we lost Felicity, long before the end of ATA, the organisation she built on their market rise and rise.

If ever 'his' pictures could undermine the comforts of the impervious in this Britain, they have lost the power now. They are admired by cultural tourists as if they were the artefacts of a culture as strange as Aztec Mexico, a culture where Socialism was hope. They are the object of curiosity and scholarly archaeology. They are more glamorous and more expensive than ever. They have died.

I suppose, in the end, neither has my curriculum vitae any need of the 'vitae' (of life – my life). It is the record of a career, a kind of life far less to be remembered. But one that is over for me too.

And the recording of these last few facts for you has made me wonder. Is what I have been writing an historical account at all? Were any of them really facts?

I don't know any more. Perhaps, after all, what I have been writing is just another fiction.